TALES OF A
Drama
Queen

TALES OF A
Drama
Queen
LEE NICHOLS

RED
DRESS
INK
TM

First edition July 2004

TALES OF A DRAMA QUEEN

A Red Dress Ink novel

ISBN 0-373-25063-0

www.RedDressInk.com

Printed in U.S.A.

SEBASTIAN, MAESENEER AND BRONSON

August 21, 2004

Re: Our Recent Luncheon

Ms. Eleanor Medina:

I regret to inform you that I was not released from the hospital until yesterday. The injuries were severe and, as you no doubt recall, I have never been a good healer.

Dr. Armitage offered the opinion that the sugar, at the time of impact, was heated to approximately 370° F. Mr. Maeseneer, Esq., was kind enough to suggest that I initiate legal proceedings against the restaurant, pastry chef and, of course, yourself. However, as you know, I would miss the *Gratinée de Coquille St. Jacques*. And, as I am well aware of the state of your finances, expecting remuneration would be more than foolhardy.

Elle, please understand that I do not regret the six long years we spent together. You are a very special person, with a great deal of vivacity, and as one chapter ends another is sure to begin. Although, if you will allow advice from a fond ex-fiancé, you might learn to curb your temper.

Sincerely,

Louis M. Ferris

Louis M. Ferris, Esquire

P.S. It has come to my attention that, during your somewhat disordered departure, you must have inadvertently removed my stamp collection with your belongings. Please return ASAP.

LMF:je

1665 Massachusetts Avenue NW • Washington, DC 20036 • (202) 555-0221

chapter 1

I got the fancy cheese grater from Williams-Sonoma. I got the obscenely fat, three-wicked candle his sister gave us. I got the cut-out *New Yorker* cartoons, saved against a rainy day for eventual decipherment. I even got the instant ear thermometer (I never get sick, but I knew he would miss it).

All was taken in manner of the break-up scene in *The Jerk,* where a drunk Steve Martin stumbles out the door, pants around his ankles, grabbing whatever catches his eye. Was proud at the time that I shrieked like a harridan for his sister's handwritten instructions about burning the candle, then deeply disappointed to read simply: "Burn no longer than one hour. Enjoy!" Have been preoccupied on flight to Santa Barbara wondering what happens if I burn longer. Explosion? Toxic fumes?

For the first time, I drink real Bloody Marys on the plane, not virgins. Concern over Death Candle melts away in cloud of drunken amiability. I delight my neighbor, a genteel old lady wearing a Laura Ashley frock, with details of my breakup with Louis. Her eyebrows beetle when I call the Iowan floozy a scheming slut. Could she be from Iowa? I assure her I don't think all floozies from Iowa are scheming sluts.

Am pleasantly surprised when old lady says there are extra seats in back, smiles kindly, and leaves in a waft of grandmotherly perfume. I scoot to the window seat and lay my head against the cold plastic wall.

Start to cry as I fall asleep to thoughts of my big, expensive, perfect wedding. And my small, cheap, flawed future.

I wake when the plane touches ground. There's a scattering of applause, and for a euphoric moment I think it's for me.

I was dreaming about trying on clothes in an endless, utopian version of the Better Dresses department of my childhood department store. The dressing room is large and shell-pink, filled with Donna Karans, Armanis, Guccis, Diors and pre-Stella-McCartney-bail Chloes. Everything I put on makes my body look like Halle Berry's. When did I get such a perfect ass? I can't stop turning and admiring it in the mirror. Like an old Labrador lying down for a nap, I turn and admire, turn and admire, searching for the best of all possible views.

Reaching for the price tag on a Missoni sheath, I can't quite make out the numbers. I ask the manager (who, oddly, is my fifth grade teacher, Mr. Bott) to help me. He says, "You never were a good reader, Elle," presents me with a gold Neiman Marcus credit card (not Robinson's after all) and says, "Take it all, you gorgeous thing." The beautiful young salespeople applaud.

I open my eyes, smiling modestly, to find a middle-aged couple across the aisle clapping. Because the plane landed. As if a safe landing is more important than a perfect ass in a Missoni.

I straighten in my seat, a crick in my neck, cranky from my nap. Doesn't help that shopping orgasm was all a dream. And that my feet have swollen to the size of pineapples, and won't slip back into my boots, forcing me to leave them unzipped.

I peer out the mini-window at the Santa Barbara airport. Looks like a Spanish hacienda. I've only been home once since college and the hacienda makes me feel nostalgic and young again—can't wait to impress my friends and family with all the brilliant things I learned at Georgetown, plus tales of my fabulous attorney fiancé and high-society Washington lifestyle. Cheered, I wander down the stairs toward the tarmac, half-expecting the whir and flash of paparazzi cameras.

It's all wrong. I'm blinded by runway lights, suffocated by fresh air, struck with sick-making vertigo. I clutch the stair-railing as I'm ambushed by the truth: I'm no longer twenty-one, all I recall from Georgetown is my relief at having graduated, my family doesn't live here anymore, my fabulous fiancé dumped me for an Iowan floozy, I never had a lifestyle—and now I don't even have a life.

I start crying again, and the grandmotherly old lady lays a gentle hand on my arm and brushes past, muttering "move it, you feeble lush."

Resolve in future to keep my airborne Marys virginal.

I've lined up my seventh suitcase (of thirteen, but some are quite small) in the baggage claim tent, when Maya bounces up. She's as cute as she was in high school, with a short tousle of blond curls, huge green eyes and a petite teenage body that belies her twenty-six years. She's my opposite. I'm taller, with long dark corkscrew hair, and more curvy than petite.

She smiles at me, and I feel dirty, tangled, big and miserable. She sees my unzipped boots and unstable expression and opens her arms. I fall into them, weeping.

"Oh, Elle." She giggles. "You're just the same!"

chapter 2

He's perfect. Brad. Maya's boyfriend.

It was ever her way. In high school, she had a string of cute, smart, loving boyfriends. My string consisted of the geeky boys in my fourth-period chemistry class. Bunsen-Burner-du-Jour and I would get drunk on Saturday night, fool around, then pretend we hadn't touched each other on Monday. I got a C– in chemistry.

Perfect Brad. Charming, handsome, always says the right thing. Not in an Eddie Haskell way, but as if he really cares. For someone like me, who's fairly certain no one would hold a funeral if she died, the effect is…effective. Okay, it's cataclysmic. But I decide not to fall in love with him, on the grounds that it would be incestuous—and, honestly, if you're living with Maya, why switch to Elle?

He is waiting when we get home from the airport. He gives Maya a welcome-home kiss, and me a nice-to-finally-meet-you peck on the cheek. He offers a nightcap. I take a ladylike slug of bourbon while they sip wine.

"You must get a good price on alcohol," I say, because Maya owns a bar downtown with her father.

She yawns before agreeing. "Yep. We drink wholesale." She sits on the couch with Perfect Brad, curled into the crook of his arm. It's late and I know they're ready for bed, but I don't want to be alone. I knock back my bourbon so I can ask for another before they finish their wine and leave me.

They look so content and normal that I don't know what to say. The price of liquor was my only conversational gambit. And I'm afraid that Maya's going to ask about my life: what happened to Washington, what happened to Louis, what happened to the aborted wedding and the non-existent career? Certain she's going to pounce, I distract her with *Fodors*-type questions about new restaurants in town.

"There's a neat tapas restaurant on the Mesa," she answers. "And a couple new Mexican places on Milpas. Superica's still there, but the line's around the block. L.A. people discovered it, so—"

I blurt: "The breakup was fine."

She looks at Perfect Brad. He refills my glass. They've been talking about me.

"Good," Maya says. "I'm glad."

"I mean, perfectly amicable, reasonable, mature..."

"Okay, Elle. What happened?" she asks.

See? I *knew* she was going to ask.

"We realized we'd been growing apart. We had different goals, different priorities." Like I wanted a wedding, and he wanted an Iowan. "It was very, he was very, I was very, *we* were very...civilized!" I gesture wildly with my drink, and a bit sloshes out. I clean the side of my glass with my tongue. *Klassy*. "Anyway, there's nothing to say, really."

They look at me, faces wreathed with pity and sympathy. I manage not to bawl.

"What about the wedding?" Maya gently asks. "We were all set to come..."

"Oh, that. It's nothing." I dismiss it with a wave of my hand. "But it *was* going to be beautiful. The flowers were hot-house peonies, the linens pale peach, the confetti cannon was rented." Tears come to my eyes. "I'd even hired Mr. Whistle to cater."

"Mr. Whistle?"

Yeah. Mr. Whistle.

It happened at Citronelle, in Washington, D.C.

I love Citronelle—the glass-front kitchen, the witty food, the elegant people. Plus it's fun to say chef Michel Richard's name with a cheesy French accent: Meeshell Reesharrrd.

I sat at one of the few tables with a view of the kitchen, sipping iced tea and watching one of the cooks fry shitakes, waiting for Louis. I'd come from Mr. Whistle's, where he and I had discussed the wedding menu. The oppressively expensive menu I couldn't afford. In fact, Mr. Whistle was *this* close to canceling my catering reservation. He'd run my credit card—never a good idea.

Which brings us to Louis, who is an attorney and makes buckets of cash. His buckets were the only reason Mr. Whistle had agreed to see me. I'd left him with a promise that I'd return after lunch with Louis and his platinum card.

Problem: Louis didn't know he was paying for the wedding.

I'd tried to get my father to pay. But when I'd called him with the news, what did I get? No "congratulations, darling." No "when's the date?" Not even an "it's about time."

I got: "I hope you don't expect me to pay, Eleanor. I've spent enough on marriage. Why don't you elope?"

Dad's had five wives, and is never so generous as during divorce proceedings.

Louis, on the other hand, is *always* cheap. But he's almost an associate partner, so paying for my perfect wedding wouldn't financially wound him—just sting a bit.

I was watching the shitakes sizzle when the maitre d' showed Louis to our table.

"Allo, Lou-ee." I always pronounced his name the French way when at Citronelle. I kissed him with a bit more oomph than usual. "I missed you," I said.

He'd been in Iowa for two weeks on business, and I'd been lonely. Worth the sacrifice though—I knew nothing about the deal, but his bonus was meant to be significant. Maybe enough to cover the wedding.

"Hi, Ellie." He hugged me, *sans* oomph.

It was good to see him. Tired and rumpled, his presence was an immediate comfort. He was my personal grounding rod: solid and true. He made me want to be a good wife, like, say Barbara Bush. Though, obviously, not so conservative, curly white-haired, or, well…old.

"Ellie. Are you listening?"

"What?" Oops, good wives pay attention. "Yes! I'll have the chicken."

"I said I've been trying to call you for a week. You never answer."

"They have scallops today," I said—his favorite. I didn't want to tell him I'd been avoiding the phone because a credit card company or two might be wondering about payments. But his face clouded, and I knew he wouldn't let me change the subject that easily. "Sorry I didn't call back," I said. "I've been so busy planning."

"Planning?"

"Helloooo." I laughed. "Our wedding."

"Oh. Right. Um, listen—"

"Will you come to Mr. Whistle's after lunch? We need to finalize the menu, and I want your opinion." And your wallet.

"No. I can't go to the caterer."

Nuts. "Have to get back to work so soon?" Maybe I could

slip his Visa from his wallet when he went to the bathroom. The scallops are spicy, and he always visited the men's room to blow his nose after eating them. But how could I get him to leave the wallet?

"Ellie," he said. "I've met someone else."

Should I ask him to leave his wallet, so I could pay the bill? Maybe I should pretend I wanted to check he still had my picture—*what?*

"You *what?*"

"In Iowa. I met someone."

"In Iowa you did *what?*"

He flushed. "I—I met someone else."

"A woman? You met a woman?"

"We can't get married, Elle. I'm sorry."

A deep breath. Calm, calm. Six years is a long time, it was only natural he'd be getting cold feet. We'd laugh about this in a month. After he paid dearly.

"Of course we can still get married. Don't be silly. It's only one last flirtation." The word *flirtation* stuck in my throat, but I refused to let the groom ruin my wedding.

Louis shook his head and mumbled.

"I understand, marriage is scary." I patted his hand. "No matter how committed or in love two people are. So you met another woman on your trip. It's nerves, of course, you—"

"I didn't just *meet* her, Ellie."

Something cold dripped down my spine, but I ignored it. The wedding dress had been purchased. The Wedgwood pattern (Classic Garden) chosen. "So, you slept with another woman." I gulped my iced tea, feigning calm. "I'm extremely disappointed in you. But our time together means more than some one-night stand."

"No. Ellie, I'm sorry, but—"

"If it makes you feel better, *I'll* sleep with another woman." A joke to lighten the mood, despite the anger I felt simmering.

"*Elle.* Listen to me. We didn't just sleep together. We got married."

"Married?!" I slammed my glass on the table. "What about Mr. Whistle?"

"And that's when I grabbed the crème brûlée," I tell Maya and Perfect Brad. "It was passing by on a dessert tray."

I drain a third bourbon before Brad takes my glass and returns the bottle to the kitchen. I slobber shamelessly and tell Maya how much I love her. I yell to Brad that I love him, too.

"Is she gonna be all right?" he calls to Maya.

She tells him she's seen me like this before, tucks me into my bed on the living room couch and follows Brad to the bedroom. I wonder if they're going to have sex. I wonder how long it will be before anyone wants to sleep with me again.

I stare at the two towers of suitcases stacked next to me in the dark. Why don't they make skyscrapers out of nylon, Velcro and wheels? Lightweight and durable. Suitcase apartments with zipper closets…

An hour later, I abruptly wake and lurch to the bathroom. Careful of my hair, I retch two gallons of Bloody Mary mix and Maker's Mark, and seven little bags of honeyed peanuts. I flush as Maya knocks on the door.

"Elle? Are you okay?"

I open the door. "Better now."

"Still a puker? Some things never change."

Which is exactly what I'm afraid of.

chapter 3

I wake with the Sunday edition of the *Santa Barbara News-Press* on my belly. I'm depressed and hungover, and unsure how to take the newspaper delivery. Helpful encouragement, or a hint that I'm not welcome for long?

The headline of the Lifestyle section is about Oprah buying a fifty-million-dollar house in Montecito, the über-rich suburb of Santa Barbara. Eager to jump into the job and apartment hunt, I make a list to evaluate my present situation:

Oprah: Recently moved to S.B.
Me: Recently moved to S.B.
Even Steven.
Oprah: Between forty-five and fifty.
Me: Twenty-six.
I'm ahead!
Oprah: Famous and beloved.

Me: Not so famous. And even my lovers don't belove me.

Back to even?

Oprah: Offers wisdom, advice and companionship on nationally syndicated hugely successful talk show.

Me: Interviewed once on the street. Local newswoman asked what Christmas gift I'd give the world. I said, "Miatas."

Oprah slightly ahead.

Oprah: Owns her own magazine: *O.* Graces cover each month in cheerful, feel-good outfit.

Me: Own many outfits.

Gap widening.

Oprah: Never lost fiancé to Iowan Floozy.

Me: Lost fiancé to Iowan Floozy.

Oprah shoots forward.

Oprah: Billionaire. Driven, smart, self-made.

Me: Credit risk. Coasting, smart, self-conscious.

Can taste Oprah's dust in my mouth.

Oprah: On the chubbier side.

Me: The less chubby side.

Cold comfort.

Maya enters, bearing fresh coffee. "Did you see Oprah's moving to town?"

"Is she?" I take a life-giving sip. "Where's Brad?"

"Working."

At SoftNoodle, a post-dot-com dot-com. They wanted a name that evoked both software and brains. Instead, they got impotence. "He works Sundays?"

"All the geeks do."

"He's not geeky. He's perfect."

"He's not perfect!"

"He looks, talks, tastes and *is* Perfect Brad."

"Tastes?"

"You know what I mean. Name one way he's not perfect."

"He's not Jewish."

"Oh," I say. "That."

Maya and I have been friends since we were twelve. She always celebrated the major Jewish holidays, unless she had other plans, but that was the extent of it. Maya's mother, on the other hand, was really observant. She died of breast cancer last year—her funeral was the one time I'd been back since college. Since then, Maya has taken religion more seriously. Not that she's started attending synagogue or anything, but she knows her mother wanted her to marry someone Jewish.

"So no wedding bells?" I say.

Her face clouds. "The wedding bells were supposed to be for you and Louis." She sits next to me. "Did he really hurt you, Elle?"

I'd been thinking about that, between bouts of obsessive eating. "Other than my pride? No. C'mon. Of course not." I take another sip of coffee, wishing it were a pint of Ben & Jerry's Chubby Hubby. The name of the ice cream makes my heart hurt. "Yeah. I guess he did. I miss him. I liked him. I really—he was solid. We really knew each other—little things, you know? The stuff that doesn't matter, but that's all that matters. And he was…well, he was there. That's important in a fiancé."

"He was there." Her tone says, *you don't sound like a woman in love.*

"Do you remember in high school, when we wanted to be mistresses?"

"No."

"Maybe that was just me." I'd seen a special on *20/20* about Kept Women. It had made an impression. Your own house, designer clothes and an allowance. All you had to do was have sex whenever he wanted. I liked sex—it didn't seem like a hardship. "That's pretty much what I had going."

"You were his mistress?"

"Well, we didn't have sex whenever he wanted. But I lived

in an apartment he paid for, I didn't work, he bought me clothes." I look at her. "I should've asked for an allowance."

"Do you love him?"

"Sure. That's what kept it from being tawdry." I finish my coffee. "I know you must've thought I led this exciting, sophisticated, romantic life..."

"Not really."

"But to tell the truth it was kind of—" I look at her. "What do you mean, *not really?*"

"You never sounded happy. Just sort of...empty."

"Empty? I wasn't empty. I had the shopping and the lunches and the...the...museums. It was full. *Very* full. I was settled, Maya—I had it all. A man I loved, a lifestyle, friends..."

Maya gives me a look.

"I had friends! People from Louis's work. I could've stayed with one of them, but it would have been—you know. More comfortable for everyone if they stick with Louis. Besides, I wanted you."

"Good. They can stick with Louis, I'll stick with you."

I feel sort of weepy, and Maya gets that pitying look in her eyes again, so I ruffle the newspaper and say, "You think I should get a place downtown, or on the Riviera?"

"You might not have a choice. How much can you pay?"

I look around her apartment. "What's the rent here?"

"Take a guess."

It's the second story of a cape in a nice neighborhood—the upper eastside. Hardwood floors, white walls, a big kitchen with tile counters. Maya's always had good taste, and the decor is mostly minimalist with Asian and Jewish accents thrown in. A Chinese lantern hangs over the dining room table and the mantel displays her mother's collection of antique menorahs. "I don't know," I say. "Nine hundred?"

Maya snorts. "Try sixteen."

"But it's only got one bedroom, and no dishwasher!"

"Dishwashers are two hundred a month extra."

"Oh. Well..." I don't know how to tell her, but she's been had. I bet this was the only place they looked at. Not everyone is good at this kind of thing.

"You'll find something," she says, and hands me a set of keys. "Use my car. Brad and I are sharing. You want to come shopping?"

I brighten. "Shopping?"

"Groceries, Elle," she says, laughing. "Then I have to stop by the bar."

"Oh. No. I should start the apartment hunt."

"Back in a few hours, then." She closes the door behind her, and I have a brainstorm: I'm gonna find the perfect apartment before she gets back. This is my new life, this is the New Elle—if Oprah can buy a fifty-million-dollar house without breaking a sweat, I can find an apartment in the time it takes Maya to buy detergent and cottage cheese.

I'm into the last ten minutes of Davey and Goliath when a key turns in the front door. I hit the off button on the remote a moment before Maya enters. I wish she'd come later. Goliath had disobeyed Davey, and I'm pretty sure he had a lesson coming.

Maya glances at the TV. "What were you watching?"

"Mmm? Oh, the news."

"What's going on?"

"Lot's of...bad stuff. The usual. You're back quick."

"I've been gone four hours, Elle."

"Well, I'm going to look at an apartment." I point to the classifieds crumpled on the table. "There's an open house, at one o'clock."

She checks her watch. "It's twenty after, sweetie."

So I lolled around watching Davey and Goliath reruns and missed an open house. So what? It's only Sunday. I've been in California less than twenty-four hours. I'm supposed to have accomplished something by now?

It's not like I don't have goals. Of course, I have goals. They are, after much soul-searching:

Apartment.
Car.
Job.
Man.

And, of course, the complete obliteration of Iowa, by Act of God, Hanta Virus or Crème Brûlée. I'm not particular.

I have assets as well as goals, by the way. I got $1,100 for my Vera Wang wedding dress. Was going to sell it on eBay, but began weeping when I wrote the header: Vera Wang Wedding Dress: Never Worn. Sold it to a local wedding boutique, instead, for their first offer. I would have talked them up, but it cost Louis $4,800, and I wanted him to suffer. If he ever learns how cheap I sold it for, I mean. Which he won't.

So $1,100 plus the roughly $4,000 in our household account, which was by all rights mine. Plus the triple-wick candle and instant ear thermometer, and so on.

I'm flush. A single girl in Santa Barbara with five grand and change. It's a monster stack of cash, burning a hole. The future lies before me, full of abundant promise and happy surprises, like an endless sale rack at Barneys.

chapter 4

Monday. Would prefer to remain wallowing in self-pity, comforting myself with treacley *Facts of Life* reruns and family-size pizzas, but I'm afraid to appear as encroaching houseguest. Normally, I'd go shopping to kill time, but I need to conserve my monster stack of cash—my credit card companies have all fallen victim to some sort of computer virus. Technology. Just goes to show you.

I muster myself into a feel-good outfit and head downtown. Window shopping is just as satisfying as buying.

Except Santa Barbara didn't used to be such a retail Mecca. When I was growing up, there were three local boutiques, the best of which specialized in sequins and appliqué. Now there's Nordstrom, Bebe, Aveda and Banana, plus a Gap and Limited for when you need a single strap tank for the week that it's in. Across the street is Bryan Lee (*très* L.A.), and down toward the beach are vintage shops catering to girls half my age—but I still manage to find a YSL suit I can squeeze into.

Fleeing temptation, I escape into the newish Borders Books, grab a *Vogue* and settle into a purple velvet chair.

A feature on Antonio Banderas takes a while to get through—kept having to pause and take deep breaths. Maybe my new man should be Latino. There are lots of Latinos in Santa Barbara. Suspect they are good family men, too.

I turn to the last page, "The Ten Best Satchels in America," and compare them to my ratty old Coach tote. Everyone else is carrying satchels this year. Not tatty ancient totes. I want *Vogue*'s number one pick—the Fendi. It's only $1,650. I wonder how much I'll get paid at my new job. Louis billed three hundred an hour, last I checked, which was years ago. Surely I'll make enough to afford a simple handbag.

I return *Vogue* to the rack and grab *Cosmopolitan*. I haven't read *Cosmo* since college, but I'm single now. This month promises "A Dating Diary," "How to Perfect Your Stripping Skills on Virtual Boy-Toys" and some advice I could really use: "Land That Man, Ace Your Job and Look Your Sexiest Ever."

Standing in the check-out line, I read "Ten Girlfriend Goof-ups" and discover I've girlfriend goofed in every way. I could have kept Louis if I'd cooked hearty dinners, wore sexy underwear, feigned interest in his work and allowed him time "in his cave."

"I can help who's next," the cashier calls. He's California cute, with dark hair and a tan. That's one thing about Santa Barbara—it's packed with beautiful people. Dumb, but beautiful. I know. I grew up here.

"Do you have a girlfriend?" I ask Surfer Boy as I hand him the magazine.

"Uh, yeah." He looks nervous. "That'll be $3.79."

I dig in my repellent, prehistoric, possibly-infectious Coach tote for my wallet. "I'm doing a survey. Does she cook you hearty dinners?"

"She makes pot roast sometimes."

"Uh-huh." I give him a five. "Does she wear sexy underwear?"

His eyes light up.

"Give you time in your cave?" I ask.

"Huh?"

"I don't get that one either. You think you'll ever break up with her?"

He doesn't hesitate. "No doubt."

See? *Cosmo* is wrong. All the peek-a-boo bras in the world wouldn't have saved me and Louis. Which means it's not my fault. It'd be Louis's fault, but he's clueless. That only leaves one person: The Iowan Floozy. I consider throwing *Cosmo* in the trash, punishment for misinformation, but decide against. Floozy probably has perfect stripping skills. I need a virtual refresher.

chapter 5

A five-day crying binge, interrupted briefly with bouts of piggery and compulsive TV watching, and I'm ready to look at apartments.

I make several appointments for walk-throughs, feeling like the heroine of my own Lifetime Television movie. Against all odds—puffy eyes, bloated ankles, damaged brain cells—Elle Medina finds herself an apartment. But can she find love amid the rubble?

No. But she can sure find rubble. Thirteen apartment impossibilities later, and I'm back where I started.

"You wouldn't believe these places," I tell Maya one evening before she heads to work. We're in the bathroom. I'm sitting on the toilet, downing a beer. She's applying makeup.

"Like what?" she asks.

"Like a shack, with a toaster oven for a kitchen, mildew

in the bath and heinous red carpet. Guess what they're asking."

She shrugs. I tell her she needs more eyeliner.

"I don't know," she says. "$700?"

"No, they want...well yeah—$700. It's insane. Remember that set we built for the school play?"

"We didn't build a set. We built one doorway."

"That doorway was architecturally sounder than this place. I'd pay $700 a month for that doorway and be getting a better deal."

"It was a nice doorway."

"Then I saw a fantastic place in Hope Ranch."

"Oh?" She lifts a brow. Hope Ranch is home to Santa Barbara's nouveau riche—the old riche live with Oprah, in Montecito.

"A guest house. Beautiful white couches. Landlady wearing JP Tods. The ad was a misprint—they want $2,600 a month. Then there's the place that smelled like cat pee, and the one where I'd have bathroom privileges. Since when is sharing a bathroom with two teenage boys a privilege? And all the places that won't rent to you if you're unemployed—which I'm not, I just don't happen to have a job. And the places that won't accept dogs and the—"

"You don't have a dog."

"Not yet."

"Ellie..." she says, washing her hands and leaving the bathroom.

"Well, how can they hold my future dog against me, but not give me credit for my future job?" I follow her to the front door. "Seriously, I don't think I can find a place." I point to the mess I've made of her living room. "I may be permanently ensconced."

She looks slightly alarmed. Possibly at my vocabulary. "Maybe you need a roommate. Then you could afford something better."

"I don't know, living with a stranger. It's too bad you don't have an extra bedroom here."

"Yeah," she says, as she closes the front door behind her. "Too bad."

That evening, with Maya at the bar and Perfect Brad working late, I decide to clean their apartment. Because I'm a good houseguest. Plus, if I clean I can snoop in their drawers.

I do the kitchen before the bedroom, to establish my noble intentions. But washing dishes by hand always makes me think. If my world had flashback wiggles like in old movies, they'd pop up every time I did dishes by hand.

I wasn't flashing back to falling in love with Louis: walking hand-in-hand on a cherry-blossomed path at the Jefferson Memorial, going on our first real date to Emily's, greeting him in an apron and stilettos after he took the Bar (See? I *used* to be a *Cosmo* girl!). No, I was thinking of that shack-landlady, her hollow voice reverberating in my memory, "first, last and security...first, last and security." And she wasn't the only one, it seems everyone requires obscene amounts of money before they let you move in. I'm not sure my monster stack is going to cover first and last...and security? I wish.

I dry my hands and call my mother.

"Hi, it's me," I say, when she picks up.

"Me who?"

"Me, your daughter, Mom." She never recognizes my voice. Sometimes I make her guess who it is. She got it right on the first try, once.

"Elle, thank God. I was worried. I got your message. I don't understand. I called yesterday and Louis told me you'd already left. Santa Barbara? You'll be back before the wedding, won't you? I've already made my plane reservations. I still don't—"

"Mom."

"—know what I'm going to do about the hotel. The cheapest one you suggested charges one-fifty a night! That's too expensive. Why can't I stay with—"

"Mom—"

"—you and Louis. I won't be in the way. You know the store takes every spare penny, and I—"

"Mom! Listen to me."

"I *am* listening, darling. What do you think I'm doing?"

"Louis and I broke up."

"Yes, that's what he said. But I already made my plane reservations. The tickets, darling—they're nonrefundable. I told the girl—"

"Mom—focus, please!"

"Well, you and Louis have broken up before." Which is utterly untrue. She thinks that because we weren't speaking after the Mizrahi couture incident, we were broken up. "It's only pre-wedding jitters. You'll just have to go back and make up."

"It's a little late for that. He married someone else."

"He did *what?*"

"An Iowan."

"He married an Iowan? When did he—how did he?" She pauses for a fraction of a second, which means she is truly shocked. "Well, are you gonna kick her ass back to the corn fields?"

Mom watches a lot of daytime TV. I often wonder what her New Age customers would think if they knew. She owns a crystal and herb shop in Sedona—she moved there when I went to college. She gives off an Earth Mama vibe, and a lot of her customers come in to ask for advice. Little do they know that the wise and evolved spirits she's channeling are Montel Williams and Jerry Springer.

"Mom, I haven't even met her."

"Well, maybe you should. I was watching *Ricki Lake* this morning—you know she's lost weight again—and there was a woman on who'd never confronted her mother when she stole her brother's girlfriend…"

And she's off. Why do I bother? She always makes me feel like this. Like the people on *Judge Judy* are more important than me. I don't know why I called, why I—oh, right. Security. As in deposit. She marks up those crystals four hundred percent.

"Mom! Louis dumped me, and I'm living on Maya's couch, and I don't have an apartment or a job or a car or anything. I don't care about intergenerational love triangles."

I must sound desperate, because she actually responds. "Oh, Elle, honey. You should have come here, where I could take care of you."

I feel my eyes water. "Yeah, I sh-should have..."

"I would've made you scalloped potatoes and Boston cream pie."

I wipe my nose with the wet dishcloth. "B-better than chicken soup."

"Hop on the next plane, darling. The red rocks here cure everything. Broken hearts included."

She sounds so sympathetic, I'm almost tempted. Cake and sympathy and reversion to childhood. But it wouldn't be like that. Ten minutes after I got there, everyone would know it was my fault that Louis married someone else. Which it *wasn't*. And she'd rope me into her shop for horoscopes and palm reading; she decided when I was eleven that I had the Gift, even though I always thought Capricorn was the bull.

"In fact, I wrote a letter about that to Oprah," she says. "She should do her show from here. In Sedona. For the healing energy. It's a nexus, Elle—and Oprah's a wise woman, like the wise women of old, imagine if she tapped into the—"

"Mom!" I cut in. "I need to borrow some money."

Silence.

"I didn't realize how expensive things are, when you don't have any money. And my credit cards...well, Louis was going to pay them off after the wedding. But now..."

"Are you in trouble with credit again?"

"I am not in trouble!" And I'm not. Because I've moved. How are they gonna find me in Santa Barbara? "I just need a little cash."

"You're welcome to stay with me," she says. "The café next door is looking for a busboy."

"Thanks, Mom. But couldn't you at least…"

"Why don't you try your father?"

Bad sign. She never mentions him. Her friends in Arizona think I was an immaculate conception.

"You know how Dad is…"

"I do know. I saw a segment on *Jerry Springer* about deadbeat dads, and just because your father never missed a payment doesn't mean he's not a deadbeat. There was this man, a yacht repairman, something with yachts, maybe a designer, I don't know, and he had seven kids—well his wife did, but he said only one of them was his—but *she* said at least four of them—"

I hang up, mid-story. That's just ducky.

chapter 6

So crossing off "apartment" on my little list isn't so easy. But a car's a car. Unless the license plate says 666 or there are dismembered body parts in the trunk, you get what you pay for. Besides, I think Maya's getting a little sick of carting Brad to work every day.

I've decided a Passat is the way to express my new self. Elegant, but not flashy. High-quality, but not ostentatious. That's the New Elle.

The VW dealership is downtown, and it's where I make my first new Santa Barbara friend. Bob, the car salesman. He's instantly smitten with me. I can always tell. And truth is, he's not bad. I mean, he's a used car salesman, which is hardly a Prince Charming job. But he's tall enough, and has a good smile and nice eyes. I fill out a form—which, I notice him noticing, includes my home phone.

I decide that when he calls, I'll tell him I just want to be friends. Because that's the sort of thing the New Elle does. No reason to jump into a relationship with the first cute-ish guy to come around.

I tell Bob I'll settle for the bottom-of-the-line GLS model, but he says everyone who bought one wishes they spent a little more for the GLX.

Well! I love it when a salesperson gives you their personal opinion. It means they like you. We start in a Black Magic GLX with black velour interior. A quick drive, and Bob and I know it is too masculine for me, so we take the Mojave Beige with beige velour interior for a cruise to the beach.

"You look good in it, Elle," Bob says.

"It feels a little soft," I say. "Like I'm a soccer mom, Bob." Bob. *Bob.* It's a funny syllable.

I'm beginning to wonder if I'll be happy with a Passat, when I see it across the lot. Silver. Curvy. Beautiful.

"That's the W8," Bob says. "Top of the line. Eight cylinder engine, leather interior, sunroof, five-CD changer..."

The minute I sit in it, I know. I'm like Goldilocks. This one is *just* right.

It's late, and the dealership is closing, so I give Bob my information and he promises me he'll put a deal together tomorrow morning. He smiles, and I mentally rehearse: *I really like you, Bob, but I just want to be friends.*

When I get back to Maya's I check my little list:

Apartment. Not living in moss-walled shack or sharing toilet with teenage boys, so I'm ahead of the game.

Man. Will reject Bob with grace and tact. Apparently the streets of Santa Barbara are paved with eligible bachelors.

Car. Gorgeous Silver Passat! Will be stunning with new, employed-Elle wardrobe, and new, Antonio-Banderas-looking boy toy. It's a W8, too. I like the sound of that, but must remember to ask Bob what it stands for.

Job.

Job.

Job…

The problem with my employment history is I have none. My mom sold real estate while I was growing up, and made tons of money, so I never got an after-school gig. It wasn't until she bought her vitamin-and-runes store that she started getting tight. Plus, my dad sent her money for my upkeep when I was a minor. Now I'm a major, and I've never had a job.

Well, there was a brief period the summer after my second year at Georgetown. My roommate, Angela, convinced me it would be fun to join the team at the Colonial Williamsburg Foundation in Virginia. I got hired as Martha Washington in a historical reenactment, while Angela got stuck with wench duty at one of the taverns. After two weeks, the administrators decided the public preferred a white-haired Martha to a young bride, and I was ousted by a retired flight attendant. I was a better Martha, though. At least I refrained from pointing out the emergency exits to George. Angela kept wenching while I slunk back to Washington. That's when I moved in with Louis. I spent the rest of the summer womanning phones for EMILY's List, but that was volunteering, not employment.

I'm home alone, halfheartedly scanning the want ads, when it hits me: What I need is a starter job. Preferably a starter job that pays well. And that's not too demanding. Like, say, being a bartender. The neat thing is, I have this friend who owns a bar. Maya *has* to hire me, right?

"I need help," I say when Maya answers the phone at the bar.

"What? The remote stopped working?"

"No, it works fine." I click off *Entertainment Tonight.*

"So what's the problem?"

"This job-hunt thing…"

"Yeah?"

"I don't quite know how it works."

"Oh. What part don't you understand?"

"Um…" I look at the paper. "Take this one, for instance. Development Director wanted for World of Goods, a nonprofit organization dedicated to sending relief supplies to countries in need. Qualified candidates will have demonstrated experience managing others, working with board members, facilitating meetings, monitoring budgets and in all aspects of development." I give Maya a moment to take it in. "What is *development,* exactly? Developing what?"

"It means fund-raising."

"How hard can that be? It's just asking for money. I did that all the time with Louis. It pays forty thousand a year. And it's in tune with my values."

"Louis ever find out how much of his money you were giving to the ASPCA and NOW?"

"Not yet—pledge cards don't come 'til the end of the month. Anyway, World of Goods also gives you a housing stipend."

"I suppose that's what attracted you."

"A little," I admit.

"They offer a company car, too? That, a company charge card and a company boyfriend, and you'd be able to cross everything off your list."

I make a rude noise.

"Forget anything with the word 'director' in it, Elle. Do you know how to type?"

"I know all the letters are on the keyboard and you push them to make words."

"How did you get through college?"

"Hunting, pecking and oral presentations."

"So secretarial, and basically all office work, is out. What else appeals?"

Ah, now we're getting somewhere. "What I need is something that uses my natural charm and vivacity. Dealing with people, you know, in a sort of social setting."

"Prostitution won't work for you, Elle—you'd hate the dress code."

"I don't know," I say. "I have demonstrated experience as a mistress."

"Don't even start. Seriously. What do you like?"

I decide against saying alcohol, and instead go for the real truth. "I like shoes. Maybe I could design shoes."

Maya doesn't say anything.

"I like people. And animals. You know how I like animals. Maybe I could be a vet or something."

"You know who became a vet?" she says. "Anna Van der Water."

"Yuck!" Anna Van der Water is this creepy girl we knew in high school. She wore cheap plastic barrettes in her hair—before Drew Barrymore made it cool—and her calves were bigger than her thighs. "Anna Van der Water, a vet. You know, I think maybe she was smarter than me."

"I. Smarter than I. And are you kidding?" Maya says, loyal to the end. "Twice as smart."

I hear glasses clinking at the bar, and am wondering how to get the conversation moving in a maybe-you-can-work-here direction when she says, "Listen, why don't you come down and have a drink. My treat."

See? A little patience, and it falls into your lap. "I'm kind of busy," I say. I don't want to sound desperate.

"Elle," she says.

"Be there in twenty minutes."

The bar's located a block off State Street on one of the lower downtown side streets. There are no front windows, just a closed door with the name of the place in neon over it.

Shika.

The bar has never done well, and I blame the name. Well, it's one of many reasons. It means "drunk" in Yiddish, I guess, which is Mr. Goldman's little joke. (He once explained it's actually "shiker," not "shika," but he went phonetical. I like Mr. Goldman.) Problem is Shika looks Japanese, and people find it disconcerting when they expect saké and rice-paper screens, but get photos of old Jews and every conceivable flavor of schnapps.

Inside, two men perch at the bar. Mr. Goldman is one of them, and the other is a man a decade older, dressed to kill. Other than them, and Maya behind the bar, the place is empty.

Maya offers me a margarita as I give Mr. Goldman a hug. He doesn't look good—his health has been bad since Maya's mom died—but it's still good to see him. As Maya mixes the margarita, we chat about my return to Santa Barbara, and my apartment and job hunt. I keep waiting for Maya to jump in and explain that I'll be working at the bar, but she plays it coy.

Mr. Goldman and I cover the weather in Santa Barbara vs. D.C., and our conversation dwindles to nothing. So I turn to Maya. "I was thinking about my career. I think I'd be good in a service-industry-type position."

She looks skeptical. "You're more served than serving, Elle."

"I've served!" I protest. "Does the name Martha Washington mean nothing to you?"

Maya explains my previous employment to her father and the other man, including some details I don't remember telling her, and I realize maybe this isn't the best time to discuss the bartending job.

"How about this?" I say. "I'll start my own magazine, like Oprah. I'll call it *E*."

"Like the *Entertainment* network?"

"Oh, no. Well, I can't call it *Elle*." This stumps me. The best thing about the magazine idea is calling it *E*. I like the letter *E*. Plus, it has the bonus benefit of standing for e-mail and other electronic stuff: very *now.* "How about *L*—just the letter *L.*"

Maya makes the "*L* is for Loser" sign on her forehead.

Enough said.

"Want another margarita?" she asks.

I look down, mine is somehow empty. I have a flash of genius. "Let me make it," I say. "I'm a whiz with blended drinks."

"I usually just mix them," she says.

"See that's where you're wrong. Where's the blender?" I eagerly pop behind the bar.

All I want to say is: I *know* the top was closed firmly before I turned the blender to pureé. Must have been some kind of malfunction. Anyway, it was just a couple ice cubes and strawberries. And Maya *was* standing too close. A pity she was wearing white, that's all.

chapter 7

The next day, desperate for an apartment, Maya (who's in an uncharacteristic tizzy: probably fighting with Perfect Brad) persuades me to relax my standards and see a place in... *Goleta*. The ad promises a "one bedroom charming garden paradise with fourteen-foot ceilings," and the price is too good to dismiss—$650 a month.

"But it's *Goleta!*" I wail. A suburb fifteen minutes north of Santa Barbara, teeming with strip malls and big box stores.

"There are nice parts of Goleta," Maya says.

"Where?"

"People like it there," she replies, vaguely.

"Who?"

"Oh, stop being such a snob, Elle, and look at the place."

Well, it does say "garden paradise." I will be the consummate country party hostess. Fabulous friends, whom I've yet to meet, will escape the city late Friday night to my oasis in Goleta. I'll serve negronis and martinis—anything but margaritas—and prepare fabulous fresh meals from my kitchen garden. Olive trees and lavender will dot the rolling hills, and all for the pittance of $650 a month!

By the time I arrive at the house, I've persuaded myself that I'm on my way to Provence. I'll be garden fabulous.

Then I turn into the dirt driveway. Dust billows into the car, and through watery eyes, I see the house. Bluish, with water marks streaming from the windows, giving it the appearance of a weeping cartoon house.

I put the car in Reverse, and a man bangs my hood in greeting.

He has long hair and a longer beard, à la ZZ Top. He wears black jeans on his stick-skinny legs, over which is an enormous belly not quite covered by a tank top.

"Here about the apartment, right?" he says. "It's around back."

I want to ask what happened. I want to ask why his house is crying. I want to ask if he needs help, if there's anyone I should call. Instead, I obediently follow him toward the backyard.

ZZ stops in the garage. The concrete floor is partially covered with bronze carpeting—a deep, oil-stained shag. The walls are unfinished, revealing two-by-fours and assorted wires and pipes.

"So," he says. "Any questions?"

"Well, one," I say. "Where's the apartment?"

"You're standing in it." At least ZZ had not lied in the ad. The ceilings are indeed fourteen feet high.

I'm describing my garage-for-rent experience at ZZ's to Perfect Brad and Maya, only slightly crowing that I was right about Goleta, when the phone rings. Maya answers. "For you," she says, a little incredulous.

My very first call in Santa Barbara! Possibly a job offer,

though I haven't actually applied for anything yet. Still, stranger things have happened.

"Hi, Elle. This is Bob. From the Volkswagen dealership?"

"Bob! Hi! How are you?" Oops, don't want to be too nice. Think *just friends.* "I mean, um, hello."

"Well, I ran your credit report and you don't qualify for the Passat W8."

"Oh, no." I'm not too surprised, though. I mean, I do have *some* concept of reality. "We'll have to settle for the GLX, then? A softer image isn't such a bad thing."

"Not the GLX."

"Oh. The GLS?"

"Not even close."

"Um…a Jetta?"

"No."

"A Bug? They're pretty cute. And I don't need four doors. After all, I can only use one at a time!" I laugh in a bright and charming fashion, and notice Maya and Brad watching me as if I am a seven-car pile-up.

"Nope."

"How about an, um…like a Focus or that other one. The Echo?"

"Those aren't even VWs."

"Right. VWs. Well, a Golf?"

"Not even a used Golf."

"So…?"

"So I told you I'd call. I called."

"I see. Yes. Thanks for calling. And is there, um, anything else you want to ask?" Because I may not qualify for a car, but I know when a man's interested.

"Actually, there is." His voice becomes a little warmer.

I smile and give Maya a look. The kind of look that says, *Here we go again, I'm gonna let another one down easy.* For some reason, Maya responds by passing me a box of Kleenex.

"Don't be shy," I say. "Ask away."

"If you have any friends who can actually afford a car, would you give them my name?"

"Oh, sure." I wait for it, and wait for it... *I like you too, Bob, but I think it's best if we try being friends, first. Dinner where? Piatti? In Montecito? Well, if you insist...*

"Well, good speaking with you," he says, and hangs up.

I try to be bright and charming as the dial-tone sounds. "That's very flattering," I say. "And you seem like a really nice guy. But I don't think so, thanks."

I pretend to listen as Maya gives Brad a happy-couple signal that sends him running to the safety of their bedroom. She takes the phone from my hand, hangs up and hugs me tight. I reach for the Kleenex.

chapter 8

I'm never going to be Oprah until I take control. I have to stop coasting and make it happen.

So this morning, I'm awake at 7:00. I roll out of bed. Take a shower. Fix myself. Choose an outfit in record time. Make coffee. Buy the paper, and sit down, pen in hand, determined to find a job. Because finding an apartment in Santa Barbara is clearly impossible, and we Highly Efficient people don't waste time on clear impossibilities.

I circle an ad for a Mental Health Worker and one for a Literacy Volunteer, and glance at the clock. It's 11:45.

Almost noon! I woke up *five hours* ago. I swear I did nothing more than the above listed. I didn't even turn on the TV. Not once. And five hours have passed? I'm temporally challenged. It's chronological-ADD or something. Am I having blackouts? Do I sit, slack-jawed, staring at walls? In five hours, Oprah could have launched ten books to the bestseller lists, and all I've done is shower and dress.

So I stop coasting. I take control. And two normal hours later, I'm back. I didn't launch a single book to the bestseller list, but I did spend $389 on a cashmere throw and fancy tin dog bowls.

I don't want to talk about it.

I hide the bags behind the couch so Maya won't scold me, and bury the now, uh, *modified* bowls deep in my luggage. Take an extended nap, dream of Louis scolding me for wasting postage and wake cranky. Why is everything suddenly so hard? It's not as if I have such high hopes. I want a non-plywood apartment, a job that doesn't require I pee into a cup, a running car and—eventually, though I'm rethinking this one—an adequate man. And some gorgeous new things. And a small thermonuclear device for Iowa.

Is that too much to ask? I watch TV, I read the magazines. Women everywhere are living *my* life. They have jobs like "public relations coordinator" and "fashion features editor." Their Upper East Side apartments have huge windows overlooking Central Park, and they all stopped wearing pashminas two weeks before a certain person finally bought hers.

I pull the covers to my chin and try to work myself into a genuine clinical depression. Then it'd be a brain chemistry thing, and I could courageously fight it—unable to leave the apartment, waited on hand-and-foot, but admired by all. They'd probably profile me in the *Santa Barbara News-Press,* and the local network affiliate would pick up the story.

In two minutes, the daydream fades and I'm bored feigning depression. Possibly it's more fun with an audience. My problem is, I'm surface-y. Not shallow, I didn't say that. I'm quite deep, actually. It's just that I like the surfaces of things. Surfaces are important to me. And depression's not really a surface affliction. You have to burrow deep into your head for a good depression.

I'd rather burrow into the Neiman Marcus catalog. Which I do. And after an hour, I magically feel better.

My problem, I realize, is I'm not cut out to be Sarah Jessica in *Sex and the City* although I do have similar hair, if not darker and longer. I don't need a Manhattan loft and sleek, underfed fashion-friends. I'm more Sandra Bullock, small-town-girl-makes-good. I can work as a bus driver or subway-token clerk, and it'll be okay. Except not a bus driver or a subway-token clerk, because those are disease-ridden careers, but you know what I mean.

Cheered, I take a hot shower and toss on a Sandra Bullock, small-town-girl-makes-good outfit, and head for Shika. Things happen in bars.

Things don't happen in Shika. Maya's behind the counter, the sharp-dressed old man is perched on a stool. A middle-aged couple is leaving as I enter, and that is that.

"Oh, Elle," Maya says. "I'm glad you're here."

It's been a few days since I've heard Maya say anything other than: "How's the apartment hunt? Job?" I perk up at this lavish greeting and tell her how pleased I am to be here.

"Do me a favor," she says. "Watch the bar? I've gotta go to the bank."

"The bank?" I'm honestly baffled. Do they actually make money here? "Why?"

"The bank's a place you put money you're not spending, Elle. I'll explain later."

"Ha-ha," I say, in my razor-sharp witty way. "So just…watch the bar?"

"Stay away from the blender."

"But I mean—what if someone asks for a Slippery Nipple on the Beach or something?"

Maya looks around the empty bar. "Monty's good for a while. There's a group that comes in, but usually not 'til later."

"A group?"

"Don't look so surprised. They're a bunch of people Monty knows. Just make sure nobody steals the—" she looks around trying to decide what someone might steal "—walls." She waves a bank pouch at me, says something about a night deposit, and heads for the door.

I realize this is my job interview. Maya won't make me actually *apply* for the job, so what does she do? Casually makes a night drop, leaving me in charge!

"It's all under control," I tell her confidently, heading behind the bar.

Maya hesitates at the door, an unreadable expression on her face.

I wave brightly, and she sort of squares her shoulders and leaves.

I slip behind the bar and glance at the sharp-dressed man sipping his drink. He's wearing a beige linen suit with a light-blue silk tie. It's rare to see a man so nattily dressed in Santa Barbara. Most of them slouch around, subcasual in stained T-shirts and shorts.

"Need a refill?" I ask.

We both assess his drink. It's seven-eighths full.

"Not quite," he says.

Pretending to be cleaning, I forage through the cabinets under the bar. Nothing of note, except a half-eaten bag of Fritos. I bet Mr. Sharp-Dresser would like some Fritos. I pour them into a small bowl and carefully set them in front of him.

I smile and gesture at the Fritos, like I've presented him with foie gras. Under my steely eye, he deigns to take a chip, and pops it into his mouth. Takes a single bite, and stops, Frito suspended midchew.

"What?" I say. "They're better than popcorn."

He shakes his head.

I try a chip. It has the consistency of moist cardboard. I choke it down. "Sorry. This is my first night."

He swallows and tells me not to worry—he needs the

fiber. He says he's Monty, and I tell him I'm Elle, and I'm starting the bartendress chatter when two men enter the bar.

One is paunchy, with dark hair and laugh-lines around his eyes. Sort of an approachable, teddy bear of a man. The other is tall, trim and would be sexy-handsome if he weren't a redhead. Red hair is silly on men. I mean, he looks good, walking toward Monty, a white button-down over blue jeans. But red hair? The other guy, the teddy bear, he doesn't walk so well, but he looks the sort who'd remember to put the seat down.

"You joining us tonight, Monty?" the redhead asks.

"Not tonight," Monty says. "My ulcer's bad enough."

"Ulcer?" the teddy bear says. "There's only one thing to do about the ulcer, and that's—Fritos?"

"Help yourself," Monty says, and looks to see if I'm going to object.

"Umm…" I say.

"Not the ulcer theory again," the redhead says.

"It's not a *theory,*" Teddy bear says as they move to the large booth in the corner.

"Should I see if they want drinks?" I ask Monty, to cover my embarrassment about the stale Fritos.

"Wait 'til others show up," he tells me. "Or they'll come to the bar."

"I know stale, baby, and these are not stale." Teddy bear's voice easily carries to the bar. "These are fresh. Factory fresh."

"Fresh from the factory that makes stale Fritos."

The teddy bear gets louder. "They're not stale!" He grabs a handful, shoves them in his mouth.

The redhead cringes. "Okay, okay. Because you ate them, that proves they're not stale."

"Actually, they are stale," I say, from across the room. "Monty and I both thought so. Three to one. Stale."

Teddy bear shakes his head, but can't speak for all the chewing he's doing.

"Wisdom, beauty and common sense," the redhead says, indicating Monty, me and himself in turn. "All say they're stale. Doesn't that prove it?"

I think: I'm *beauty!*

The teddy bear manages to swallow; beaten, but unbowed. "How long you think stale Fritos stay in your colon?"

"Jesus, Neil."

"Not as long as maraschino cherries," Neil says. "But way longer than beef jerky."

The redhead gives me a look, and smiles. And red hair isn't that bad, actually. Plenty of attractive men have red hair. Howdy Doody. Carrot Top. I return the smile, and the door opens again.

Three men and a woman enter and head for the booth with Neil and the redhead. I watch as they sit, wondering if I should wait on them. What would Maya do? Will they want margaritas?

"Don't worry," Monty says. "One of them will come to the bar."

And as if summoned, the redhead is here.

"Two IPAs," he says, and I even know an IPA is a kind of beer. "And two Newcastle Browns."

"Great!" I say, dripping with relief that I haven't been asked to make a Grateful Dead, Hold the Jerry, or something.

"And a Manhattan and a Cosmopolitan."

"A Manhattan?" I grab a hank of hair and tug, keeping the smile pasted on my face. "I love Manhattans. Big Manhattan drinker."

His gray eyes crinkle. They clash with his hair. "If you don't know how to make a Manhattan, that's okay. I'll just have—"

"Of *course* I know! I mean, what kind of bartender doesn't know how to make a Manhattan?" I've never heard of a Manhattan. "You want that…on the rocks?"

"On the rocks, yeah." He looks suspicious. "Tell me—what, exactly, do you put in your Manhattans?"

"Liquor. The hard stuff."

He smiles, and looks at me, and looks like he likes looking. And I like that he looks like he likes looking, and I hope that's what I look like.

I realize he just asked something that I didn't hear over the sound of my ovaries chiming like eager little bells. "The what?"

"The primary liquor. The backbone of the drink. The Broadway of the Manhattan."

"Um… Gin?"

He starts to shake his head no.

"Right! That's a Chicago. I meant vodka." I get the look again and continue: "Vodka is in the Brooklyn. You sure you don't want a Brooklyn?"

The teddy bear interrupts with a bellow about Texas grapefruit being better than any other grapefruit, and the redhead says, "Maybe you should give me the beers first. Pacify the natives."

"Two IPAs and two Nukey Browns." The Newcastles are on tap, and I overpour one, but remember in the nick of time not to clean the drippage with my tongue. Though that's gotta be a great way to get men interested. The IPAs are in bottles—thank the God of beer—and I plop them down.

"I've changed my mind," he says. "I think I'll have a Cosmopolitan, too."

"Two Cosmopolitans—coming right up."

"And, of course, a Cosmopolitan has…"

"Vodka," I say, because I actually know, and wave airily. "And the rest."

He sort of cocks his head, grins and returns to the booth with the beers.

As soon as his back is turned, I lunge at Monty. "How do you make a Cosmo?"

"No idea. They're after my time. But a Manhattan is bourbon, bitters and sweet vermouth."

"Monty! You could have told me!"

"Don't look now," he says. He excuses himself and heads for the bathroom, and Redhead is at the bar again.

"Problem with the beer?" I ask.

He smiles. "Just waiting for the Cosmos."

"Won't be a second." I reach for the vodka—and there are six bottles, all different. I grab the closest, aware that Redhead is watching me and I've never mixed a drink other than Kahlua and milk in my life. I ease two martini glasses from the rack. So. Vodka, check. Martini glasses, check. And I'm stymied. "You know what?" I tell Redhead. "Why don't you sit down, and I'll bring them to your table?"

"That's all right."

"No, really."

"I don't mind," he says. "I like it here."

"No, really." I smile, baring my teeth.

He smiles, but doesn't move.

"Go sit down!" I bark.

He goes.

I turn toward the wall of liquor. Vodka, and...Schnapps? Cosmos are sort of pink, so I choose peach-flavored. And maybe brandy. That goes with everything, right? It's the basic black of liquors. There's a bottle on the top shelf that looks like brandy, all the way in back, like Maya's forgotten about it. I splash some into a silver shaker. Adjust until the color is right, add a couple of maraschinos, and ta da! Cosmos.

"Maya should be back any minute," Monty says, taking his seat and eyeing the drinks.

"Yes, she should," I say primly, and serve the drinks. One for Redhead, the other for the normal-haired woman with the tortoiseshell glasses. I hover nearby as they sip.

The woman gags. Redhead only coughs.

"A little stiff?" I ask. "That's how we like 'em, here at Shika."

"This isn't a Cosmopolitan," the woman says.

"Not entirely," Redhead agrees.

"Let me taste that." Neil grabs Redhead's drink and takes a slug. He shivers, a full-body expression of disgust. "That sure as shit *is* a Cosmo," he says, suppressing a secondary tremor. "Never tasted better."

"Have you ever *had* a Cosmopolitan?" the woman asks, and I'm just glad she's looking at Neil, not me.

"So what if I haven't?" he says. "That means I don't know one when I taste it? Let's say the first time you tasted a Cosmo, it was really a—I don't know, let's say it was a…"

"Manhattan," Redhead deadpans, flashing me a glance.

"Yeah, a Manhattan," Neil says. "So what you think is a Cosmo is really a Manhattan. That's epistemology, baby! The limits of knowledge in—"

"That's just crap," one of the extra men says.

"It's not *just* crap," the other extra man says. "It's utter crap."

Which sets Neil bellowing again. "Utter crap? I'll tell you what's utter crap! The fact that George W was *appointed* president—"

Maya bounces over from the front door, and they all greet her with great relief. "I see Elle got you started," she says. She smiles at them, and at me, and I feel I've been anointed. Then her gaze settles on my Cosmopolitans and her smile settles into a frown. "What are those?" she asks.

"Chicagos," Redhead says.

"Well, I *ordered* a Cosmopolitan," the woman says.

Maya looks at me.

"Cosmopolitans?" I say firmly.

"You don't know how to make Cosmos, Elle."

"They're pink."

"I'll make fresh ones." Maya takes the woman's glass, and reaches for Redhead's, but he stops her.

"I like it," he says. "It's unique." He looks at me. "Sweet."

"What are you talking about?" Neil the teddy bear says. "It's awful. You can't drink that. It's not even a Cosmo."

He's shouted down by a volley of derisive hoots. Redhead sips triumphantly, and winces.

I scurry back to the bar as Maya fixes two Cosmopolitans. As she puts the bottles away, she pauses over the brandy I've pulled from the top shelf. "What's this doing out?"

"Umm..."

"Tell me," she says, fixing me with a horrified glare. "Tell me you didn't use it in the Cosmopolitans."

"Well...it's not *all* I used."

"Elle, this is de Fussigny—it's a two-hundred-and-fifty-dollar bottle of cognac. It's sitting on the top shelf so nobody opens it." She doesn't look mad so much as really disappointed.

"I'll pay for it," I say, wanting to shrink into nothing. "You know I have that monster stack of cash."

"It doesn't matter," she says, though I know it does. "We might as well drink it now. You want a glass?" She pulls out some brandy snifters.

"I'll have a glass," Monty says.

"You have to pay for it," I snap. "It's expensive."

"Elle," Maya warns.

But Monty laughs. "How much?"

"Fifty bucks. It's d'Fussy. Worth every penny."

"Ellie," Maya says.

"Hit me up," Monty says, and lays a crisp hundred on the bar. "And one for the lady." Meaning me. He's now, officially, my idol.

"I'll take a glass, too," this lovely, deep voice says from three inches behind me, and Redhead is there for his Cosmos.

"Just one?" I say. "What about your friends?"

"Don't push your luck," he says, and takes the drinks back to his table.

Maya looks harried. "It's not worth fifty dollars a glass. I can't charge—"

"Oh, shush," I say, and clink my glass with Monty's. Maya snorts—trying not to laugh—and clinks her glass and we drink.

From the booth, Neil the teddy bear bellows something

about us all living in a pentarchy while getting redder and redder in the face.

"What's the deal with him?" I say. "Cute, but kind of argumentative."

"That's what they're here for." Maya sips her cognac. "Neil has a problem with rage. His wife said she'd leave him if he didn't deal with it. He wasn't beating her or anything, she was just sick of all the yelling. So he started this club. They come every Tuesday night and argue."

"Does it work?" I ask. "Is he less rageful?"

"I don't know," Maya says. "I'm afraid to ask him."

Maybe it's the cognac, but we all laugh, and Maya tells me to watch the bar again for a sec, while she runs out back.

I panic. "No! Don't leave me—I'm not ready!"

She ignores me, so I take my post and consider wiping the bar until it shines, but decide it isn't worth the effort. Shika needs major renovation before cleaning will make it look any better. The booths are brown vinyl, the walls are painted dirty beige. The yellowing photographs of the Lower East Side of New York are fun, but better suited to a funky deli than a happening bar.

There are some good architectural details, though. The floor is hardwood, worn to a soft golden honey color. The ceilings are taller even than ZZ's garage in Goleta, there are four skylights half-hidden by dingy fluorescent lighting fixtures and the bar itself is a great old art deco piece.

I happen to glance toward Redhead—only because I'm thinking we can paint the bathrooms a lovely deep red, and want to remember what shade of red I *don't* like—and notice that he's doing what I'm doing. Looking around the room, his eyebrows raising slightly at the good bits, and lowering at the ratty booths and walls. I wouldn't mind renovating *him*. Shaving his head would be a first step, and—he catches me staring.

I'm not usually so weepy and pathetic. It's the wedding, the engagement, Louis. Being left at the altar does things to your self-esteem. Plus, starting from scratch, back in the town where you went to high school—and realizing that you've accomplished nothing since then, except maybe what you *thought* was a nice, committed, six-year relationship, and even that fell apart, and there's a man who catches you staring and he's lovely except for being a ginger freak-head, and you don't know what you want and barely know who you are, and what if he likes you and expects to see you naked, and dating is supposed to be this utter nightmare and you don't know—

Long story short: I run away. I am a blur, fleeing out the front door.

I hear Maya's voice say, "Elle?" but I don't slow down. I am gone.

Wish I'd waited one more second, though. To see which direction his eyebrows went when he looked at me.

chapter 9

Perfect Brad comes home at ten. He helps with my résumé. We finish at 10:07.

The next morning, memorizing sections A through D of the newspaper and putting off the classifieds as long as possible, I find this headline: Prize-Winning Bitch Missing.

I ponder the gratuitous use of the word bitch. You hear it on *Friends* and *Will & Grace* now, where calling any woman a bitch provokes screams of laughter. I don't get it. Why aren't they calling men assholes? Now *that's* funny.

But no. The article's actually about a female dog.

Prize-Winning Bitch Missing

A prize-winning golden retriever puppy was stolen from local breeder, Sally Ameson, last Wednesday. Ameson believes that a man claiming to be interested in purchasing one of her older dogs was responsible.

"I went into the back room to run the guy's credit card," Ameson said. "But he was gone when I returned, and Holly-Go-Lightly was nowhere to be found."

The Santa Barbara Police Department ran a credit check, which revealed the Visa card to be stolen. "I never would have sold Holly. She's unbreedable," said Ameson.

After winning a blue ribbon at this year's Santa Barbara Dog Show, the puppy was diagnosed with Clay Pigeon Disease, a rare disorder affecting a dog's nervous system. The five-month-old bitch can live a normal life, but requires regular medication. "Without it," said Dr. Van der Water of Riviera Veterinary, "she has little chance of surviving the next several months."

If you have any information about this missing bitch call the Send Holly Home Hotline at 555-5658.

Figures they'd quote Anna Van der Water. *Little chance of surviving the next few months*—what does she call that, bedside manner? At least there wasn't a picture of her with those stupid barrettes.

I enjoy fifteen minutes of revenge fantasies, deciding how Anna should be punished for having found a lucrative and reputable career, then force myself to read the classifieds.

There's a new ad, for a "unique living opportunity in Mission Canyon." And it is—get this!—only $500 a month. Unique? If $650 pays for a garage in Goleta, what can $500 possibly get you in Mission Canyon? I'm thinking a carport. With housemates.

I draw a dark blue *X* through it with my pen, and browse on. But it keeps nagging at me. Maybe what's unique is that it's a stunning one-bedroom apartment, for only $500. Doesn't get more unique than that. I decide to chance it.

Mission Canyon lies just beyond the Santa Barbara Mission, towards the foothills. At sunset, the Mission's peach walls glisten with falling light and the sky blushes a pink glow behind it. Across the street is the public rose garden. As I drive past, the scent of roses is thick in the air, and all is right in the world—if you ignore, for a moment, your little list.

I park in front of the house on Puesto Del Sol, next to the iron gate the woman on the phone mentioned. There's a kid who looks like Eddie Munster—but without the formal attire and widow's peak—tossing pebbles at a tree trunk across the street.

"You parked on my stick," he says.

I look. There are any number of sticks on the ground. It's true that I parked on some of them. "Sorry."

"You broke it."

"Oh. Which one is yours?"

He points to a stick exactly like every other stick, except broken. "See?"

It occurs to me that this is some new juvenile prank, the current equivalent of asking someone to page Mike Hunt. I smile weakly, and take a step toward the gate, and wave away a bug that whizzes by my ear. Take another step, and a second bug stings me on the shoulder-blade. Another step, another bug—on my butt.

I spin, and Eddie Munster is still tossing pebbles toward the tree trunk. Not the slightest sign of a smirk on his face. Little fucker.

I take five quick steps and close the gate behind me. Think I'm safe until a half-dozen pebbles sail though the bars and pelt my back. Briefly consider cracking Eddie Munster's head like an egg on the rim of a bowl, but the New Elle rises above. Plus, I don't have the firepower.

I step out of the line of fire and am hit with two bullets of fur. Much yapping ensues, and between barks one of the little black pugs tries to nibble my toes. After I realize this is not part of Eddie Munster's evil plan, I pat the dogs, setting their pig-tails wagging delightedly.

"Penny! Pippin!" a woman's voice scolds, and the beasts retreat. The woman is a schoolmarm, with withered cheeks, a sticklike body and white hair pulled into a bun. She wears a tailored cotton blouse and a full pleated skirt. And is that a cameo at her neck? I move in for a greeting and get a closer look. No, just an ugly piece of agate.

"Hi," I say. "I'm Elle. We spoke on the phone?"

"It's this way. I'm Mrs. Petrie." And before I have a chance to worry about what I'll find, she's off at a canter, the dogs and me trotting behind.

The walk is through a well-loved, well-tended California-English-style garden. Roses, hydrangeas, lavender and Mexican sage are all in full bloom. "Unique" is looking better and better—and I start thinking the guest house will be a delicious little truffle of a cottage. Tiny, considering the price. But the garden! And it's in Mission Canyon. There's nothing shameful about telling people you live in Mission Canyon.

There is, however, something shameful about telling people you live in a trolley. Not a carport, a trolley. It squats, sans wheels, just beyond the garden.

"That's a trolley," I say.

"Water and trash are included," she answers. She climbs the stairs and unlocks the door.

I enter behind her, and the trolley teeters a bit from our combined weight.

"Light switches, bathroom. Bed. Kitchen. I will return in five minutes for your answer." She opens the door to leave, but pauses on the steps. "There is dirt on the back of your blouse. And your skirt."

I start to explain Eddie Munster, but she interrupts with a glacial nod and leaves.

I sigh and look around, and it is still a trolley. It's carnival red, except where the paint has chipped off to reveal a coat of mustard yellow. Half the floor is covered in green carpet, the other half, brick linoleum. In the "kitchen" is an all-in-one stove/sink/refrigerator unit. It's 1950s—futuristic, and kinda cute.

The toilet, however, is less than cute, and sits directly next to the stove/sink/fridge. I'm talking ten inches away. A showerhead protrudes from the wall three feet above the toilet tank, and a drain is planted in the floor under it. There are brown curtains over the windows, and the roof is maybe two feet above my head. I've seen SUVs with more living space.

I need money. Not millions. I'm not asking for millions. I just don't want to have to choose between ZZ's garage and a converted trolley. My real apartment, I mean the apartment Louis and I lived in, has two bedrooms and…and it hits me. Louis is living in *my* apartment with his new wife. His *wife.* He *married* her. In a week. After six years with me, he married a stranger. He's married. He's somebody's husband. He has a wife. What if he hears I'm living in a garage or a trolley?

I am suddenly thrilled with the drain in the floor, because I'm gonna throw up. I make a noise like a sick cat and bend over the toilet, and Schoolmarm Petrie knocks and enters.

Apparently she thinks I'm inspecting the toilet, because she says something about the plumbing and the pipes, and sternly warns against flushing "feminine napkins."

"Well?" she finally says.

I straighten in a dignified manner. "I'll take it."

Leave messages for Maya and PB regarding my rental triumph. Do not offer specifics, due to theory that once I'm there, it will look less like a trolley and more like a gatehouse cottage à la the Cotswolds.

Have a private ceremony to officially erase "apartment" from my list. Wake up two hours later suffering from a sugar-crash and surrounded by the crumbs of a celebratory Anderson's Butter-Ring—butter pastry, marzipan and white icing baked into sugary goodness. But the New Elle does not stop while on a roll. The New Elle continues rolling. The New Elle will apply for three jobs today, three tomorrow and three more each day until she is gainfully employed.

I look through my job folder—actually a stack of clippings stuffed in my mildewed, hateful tote. Over the last week, I've cut out every job that mentions "development" or "boutique" or "team leader" but not "director" (grand total: seven). I pick one at random, and in a burst of efficiency write a cover letter, stuff it in an envelope with a résumé, and place it on the kitchen table so Maya will remember to stamp and mail it.

Despite being exhausted from use of fiction-writing muscles atrophied since college, I have two more cover letters to write. I write "To Whom It May Concern" and am debating merits of following it with a colon or a comma when it hits me: I've no furniture, I've no silverware, I've no bedding, I've no gorgeous *objet;* in short, I've nothing at all for the new cottage.

This isn't optional, this is housewares. Thing is, I started with $5,100, right? Then gave $1,500 to Schoolmarm Petrie for first, last, security. Spent $300 on assorted shopping. Well, $400. Let's call it $500 on assorted shopping, to be safe. I do a little long-division and discover that $5,100 minus $2,000 is $3,100.

I count my money: $1,773.59. Must have it wrong. Even I cannot misplace $1,300 in cash.

I count it again: $1,612.59.

Again: $1,598.59. This rate of shrinkage, I'll have nothing left by midnight, except the fifty-nine cents I'm so sure about.

I panic. I call Louis, and hang up on the second ring. I call back, and hang up on the first. I take a deep breath, and call a third time. I get a message. In a woman's voice. I hear: *Hi, you've reached the Ferrises. We're not in right now—*

I slam the phone down. The Ferrises? That is *my* fucking answering machine and *my* fucking fiancé. I call Maya at work and get the machine. I dial my mother and hang up before the call goes through.

Twenty minutes, and all the Butter-Ring crumbs later, I'm thinking more clearly: what I need is money, not comfort. I call my dad.

"Dad, it's Elle," I say when he answers.

"Hi, sweetheart." He sounds pleased to hear from me. "Guess what?"

"I don't want to guess. You got my message that I moved? I'm in Santa Barbara now. The flight was fine. I just rented an apartment."

"I got married."

That isn't my favorite sentence. I feel the throb of an impending migraine. "You already are married."

"Leanne? We divorced months ago. I met Nancy in Panama in October. We tied the knot last week in Hawaii."

I want to ask why he didn't invite me, but I know the answer: He's still upset because last time he got married I said I couldn't come *this time,* but would be sure to catch the next one. "Is she Panamanian?" At least that would be something new.

"She's a school teacher from Vermont. She quit her job and moved in last month."

"She quit her job and moved across country to be with you," I say. "Does she know there's no chance the marriage will last more than two years?"

"Eleanor, c'mon. That's a little hard on your father. Your mother and I were together seven years."

"Longer than me and Louis," I say bitterly.

My father perks up. "Oh! That reminds me. You're not going to believe this, but while Nance and I were on our honeymoon, we ran into Louis."

"In Hawaii?" He never took *me* to Hawaii.

"No, no. That's just where we got married. We honeymooned in Venice."

"Venice?" He never took *me* to Venice.

"Most romantic city in the world. Me and Louis were trying to hire the same gondolier. Small world, huh? Anyway, he's doing great. Got a huge bonus for some deal in Iowa. Gave him a corner office, too. He and his new wife were celebrating. Lovely girl. Have you met her?"

I can't respond, due to the red-hot poker that has been shoved into my left temple.

"Charming girl. Pretty. Reminded me of you. Except not so...you know."

"No, I don't know. Not so *what?*"

He laughs weakly. "Oh, nothing."

I take a deep breath. "Dad, I need money."

Silence.

"Dad?"

"Louis said you took three thousand out of the household account. He thought that was very fair."

"*Three* thousand?" I thought it was four. So I didn't misplace $1,300. Only $300. I'm oddly relieved: misplacing $300 is easy.

"That's what he said. Oh, and he asked about his stamp collection. Apparently got mixed in with your things."

"I don't want to talk about Louis. I want to talk about me. I'm running out of money. I don't have a job. I just rented an apartment and I need a car."

"Honey, I'd love to help. But you know how strapped I am."

"You managed to scrape up the cash for Hawaii and Venice," I shrill. "And to pay four alimony checks a month."

"And that," he says, "is why I'm strapped."

chapter 10

The next morning, in what she undoubtedly intends to be retail therapy, Maya and I go shopping. Housewares, remember? Our first stop is Indigo, a shop on State Street, past the Arlington Theater. It has gorgeous, gorgeous, just delicious Asian and Asian-esque couches, tables, fabrics, lamps, chairs, rugs. Maya checks price tags and drags me outside.

We try Living, Ambience, Home and Garden, and Eddie Bauer, and I am dragged from each. Maya finally snaps and grabs the car keys. An hour-and-a-half later, in Burbank of all places, I see the light.

Love Maya. Love IKEA.

I used to think it was the Wal-Mart of home furnishing stores. But there are endless rows of lovely things I always *knew* could be made at a reasonable price. And everything has these lovely foreign names like *Hemnes* and *Beddinge.*

Four hours, and Maya had to bribe me away with Swedish meatballs at the cafeteria.

Best part: Their computers were down, so it was a snap to get an IKEA card with a fifteen-hundred-dollar limit, using my other (useless) credit cards to secure it. I was slightly over though, and had to put back assorted lamps, an IKEA teddy bear and one of the welcome mats. And the Persian-rug mouse-pad. Maya reminded me that I don't even own a computer. Well, I'll never own one at this rate, will I? Still, I returned the mouse-pad.

"The toilet is in the kitchen," Maya mentions helpfully, as if I hadn't noticed. I couldn't convince her not to come in. So I'm putting away purchases, and she's giggling at the trolley. "That takes 'efficiency unit' to a whole new level!"

I scowl and tell her to go away (but remember to pick me up tomorrow before she goes to work, so I can have the car, and to change her message to mention my new phone number, and to tell Perfect Brad that I'll need help carrying the new IKEA chair inside when they deliver it).

I can't tell if she's listening, because she's busy being fascinated by my three-utility stove/fridge/kitchen sink unit.

"Does it work?" she asks.

"Of course," I say, though I've never actually turned it on. I open the refrigerator door. Feels cold. Turn on the tap—water runs out. Click on a burner. Smoke issues forth.

"Well," she says. "That should keep the mosquitoes away."

"A fourth utility to the thing," I say. "It's like magic."

We finish unpacking, and Maya, who hasn't quite stopped giggling, has to go to work. I stop her on the way out. "Tell me the truth. Do you think it's like living in a trailer?"

"No, not at all." She closes the door behind her, and calls out: "A trailer would be nicer!"

I think of something to yell back two minutes later, but by then I'm alone. I bustle around the trolley, making it mine and trying to ignore the growing sense of isolation and the encroaching dusk. I assemble my new bureau, and then disassemble the bits that don't fit, then reassemble it and it's perfect! I glow with satisfaction at being so handy and self-sufficient, and I look up and it's pitch-black outside.

I meekly open the door, and the lovely tea-garden has been transformed into a horrible, brackish swamp. I lock the door. Close the curtains. Grab one of my IKEA knives, just in case. And curl up in my new comforter, pretending to leaf through *Marie Claire.*

The wind scratches tree limbs against the trolley, and I manage not to shriek. I often feel I'm in a movie; tonight, it's *Texas Chainsaw Massacre: The Santa Barbara Years.* I turn on all the lights, then realize this just makes the trolley a beacon in the darkness. Moths and rapists will be swarming around shortly. I turn the lights off. It's worse.

I watch a rerun of *Bewitched* on the little TV Maya loaned me. Turn the sound up all the way. Not loud enough, as a gust of wind sends the branches into a terrifying crescendo, and something slams against the trolley.

I think it was a slam. It definitely wasn't a tree branch. It could have been a knock. Schoolmarm Petrie seems the sort who'd make one sharp rap on the door, like the smack of a ruler down on an errant pupil's knuckles.

I crack the door and peek out. Nothing but menacing swampland. And something brown at the bottom of the steps.

It's a dead squirrel.

I clutch my throat in horror, like some prim Victorian lady who accidentally wandered into the *Vagina Monologues,* and debate the various merits of fainting and screaming.

A motion sensor light illuminates the Schoolmarm's gate, and I see the shadowy form of a pudgy boy recede into the darkness. Eddie Munster.

"Hey!" I yell. "You little creep!"

I'd track him down and kill him, but that would mean leaving the relative safety of my trailer. *Trolley.* My trolley.

"Squirrelly, aren't you?" he yells.

I respond with a well-reasoned string of curses, and slam the door. On TV, Samantha has black lines painted on her face. I wonder what happened to her. I wonder what's happened to *me.*

chapter 11

The telephone rings at 9:12, waking me from a Swamp Thing nightmare.

It's Bob from the VW dealership. And when you think about it, being a car salesman isn't so bad. Plus, he's actually seen my credit report, and still he calls.

"Bob," I say. *Bob. Bobbing for apples.* "Robert. Robbie. Rob. That's a lot of possible nicknames."

Silence on the phone.

I think of saying *Bobby?*

"Well, I just go by Bob," he finally says. "I've been thinking about you since last week."

"Oh, have you?" The New Elle plays hard-to-get.

"Yeah, I got this…borderline trade-in. My boss doesn't want me to put it on the lot. And I know you're looking for something affordable."

"Borderline?"

"It's a BMW, though. A Beemer. 1974. It's virtually a classic luxury automobile. Plus, it's not worth sending it down to L.A. for auction."

"So you've got a car you can't sell, and thought of me?"

"Yeah, you interested?"

This is insulting. "How much?"

"I'll let it go cheap. Fifteen-hundred."

Fifteen-hundred! That's a huge chunk out of my monster stack. But I do need a car. "Can I come see it this morning?"

"This morning isn't good. I've got real clients coming in. How about two this afternoon?"

Real clients. "Two is fine."

"Actually, three would be better."

I sigh. "Three, then."

I hang up, and immediately check my voice mail to see if anyone called while I was on the phone...and I have a message! It's not even Maya. It's a smooth, masculine voice.

"Eleanor Medina," the smooth, masculine says. "You're a hard one to find. This is Carlos Neruda. We haven't met...yet. But I've heard all about you, and I really want to talk. My number is—" he pauses, and I realize he has Antonio Banderas's voice and I'll coolly wait ten or eleven seconds before returning his call "—no, on second thought, I'll call you back. Take care, Eleanor Medina."

Ha! Take that, Bobby! You're not the only car on the lot.

IKEA furniture delivered precisely on time. Perfect Brad, too, precisely on time. Perhaps Brad is Swedish. Perhaps he is Bräd.

I bought a white linen chair. Am very pleased with the mature, adult decision to choose white. I was worried it would be like a white T-shirt: a magnet for chocolate ice cream, tomato sauce, coffee, mystery stains. I'd stared at it drooling, like a dog at a barbecue, until Maya found me. To prove her wrong, I decided the New Elle was adult enough to take care of white linen. Am pleased with the decision—it's pretty against the chipped carnival-red of the trolley walls.

"You're sure that's where you want it?" Brad says, after relocating it several times. If he weren't perfect, he'd be exasperated. But he is, so I don't worry.

"I'm sure. Thanks, Brad—you're a prince."

He stammers endearingly, and spots the bureau I assembled last night. He fixes the bits that were uneven, and puts the drawer-pulls on. He knocks together the sides and adjusts the two drawers that had refused to close.

I consider being insulted by the implication that I'm not capable of doing it myself. But honestly, men enjoy this sort of thing. Why ruin their fun? It's like shopping. Men think it's a chore, and can't understand why we like it. He can fiddle, I can shop, and we'll both be happy. Maybe I'll repay Brad by buying him a new pair of shoes.

Then I realize I have a bigger treat for him: I am forced to wheedle and whine slightly, as he wants to get back to his office. But it only takes Perfect Brad fifty minutes, and I own the Beemer for one thousand, flat. Including taxes and registration and all that. Apparently fifteen hundred was far too much.

Don't tell Andrea Dworkin, but it's good to have a man around. I consider getting weepy about Louis, and how much I miss him. But frankly, PB is better at the manly stuff than Louis ever was. And I *do* have PB around, even if he's just a loaner. So it works out fine.

I swing by to take Maya for a Beemer joyride and ask if she's interested in a time-share agreement.

"There's plenty of Brad to go around. Plus, I'll cancel out all the non-Jewish parts."

She laughs. "Don't get any *Big Chill* ideas. I draw the line at furniture assembly and car shopping."

"That is so bourgeois," I say. "If you were young and hip, you'd share."

"And if *you* were young and hip, Elle, you'd get a bunch of your tender places pierced, and sleep with girls. But, if you're still interested in men…"

"What?" I say, thinking: *Carlos? Is he a friend of Brad's? I bet he's a coder, too—exactly like Brad, but Latino.* "What man?"

"You know the guy at the bar the other night?"

Redhead! I pretend to have no idea. "Neil? Monty?"

"The one who kept going on about Chicagos? He asked about you."

"What did he ask, if I was taking my meds?"

"General stuff. He's an architect. Wondered if I'd ever consider remodeling."

I know she wants me to beg for info, so I play it cool. "Yeah, I saw him looking around."

"I told him I couldn't afford it. And Dad would pop a vessel if I even repainted. It's the only reason I haven't taken down the *shtetl* gallery. I'm thinking of having the lights removed, though. The ones blocking the skylights. And—"

"Okay, okay! What did you tell him?" I shift roughly, going up Carrillo Hill. "I mean about me!"

"Hmm?"

I glare.

She smiles. "Guess what his name is."

"Theodore Bundy."

"Here, he gave me his card." She pulls it from her purse and hands it over.

I glance down. It's a classy card. White linen, and embossed black sans-serif font, with his name, the word "Architect," and a phone number.

His name is Merrick. *Louis* Merrick.

"Watch the road!" Maya yells, as car wheels shriek.

It's a good thing Beemers are the ultimate driving machines.

After I convince the nice old man that we don't need to exchange insurance information, Maya remembers an important appointment with her living room. I drive, very cautiously, to her house.

"So?" I ask when we get there, and her color looks normal again. "What do you think? Of the car?"

"It's...really a BMW," she says.

"1974 was the first year they made square taillights," I say proudly. Bobby told me.

"Great," she says, unimpressed.

Can't she be a tiny bit excited? This is the first car I've ever bought for myself. It may not be a Passat, or even a Jetta, but it's mine and I'm determined to love it.

"It's great," she repeats, with a little more enthusiasm. "It's zippy, it's fun and Beemers are suppose to run forever."

"Thank you."

"And the color doesn't bother you?"

Okay. It's bright orange—almost a perfect match for the architect's hair—with a black interior that gives it the appearance of a low-budget float in a Halloween parade.

"I love it," I insist.

"It's charming," she says, closing the door behind her. "And it'll be October in no time. We'll get you some black cat cutouts—"

I put the car in First, and Beemer out of there. Through the open window, I hear her laughing.

Scrooge-like, I return to my lair and count my money. I'm considering having the car painted. Not because I don't like it, just to show Maya. I have $570, more or less. Which may not sound like a lot, but I have an apartment, sort of. I have a car, sort of. I have Maya's man, extremely sort of. And I definitely have housewares. Sort of.

And soon I will have a job. I called about a development position—and they want to interview me tomorrow. I'm not sure what I'll wear, though. On the one hand, I don't want to be overdressed. On the other, if development is fund-raising, they'll probably expect me to hobnob with Montecitans, so I should look the part. On the third hand—

On the third hand, there's a horrific black splotch on my

pristine white linen chair! Black as tar, a nasty Rorschach stain on the armrest. I lick a finger, intending to de-smudge it, and notice that my hand is covered in the same stuff. Black inky yuck. Oil from the Beemer? I check my shoes. There's a smudge on one of the straps, but nothing on the soles.

I retrace my steps to the front door. Check every surface. No other signs of black liquid. I open the front door, to check the car. And it's there. On the doorknob. Coated in black ink.

Not ink, I think. Anything but ink. Coffee, chocolate, red wine. Just not ink. And where did it come from? An exploded pen? I look skyward, as if expecting the heavens to leak ink, and hear a rustle in the bushes next door. I see a flash of juvie.

That little fucking Eddie Munster coated my door handle with ink.

I rocket after him. The little bastard may be roly-poly, but he's fast. I snag his T-shirt, but he breaks away. I'm about to shove through the bushes after him, when I hear Mrs. Petrie call me from her kitchen window. She tells me there's ink on my skirt…and get out of her juniper.

chapter 12

My first job interview: 10:00 a.m. at Planned Parenthood.

I dress in a lavender silk Armani suit Louis accidentally bought me in New York. Do my hair and makeup, and am ready in under fifty minutes. Which is quite good. I have fifteen minutes to get downtown. Then—and this is the shocking part—I make it to my car with no mishaps. The car starts. I find a parking space directly outside the clinic. And I'm inside, with five minutes to spare.

I beam at the beautiful Latina girl behind the little glass window—not my natural reaction to beautiful teenagers—and tell her I have an appointment. She nods and hands me a clipboard.

I sit on one of the sticky couches, next to a wicker basket filled with condoms, and pretend to concentrate on the application while checking out the competition. Another woman is filling out the same form. Her suit is royal blue, and appears to be a polyester blend. I feel sorry for her, and when our eyes meet I give her an encouraging smile and turn to my clipboard.

Name: *Elle Medina* Date of Birth: *10/21*

Occupation: *Future Developmental Coordinator at Planned Parenthood*

Marital status: *Separated from fiancé.*

Occupation: *He's a highly-paid attorney.*

Current medications: *None.*

Have you ever smoked cigarettes? Yes(X) No ( )
But just my first year of college.

Current alcohol consumption:
drinks per week: *Anywhere from 1 to ~~6~~ ~~8~~ 15*

Major injuries: *broke wrist*

If any, describe: *Wanted to prove to Jamie Erheart in sixth grade that she wasn't the only one who could do back handsprings.*

Are you on any special diets? Yes(X) No( )

If yes, describe: *Sugar Busters, Zone, Not-Zone and The Famous Overnight Hollywood Celebrity Diet.*

Do you do breast self-exam regularly? Yes( ) No(X)

Date of last Pap smear: *3 years ago*

Normal Yes(X) No( )

Are you sexually active at this time?

Yes( ) No(X)

Is your sex life satisfactory for you?

Yes( ) No(X)q *Would like to be sexually active at this time.*

How many partners have you had this year? *1*

How many partners have you had in your lifetime? *~~IIII~~ II*

* * *

This is way more personal than I expected. I guess they're looking for someone who really believes in Planned Parenthood. Someone open with her sexuality. I can be open. Maybe I'm too open. Is seven a lot of partners? Or pathetically few? I mean, six of them were between the ages of sixteen and twenty—they don't ask about that. They should have a question about average number of partners per year. I ought to get credit for being monogamous between twenty and twenty-six.

I hand the clipboard back to the receptionist, expecting her to comment on my speediness. I definitely filled it out far faster than the competition. I can see her pen still poised halfway down the first page.

"I've always been fast at forms," I tell the girl behind the counter. I have been. I'm very fast at forms.

She doesn't seem impressed. "Have a seat. They'll be calling you."

I return to the sticky couch until my name is called by a hatchet-faced woman in the white doctor's coat. I offer a professional-type smile and my hand. "I'm Elle Medina. Nice to meet you."

She cocks her head and ignores my hand. "Pleeze. Come theez vay."

"Oh, are you from Germany?" I ask. Trying to make confident, career-woman chatter as we head into a spare examination room.

"No."

It's the shortest "no" I've ever heard. Any shorter, and she would have said nothing. "From where, then?"

"You vould not know it."

"Is it smaller than Rhode Island?" I ask.

She glares, and I remember Rule One of job interviews: Do not alienate scary European prospective co-worker.

"Pleeze sit, and remoof your jacket."

The only place to sit is the examination table. "I'm fine, thanks."

"I vill be unable to take your blood prezure if you do not remoof ze jacket."

"My blood pressure?" I know they make you pee into a cup for some jobs, but this is ridiculous. I try to convince myself that blood pressure measurement is how they weed out high-stress candidates. I fail. "I think there's been a mistake. I'm here for the development job. I want that position. Not—" I point to the stirrups extending from the table "—this position."

The nurse is not amused. Happily the doctor arrives and finds the situation quite funny. He's a short, roly-poly man and we hit it off immediately.

When we finish chuckling about the misunderstanding, he gives my résumé a cursory read: "For the job?" he says. "No. We're looking for someone, um, qualified."

I tell him I'm a fast learner. I ask him to please give me a chance.

He agrees to interview me, and flips through my paperwork more carefully. "Well, I see you haven't had a pelvic exam in three years?"

I call Maya as soon as I get home. "There's good news and there's bad news."

"You got the job?" she asks, incredulous.

"You have to promise not to tell PB."

She refuses.

I consider hanging up, but then I'd just have to call back. Besides, even if she promised, she'd still tell him.

"Fine," I sigh. I explain how the receptionist mistook me for a patient, the nurse was an Albanian Cruella De Vil and that the doctor rejected me very kindly.

"So what's the good news?"

"Well, the doctor read my file."

"And..."

"And it'd been three years since my last exam."

"So you're saying—"

"I had my annual GYN checkup while he interviewed me."

There is an incredulous pause. "How *do* you do it?"

"It's a gift."

"At least the interview must've been memorable. How'd it go?"

I grunt. "It's a little hard to appear competent and charming when you've got a speculum stuck up your—"

"Pap smear?"

"He said I looked normal. He'll call me if there are any problems with the results."

"Well, that's good."

I brighten. "Yeah. And you know that kid whose been tormenting me? I stuffed my bag with condoms from the free condom basket, on my way out the door. I'm gonna fill 'em with water and peg the little bastard."

Telephones can turn hot, just like slot machines. I hang up with Maya, and the phone rings immediately. I offer a distracted "hello," still trying to figure out exactly what Maya meant by "Oh, *that's* how you do it."

"Is this Elle?" For a sublime moment, I think it's the mysterious Carlos, but the accent is all wrong.

"This is she," I say.

"Oh, hi. It's Louis. We—"

"Louis!" I hiss like an angry cat. "I don't want to talk to you. Not now, not ever."

"What? What did *I* do?"

"Fuck you! I heard about Venice. I know *all* about Venice."

"Venice? I think you have me mistaken for… We met at Shika? You served me a Chicago?"

My stomach drops. The *architect* Louis. "Oh! Oh. Oh. *Merrick.*" I cannot bring myself to call him Louis. "I've been getting…crank calls. I think it's the kid next door. Sorry."

"Uh-huh." He sounds like he regrets having phoned. "Maybe this is a bad time?"

"No—no. I'm happy you called." That sounds too eager. "Long as it's not a crank call, right?" Stupid, stupid, stupid. I press my fingers to my temple.

"Right."

There's a long awkward silence, and I feel bad for the guy. He's just being nice, he doesn't expect to be dragged into my emotional morass. On the other hand, why is he being so nice? As far as he knows, I'm just a desperate bar-wench who can't mix a drink. And now he's trying to figure how to avoid asking her on a date. I should put him out of his misery. "Listen, I have to go," I say.

For some reason, he laughs. "Go where?"

"Umm…out?"

"Do you want to have coffee with me? Maybe tomorrow?"

"Coffee?"

"Tomorrow morning. Is ten all right?"

"Ten? Tomorrow morning?" Must stop repeating everything he says.

"There's a place called Bread and Water, down on Haley."

I manage not to say "Bread and Water?" I say: "Sure. Bread and Water. On Haley."

"Ten o'clock, then? I'll see you there?"

I tell him he will, already wondering what I'll wear. This is a morning coffee date? Do men *do* this? Make a woman put herself together before noon, for a date? You'd think someone would tell them it's not a good idea.

"Great," he says. "Oh—and just so you know? I've never been to Venice."

chapter 13

Bread and Water is far more stylish than you usually see in Santa Barbara. The countertop, windows and walls are all a bit askew, giving it a Cubist feel—but not unpleasantly so. The colors are muted greens and grays that match the natural wood of the tables and beams. A showy yellow orchid sits on the counter in a jade green planter. It's lovely.

The architect—Merrick, whom I will not call Louis—is wearing a celedon linen shirt and khakis, which match the decor perfectly. Except his red hair clashes horrifically, of course. I've never seen him in full daylight and I'd not have thought it possible, but his hair looks even more like something out of a special effects department.

He's chatting with a young blond waitress when I approach. I'm only a few minutes late, maybe ten, and he's already hitting up another woman? Waitresses and barmaids: I detect a pattern.

We smile hellos, and both order lattes, and Merrick asks the waitress if she could tell him what, precisely, they put in their lattes.

She's a wholesome-looking girl in jeans and sneakers and a T-shirt that says "Meet the Breasts." I wonder if Merrick has met them. "The usual," she drawls. "Espresso and steamed milk. Unless you want something sprinkled on top?"

We both say no and she and her breasts swing off. He says: "Boring. If you were making them, they'd have ice cream and cherry syrup, sprinkles."

"Or hundred-year-old scotch."

"Cognac," he says, smiling.

"I guess those Cosmopolitans were pretty bad, huh? I don't really work there."

He asks what I really do.

"I'm looking for something in non-profit development. I spoke to the people at Planned Parenthood, but I'm not sure the position is right for me." Certainly the stirrup position was wrong.

"Really? I have a friend who works for an NGO out of L.A. He does mostly estate-planning in conjunction with the development board. Living trusts, endowment funds, that sort of thing."

"Sure. Endowments." I'm in way over my head, so I say, "I'm also thinking of starting my own magazine."

"Your own magazine?" He gives me the crinkly eyes again. If only I didn't have to look above his forehead, he'd be really cute. I want to ask about the carrot freak-hair, but I'm beginning to suspect it's a vitamin deficiency or genetic disorder, and I don't want to embarrass him. But from the forehead down, he's sexy, especially the crinkly thing with the eyes. "Have you worked in publishing?"

"Not in publishing, *per se.* I just moved back to town. I haven't fully explored all the facets, the implications, the, um, and so forth, of starting a magazine." Please God—shut me up. "I'm going to call it *L,*" I hear myself saying.

"Elle, isn't that already taken?"

"Isn't what already taken?"

"*Elle.* I thought it was a fashion magazine."

"Oh! I thought you were saying, like, *Eleanor, isn't that already a magazine?* But you meant it more, *Elle*—" I make a pausing dash with my hand "*—isn't that already a magazine?*"

He nods solemnly. "Right. I meant it with one of these." He makes a pausing dash. It looks good when he does it, though—more of a dashing pause.

"Anyway," I say. "Mine would just be the letter *L.* You know—" I make the Loser sign on my forehead. "It'd be like Oprah's magazine, except not so relentlessly upbeat."

"So you're going for depressing and hopeless. For people who identify as losers."

I smile. "It's a big market."

We fall silent as the waitress brings our coffees, so I ask if he's from Santa Barbara.

But he doesn't want to talk about himself, which flies in the face of everything I've heard about dating. Instead he asks more about me, and I tell him I grew up here, went to college back east, and in about two minutes I'm utterly bored with myself. I wind it down: "…then I broke up with my fiancé, and here I am." Manage not to mention that my ex-fiancé's name is Louis.

"Did you leave him at the altar?"

"No, no. It was one of those mature, adult, mutual-type breakups. We're still good friends. So anyway, I'm back and in the market for a new job." I stress the word *new* like I had a job before.

"Until you start your magazine," he says.

"Right. Until then. Or get a development gig. But actually, I'm looking for anything right now. To pay the bills while I do the career search thing."

"Oh, yeah? I'm looking for an assistant."

"An assistant?" I don't know much about blueprints, but I suspect I could design a villa or two.

"More of a receptionist. To make appointments, keep the office organized."

I think about the apocalyptic mess I've created in the trolley. "Organization happens to be one of my *fortes.*"

"Fort," he says.

"What?" I say.

"Apparently it's pronounced fort. Not fort-tay. One syllable, as in Knox."

What a jackass. "Are you sure?"

"Yeah," he says, with a smile that redeems him from jackass-hood. "I pronounced it fort-tay on a conference call to New York last year, and haven't heard the end of it. They say they're gonna take me to court-tay for my sins."

"So, organization is my *fort?* I don't know if I like the sound of that." Chastened, I sip my latte and ask him how long he's been an architect.

He tells me about his work. He's amusing and charming, and despite the early morning hour, I realize I'm having a good time. Then he checks his watch, says he had fun, but should be going.

He stands. I stand. And I think: *who's gonna pay for the lattes?*

I open my rank and fetid tote extremely slowly, and he says, "Don't worry about that. I have a deal with the owners. They still owe me for designing this place."

"You designed the café?"

"Yeah."

"No way!" It's gorgeous—and entirely devoid of bright orange.

"You like it?"

"Get out. You did *not.*"

He smiles. He actually did.

"It's beautiful. Wow. Maybe I'll stick to—whatever—instead of designing villas. I could never compete."

He steps closer to me and touches my arm. "Listen, if you

want, you could do a little temp work at the office. Phones and filing...?"

I want to haughtily refuse, to tell him filing is not my fort. But I also want to have more than $500. "Well, I do have my résumé with me..."

I dig in my tote for a résumé, and yank it out. Five tea-bags burst out with it. Tea-bags? I don't even drink tea. They hang suspended in mid-air as it hits me. They are not Earl Gray. They are neither chamomile nor Irish Breakfast. They're condoms.

Little plastic squares, hovering above my tote like a swarm of mortification. The condoms from Planned Parenthood—yellow and blue and gold and red, their jagged edges catch the light, they spin and twirl in the air between me and Merrick.

Time kicks back in, and three condoms skitter across the floor. One lands with a *plunk* in the dregs of my latte, and one bounces off his celadon linen shirt.

I die.

Merrick casually hands me the condom that hit him in the chest. "Ribbed," he says.

Being dead, I cannot respond.

Rigor mortis sets in, freezing me with one hand in my tote—this would not have happened, by the way, if I'd had the Fendi satchel—and the other suspended useless in the air, having managed to catch not one of the cavorting condoms. I wait for a white heavenly tunnel to appear or, failing that, a fiery chasm to open in the earth.

Instead, Meet the Breasts suddenly reappears. Still blond, still young, still wholesome...and wanting to remove our empty lattes. In a frantic attempt to keep her from taking the cup with the floating condom, which for some reason seems the worst possible thing, I lunge forward. My hell-tote slings from my shoulder to my wrist and upends.

A rainbow eruption of multicolored rubbers spews forth. Dozens of them, in every flavor, texture and tip. Hundreds.

Thousands. Like I'm a malfunctioning condom vending machine. Like I've hit the biggest jackpot in Vegas history, and am being paid in prophylactics to the accompaniment of shrieking sirens and flashing lights. In an instant, I am up to my knees in condoms. Children and small dogs are lost in the torrent. A house floats by.

Silence descends upon the too-hip café. All eyes are upon me. Merrick says something, but I cannot hear over the deafening thrum of humiliation.

I would run away, but my wallet and Chanel lipsticks are scattered among the condoms. I drop to my knees and shovel everything back into my purse. If I were not dead, I would no doubt hear the comments of amused onlookers.

I stand and turn to Merrick. He holds his hand out to me. For comfort, for support, in a gentlemanly gesture of solidarity?

No. His hand is full of condoms.

I flee.

Lunch with Maya to lick my wounds. She invites Perfect Brad. Why? Because they are a happy-loving-couple.

I hate them. But because I'm a friend, I will not stick my fork into the back of PB's neck; it's not his fault he was born with the X chromosome. Or the Y. Whichever it is.

Besides, I'm fairly certain that Maya came through, and didn't tell him about the Planned Parenthood Fiasco. So I fill them in about the debacle *du jour,* and after spurting their iced teas over the table, they are quite sympathetic.

"Men are off the list," I say. "But what am I going to do about a job?"

"Just don't apply at an orthodontist's office," Maya says. "You'd look silly in braces."

"And beware of jobs at a tanning salon," Brad says knowingly. "Go in for an interview, come out glowing orange."

"And watch out for tattoo parlors."

Okay, so she told him. I glower, but it *is* funny, and I suspect they're only trying to cheer me up. This works, until I realize that not only is my sure-thing job (Shika) not going to happen, but I have precisely zero prospects.

"How many résumés have you got out?" Maya asks. Should I lie? I hesitate a fraction too long, and Maya says, "Just the one, huh?"

"I wore my Armani," I say.

"Hey, you know what you should do?" Brad says. "Go to a—what's it called?"

"A therapist?" Maya asks.

"No, no—an employment place."

"A temp agency," she says. "That's a great idea. There's got to be a temp job for you, and once people know you they'll want to hire you permanently."

"Maybe reception?" I say. Because, now that I've considered Merrick's offer, it seems a good starter job. I can answer phones and take messages and look sleekly attractive behind a massive mahogany desk at an upscale entertainment lawyer's office. Only not a lawyer. Or an architect. Maybe a Hollywood producer…

Maya says this is a good idea. Brad says he'll ask if they need anyone at SoftNoodle, though I inwardly cringe at the thought of spending my days saying, "Good morning, SoftNoodle, how may I direct your call?"

After lunch, I head back to the trolley and iron my Armani, which got a tad wrinkled at Planned Parenthood. It's 4:00 before I make it downtown to Superior Employment. Had to wash hair, apply makeup and listen to latest message from Carlos, mysterious Latin admirer, over and over again.

I clump upstairs to the office, thinking about my new career. Reception is fine, but the New Elle shouldn't set her sights too low. I should aim for a position I really love. Such as interior designer. I have a flair for design. Or maybe *I* should be a therapist. I love other people's problems.

"I'd like to apply for a job," I tell the receptionist.

She hands me a clipboard with a stack of papers attached. "You can start by filling this out."

"Sure, thanks." I start towards one of the chairs before hesitating. "Um—this is a job application, right?"

"What else would it be?"

"You'd be surprised," I murmur.

Pen in hand, I quickly complete the application. Least I haven't lost my touch with forms. The *previous employment* section does not take long, though it turns out that Martha Washington did ten-key, reception, filing and artistic development. In addition to managing others.

The receptionist tells me I'll be working with Sheila, and introduces me to a woman with an uncanny resemblance to my grandmother, with tawny hair teased into a bun, and a nice camel sweater set on over a matching three-quarter length skirt. We sit in her office while she goes over my application.

"Not a long employment history, is it dear?" she says.

I love being called dear. "I've been in school, mostly."

"Well, at least your duties were varied. We'll go ahead and give you the ten-key and typing tests, shall we?"

They *test* you?

Sheila leads me to a small room with a computer and an adding machine, then leaves me alone to struggle valiantly.

She reappears in five minutes. "All finished dear?"

I've barely had time to adjust the seat. I glance at the clock. It's been fifty minutes.

She checks my work with a subtle sigh. "That's all right, dear. Everyone exaggerates a little on their application. We'll put down you recognize an adding machine. And how many w.p.m.?"

"Umm…?"

"Words per minute."

"Oh." I glance back at my typing score. "Sixteen. That's not *too* bad, is it?"

"Yes, dear. It is." She leans conspiratorially towards me. "I shouldn't really ask this...but have you considered marriage? I know young women feel differently these days, but a pretty girl like yourself, without any job skills..." Her voice trails off as tears spring to my eyes. She pats my hand. "I'll see what I can find you, dear. But honestly...don't hold your breath."

Takes a surprisingly long time to fill the condoms with water, but I eventually get the hang of it. Consider filling some with glue, ink or wine, but am too mature to stoop to Eddie Munster's level.

Still, wine sounds good. Half a bottle of Prosperity Red later, and I am curled weepily under my duvet. What kind of twenty-six-year-old woman has never had a real job? Even women in the 1940s were gainfully employed. Rosie the Riveter and such. Possible I would enjoy riveting?

If the wedding had gone as planned—or even if it had gone disastrously, just as long as it had *gone*—I wouldn't be in this mess. I'd be in a lovely apartment, and half of everything Louis made would be mine, and I'd spend my days shopping for lovely things, bored out of my fucking mind and so lonely that I slept fourteen hours a day.

I'm suddenly sober. Where did *that* come from?

Because it's not true. I was happy. I was happy-ish. I was as happy as can be expected. I was quite happy. I shopped and went to shows and exhibits and had lunches. I mean, I didn't even have to clean house; we had a nice Ecuadorian woman, named Columbia, come in once a week. I always liked that, and wondered if there was a Colombian woman named Ecuadoria, somewhere. Of course, I always vacuumed and dusted and straightened before she came, but that's just polite.

Instead of counting sheep, I count names of places which are also names of people. I am not thinking at all about the Planned Parenthood disaster, the condom disaster, the ten-key disaster or any of the other assorted disasters. I fall asleep to thoughts of Jordan (as in Michael), Paris (as in Hilton), Georgia (as in O'Keeffe) and Chicago (as in Merrick).

chapter 14

Get Paid to Shop!
Apply in Person
Anacapa Building
Suite 202

The address listed in the classifieds is an old office building just off the main drag. I stumble through hallways which house various small businesses—a mediator, a barter network, a tailor—until I reach Suite 202. The plaque on the door reads *James "Spenser" Ross, Investigative Services.*

Inside, I discover Tony Danza's doppelgänger. He introduces himself as Spenser and I tell him I'm Elle, here about the ad. We sit down at the avocado-green Formica kitchen table he uses as a desk.

"So," he says. "Think you got what it takes to be a private dick, do you?"

"Well, I saw your ad, and…" And I didn't know it was a private detective firm. I thought it'd be a private shopping firm, and I will ignore his use of the word *dick*. "…and I'm good at shopping. *Really* good."

"Shopping? You think they come to Spenser for shopping? You think it's about the shopping, you might as well walk out that door, 'cause this business ain't one inch about shopping." Any resemblance to Tony Danza is fading fast.

"Maybe I've made a mistake." I hand him my newspaper with the advertisement circled.

"Is it a misprint?" I ask. Please don't let it be a misprint. When I'd spotted it this morning, wedged between ads for a Machinist and a Line Cook, it'd been like a religious experience. I could get paid to shop!

"Well now, you tell me." He leans back in his chair and clasps his hands behind his head.

I know this is a test, and it's one I should try to fail, so I can get out of this freak office. But I *need* a job. Thick stack of cash has become thin stack. If I don't get this job, I'm going to be kicked out of my trolley, living in my car (parked outside Maya and Brad's, of course) and forced to shoplift groceries….

"You catch shoplifters," I say.

"Well, now, ladies and gentleman," he says. "Spenser's got himself a live one. Most of it is employee theft—that's the biggie. But I've got me a customer right now thinks they're losing too much money to two-bit sticky fingers. That's where you come in. You shop, keep your eyes open. You see a palmer, call security. Only thing to remember, wait until they're out of the store—otherwise it ain't shoplifting. Think you can handle it?"

"Perfectly. No problem."

He shuffles some papers around on his Formica. "Customer is Super 9. You can start tomorrow?"

"I got the job? I mean—you're hiring me? I'm hired? You're hiring me?"

He stares. "Any reason I shouldn't?"

"No! No—this is…I'm just so pleased." Though, in fact, I hate Super 9. I can't stand five minutes in that superstore discount hell. How am I gonna last a whole day? "Working in investigative services. Catching, um, sticky fingers."

"You watch yourself. Some of these guys are professionals. It's a billion dollar industry."

I nod in agreement, and we go over my wages (low) and benefits (none). He asks for my driver's license and slides me a W-2 form. Deductions, dependents…all very mystifying. I puzzle it out—probably in record time—and hand it over.

"Any questions?" he asks.

"Well, there is *one* thing." I smile winningly. "Your nickname? They call you Spenser because of the books?"

"What books?"

"You know, *Spenser for Hire,* the private detective. Robert Parker, I think. There was a TV show, too."

He looks blank.

"Starred Robert Urich?"

"Oh, you mean Dan Tanna. What's that got to do with me?"

"Umm…" Not worth it. "Nothing, I guess."

He tells me to report to Phillip, the head of security at Super 9, tomorrow morning, and asks if I'm ready to start watching my training videos. I am, but I worry that we haven't bonded. I mean, if I'm gonna be Elle Medina, Girl Detective, I ought to have some rapport with my boss, right? So I ask if he's got any interesting cases.

He lights a Marlboro Red with his silver lighter, and I can tell he's pleased with the question. "Nothing new under the sun, Medina. Divorce, background checks and industrial security. Well, and a little something else. You heard about Holly? The bitch that went missing?"

I'm a quarter-second from snapping that I'll sue his aging-Tony-Danza-ass if he calls women "bitches" in my presence, when I remember: "The golden retriever puppy who needs her medicine?"

He blows a smoke-ring and nods.

"Do you have any, um, leads?"

"Nothing but dead ends," he says glumly.

"I'm sure something will turn up," I say. "If Ace Ventura can do it, so can you."

"Ace who? Never heard of him."

I try to explain, but he doesn't believe Jim Carrey was in anything other than *The Truman Show, The Majestic* and, for some reason, *Ocean's Eleven.* Then he sits me down in front of his VCR for four hours of investigation instructional videotapes from the 1970s. They're groovy, man. Shoplifting is a bad trip.

"What on earth is that?" Mr. Goldman asks as I heft the gigantic orchid (just like the one at Bread and Water) onto the bar.

"It's a gift. For Maya. For everything."

"Ellie," she says. "It's beautiful. You didn't have to—" Then she gets suspicious. "Where did you get it?"

"At that cute little garden shop around the corner."

"You mean Honeysuckle? They charge twelve bucks for a single rose."

"I know, everything is *gorgeous.*"

"What did it cost?"

I refuse to tell. I'd lie, but she'd check.

Mr. Goldman chuckles. "You girls, always the same since you were this high. I'll see you tomorrow." He waves goodbye, and leaves out the back.

"I love your dad," I say, to distract Maya.

"Elle," she says. "You can't spend money right now. Do you understand this? Money is not for any passing whim, for anything that catches your eye, you have to plan and you have to budget, and you—"

She enlarges on this theme for five minutes, not pausing for breath until Perfect Brad comes in.

"Hey," he says, leaning over the bar to kiss Maya. "Where'd the tree come from?"

"Elle," Maya says. "The real question is, how did she afford it?"

They look at me, and after a dramatic pause I say: "I got a job."

I am hugged and kissed and exclaimed over, and I eat it up with a spoon.

"Well, who's the lucky boss? Where are you working?"

I brace my hands on the bar. "Grab hold of your barstools, boys. There's a new sheriff in town."

Maya giggles. "What?"

"You're working for the Sheriff's Department?" PB asks.

"Better. I'm a private dick."

"Elle, those badges in Cracker Jack boxes aren't real."

"Hold on, hold on," Brad says. "Are you investigating, or being investigated? If it's anything like Planned Parenthood..."

I flick a cocktail straw at him. "I am working for Ross Investigative Services, thank you very much."

"Do you get to go undercover?"

"As a matter of fact, I do." I brief them on my duties.

"You're getting paid to shop," Maya says, wide-eyed. "*You* can do that." She makes it sound like a chipmunk would be overqualified.

"Thanks, Maya."

"No, really. You actually did it! This calls for a celebration."

I wag in my chair. That's more like it.

Brad says, "We'll take Elle to dinner when the new guy comes in. Go to Shanghai and drink too much Tsingtao."

"What new guy?" I ask.

"New bartender," Brad says.

Maya shoots him a look. "He's not really *new,*" she says. "He used to work here, and Brad's been after me to get some help, and I promised this guy—who worked here before—"

"You already mentioned that part," I say.

"Elle, you wouldn't have liked working here. You need to do something that's yours, not Louis's or mine or anyone else's." She's gentle and sympathetic. "And I promised the guy I'd hire him again if I could."

I finger a ring of condensation on the bar. "It doesn't matter. I didn't expect you to hire *me.* I'd be a terrible bartender."

"Come have Chinese with us," she says firmly.

"It's a fantastic place," PB says, apparently trying to cover his faux pas. "Robert Zemeckis goes there."

His awkwardness makes me realize that Perfect Brad has actually stuck his foot in it. I'm elated. He's *not* perfect! Then I think: if he were *always* perfect, he'd be unbearable, thus making him imperfect. So, the fact that he screwed up makes him even better and more perfect. And not only is *he* perfect but their relationship is perfect. And it does hurt that Maya didn't want to hire me. I know it's silly, but it does.

"Sorry—just stopped in to drop off the orchid," I say, suddenly wanting to be alone. "I have places to go, people to stake out."

I almost run over Monty on my way out the door. He greets me in a courtly manner—he's natty as ever in a beige linen suit with a yellow silk tie—and I remember what I forgot to tell Maya and PB.

"Oh, and guess what his name is," I call back to them.

"Louis," Maya says.

I laugh. "No, that'd be too Russian novel. His name's Spenser."

"What's wrong with Spenser?" PB asks.

"It's a private detective series. There's like a thousand books."

"Robert Parker," Monty says, taking his usual stool.

"See," I gesture to Monty. "Monty knows. Robert Parker."

"Never read him," Brad says.

"There was a TV series with Robert Urich, and the big black guy, Hawk?"

"I thought you said Robert *Parker,*" Brad says.

"That's the *author,*" I say, exasperated.

"Was that the one that was like in Vegas or something?" Maya says.

"That's Dan Tanna." I shake my head in disgust. "Just forget it."

I bump the door open with my hip and…

…the dame stepped out of the juke joint like a crime wave waiting to happen, her shapely gams seductive as a pair of Manolo Blahniks on the 50% off rack. It was early Wednesday evening, but she was dressed like late Friday night, in a suit black as widow's weeds and sexy as Marilyn Monroe's whisper. Sure, she was hurting. Who wouldn't hurt, stabbed in the back with a jade dagger by the orchid woman who owned the juke? The orchid woman who had a hunk of man wrapped around her little blond pinky, while the dame had nobody except a mysterious Mexican with a hypnotic voice, and Babyface Eddie Munster hot on her tail. But as she walked to her jalopy, a smile played around her ruby lips….

I'm going to be a private detective! My first real job.

I plan on going straight home to condition my hair for the big day tomorrow, but get sidetracked by the mall.

Barnes and Noble has a surprisingly well-stocked section on private investigation. Three books. On the cover of one is a woman P.I. holding a gun. Sexy, in a woman-with-a-gun sort of way. Perhaps P.I. Elle will need a gun. First, however, I need a credit card, so I can buy the book. I shoot thanks-but-no-thanks to the cashier with my finger pistols, and head to Nordstrom.

I ponder shoes while wondering where people buy guns.

Pawn shops? There must be gun shops, of course, but—ooooh, Cute BCBG heels. Only $145. I got a job, I deserve a new pair of shoes. I ask salesgirl to bring me a pair. Notice violet Charles David mules while I'm waiting. Girl brings me BCBGs, and begrudgingly heads back for the purple mules.

I strut the BCBGs in front of a full-length mirror. They're cute, but...what will the other girls be wearing? Will there be other girls?

"You look good in those," the salesgirl says, as she plops the Charles Davids on a bench.

"Do you think I could run in them?" I ask. What if I have to chase down a shoplifter?

"Ummm..." she says, and wanders off to help another customer.

I try on the Charles Davids. Then the BCBGs. Then the CDs, then the BCBGs again. Hard to decide. The BCBGs have a strap, though, which might make shoplifter-apprehension easier. I glance around to see if anyone is watching. Free and clear. I do a quick skip and start running. Just a couple steps, to see.

Unfortunately, I'm aiming toward the front door.

"Stop her," the salesgirl shouts. "She's wearing our shoes!"

My fear of being tackled by the perfume girls overcomes my fear of having to deal with this, so I skid to a halt, to explain. Explanations are not forthcoming, however, as my right heel snaps off, and like a track star who's missed the hurdle, I wrench my ankle and sprawl to the tile floor.

I check to see if only my pride is wounded, not my ankle, and look back to find a pair of Bally wingtips standing in front of me.

"Can I help you, ma'am?" the wingtips say sternly.

"I was only—"

"She asked if I thought she could run in them," the salesgirl says. "I never thought she'd try to steal them. Sorry, Todd."

I struggle to my feet and face Todd.

I know him. He was in my high school chemistry class. We dated briefly. Great. Can this get more embarrassing?

"Todd? It's Elle. Elle Medina? From high school?"

"Elle? What are you doing stealing shoes? I thought you lived in D.C. or something."

"I wasn't stealing. Honest. I was just—running."

The salesgirl snorts.

"It's all right, Celia," Todd says. "I'll take it from here." He points to my tote and shoes, which look forlorn sitting on a couch surrounded by shoeboxes. "Are these yours?"

I nod, and he grabs them. "My office is this way."

I hobble after him. "It's good to see you," I say, as though we've met over lunch. "So, you work at Nordy's now?"

He doesn't feel like chatting until we're in his office. "Technically," he says. "We can't charge you with shoplifting, as you never left the store, despite your intentions." He's serious and officious. Whatever happened to the goofy seventeen-year-old who said he wanted to join the Mafia when he grew up?

"Todd, my intentions were completely innocent. I wasn't trying to steal the shoes. I just..." I just don't know. How does it happen? The Planned Parenthood Fiasco, the Coffee Condom Catastrophe, and now this? I begin to think my mother is right, and these disasters are the world's way of telling me I'm on the wrong track.

"Can't think of an excuse, huh?" Todd says.

"I don't need an excuse. I was—"

"Doesn't matter, I'm not going to press charges." He gives me a lopsided grin. "Funny way to run into each other again, huh?"

He's flirting with me! Maybe this is the answer to boyfriend problems. Think about it: a) we sort of know each other already, b) he's seen me at my worst (almost) and is still flirting, and c) he works at Nordstrom, and undoubtedly can get me a HUGE discount!

I twirl a curl behind my right ear.

He smiles. "I thought you were in D.C., married to a lawyer."

It's times like these I wish I knew a good lawyer joke. "Actually, I just moved back. I'm working as a—I do investigations. Private investigations."

"Like Kinsey Milhone? E is for Elle." He's definitely interested in me. "How'd you get that job?"

"I sort of fell into it. That's what I was doing with the shoes." I make pumping notions with my hands, as though jogging in place. "In case I have to chase down perps." The word "perps" comes out funny, like maybe I should excuse myself. I stop pumping my hands.

"You have any interesting cases?"

"Nothing new under the sun, Todd," I say. "Divorce, background checks, industrial work. How about you? Worked here long?"

As he tells me the story of his career, confirming everything I've been led to believe about dating, I have plenty of time to casually grab my things, remove the BCBGs and put on my own shoes. "Hey, good seeing you, Todd." I look at the clock over his desk. "But is that the time? I've gotta go."

I step towards the door.

"Wait," he says.

I pause, my hand on the doorknob. Should I give him my phone number? I think I should. I know he's not an axe-murderer—I mean, I've met his parents. And a shoe discount is always appealing…I turn and give him an encouraging smile.

He returns the smile and gestures to the mules I've left lying broken on the floor. "You'll have to pay for those."

chapter 15

Stayed up late watching *Charlie's Angels* rerun—with the original angels. The episode where Cheryl Ladd shoots and kills a baddie, and is so stunned that Sabrina has to ease the gun from her hand. Was food for thought, for those of us in law enforcement, so I did not fall asleep easily. A good thing I don't have to be at Super 9 until ten.

At precisely ten o'clock-ish, I step into the Super 9 security office. I feel distinctly out of place in the mazelike Employees Only area, wandering the cracked cement floor looking for the office. Gigantic boxes of All-Temperature Cheer, Billy's Pork Jerky and Brawny Paper Towels make me feel like Alice in bunnyhole.

Phillip does not help. It's the first day of school all over. He's a surly, toad-faced middle-aged man with an obvious toupee. I tell him I'm Elle Medina, from Ross Investigative Services.

He says: "Yeah? So?"

I shift uncomfortably. "So, um, Mr. Spenser told me to report to you."

"Yeah? You're not gonna do me any good back here. Get out on the floor. You see anyone stuffing anything up her shirt—" he pauses and leers "—or down her pants, you let me know."

Am flushed and mortified as I push through the swinging doors onto the sales floor. Spenser said check in, so I checked in. I know I'm supposed to be on the floor, looking for shoplifters. I just did what I was told. I hide behind a display of Oreos, and want to cry. Also want to stuff entire package of Oreos into my mouth.

I pull myself together. The New Elle may have a really stupid job, but she'll do it better than any previous Retail Loss Reduction Associate ever has.

I grab a cart and wander aimlessly. This is too obvious, so I trickle through the $1.99 CD bin until a salesboy asks if he can be of assistance. Embarrassed, I randomly grab *Thom Jonez: How Do You Like My BSD?* and say I found what was looking for.

Drop *Thom* on a display of tube socks. Pretend Louis hasn't married Iowan floozy, and eye men's underwear as if buying tighty-whiteys for my loyal, loving husband. Carefully scan all underwear packages to determine if the models are gay. They are.

I glance around investigatorially, but it doesn't look like anyone's shoplifting. Decide my fictional husband wears boxer briefs, not tighty-whiteys, and agonize over the color combinations of the 3-packs. Would prefer a pack with purple, berry and green, but the berry and green only come with navy, and the purple only with black and white....

After underwear and Big & Tall, I hit the toy section. My trained eyes detect no shoplifters. Not even a punk kid. I have an extended fantasy about catching Eddie Munster shoplifting, and sending him to a bleak, violent prison for his formative years. Then:

Inspect bicycles for sale. Banana seats seem to be less popular than I remember. Several models have very cute baskets. One has a horn, which honks far louder than expected. No shoplifters.

Consider the purchase of a barbecue, for use during garden party. Fictional husband will grill. No shoplifters. (Realize it would be difficult to shoplift a GrillMaster 2000, but a cunning sticky fingers might walk off with a hibachi).

Examine quilt sets. Choose my favorite. Choose my least favorite. Change my mind. Change it back. No shoplifters.

Decide to lurk where the money is. Choose a diamond ring at the "better jewelry" department. Wonder why it is called "better." Better than what? Where is the "worse" jewelry department? My fictional husband reverts to a fictional fiancé, due to the lack of ring on my finger. Possibly should *not* have flung engagement ring at Louis while he was howling and covered in warm-ish crème brûlée. Jewelry department seems good place for crime spree, but no shoplifters in sight.

Consider going back to underwear, to look at the gay men with perfect bodies again. But I'm exhausted. I check my watch.

10:54.

I've been here forty minutes. Seven hours left.

Wonderful.

Days two through three. Feet hurt. Head hurts. Am avoiding Maya.

Don't want to talk about it. Day four. I'm in frozen foods, shopping for dinner, when I finally spot one. A shoplifter. I'm so excited I nearly drop my pot pie.

She's in woman's clothing. After four hell-days in Super 9, I am intimately acquainted with every item in that department, and even from here I can tell she's stuffing the worst of the lot into her gym bag.

I observe her criminal acts with a dispassionate and professional eye. She's a mousy little thing, about five-two, with sandy blond hair halfheartedly pulled into a scraggly tail. There are deep circles under her bleak eyes. She's in her late forties, and looks like she needs an electric blue rayon blouse far more than Super 9 does.

But I have a job to do. I stealthily approach. "Excuse me," I say. "I couldn't help but notice—"

"I'm sorry," she whispers hopelessly, crumbling in the face of the accusation I didn't have time to make. "I'm so sorry. I didn't mean to…"

"I have to look in your bag, ma'am."

She meekly hands it over. Inside are three polyester blouses festooned with laces and bows; one puce T-shirt from the Li'l Missy Department; two poly-blend beige skirts from the Li'l Dowdy Department; one box Rembrandt extra-whitening toothpaste; one Sonicare electric toothbrush; and a jumble of dental flosses, mostly mint.

She smiles in apologetic terror, and her teeth are horrible. She needs those dental products in the worst way.

"Shoplifting is a crime," I tell her sternly. "It is the policy of Super 9 to prosecute to the full extent of the law."

She cowers, and I almost snap and tell her that I stopped her inside, and she has nothing to worry about. Because this woman is clearly not part of an international ring of billion-dollar shoplifters. She is a woman with terrible teeth and a little daughter whom she dresses in puce.

But I do not snap. I speak harshly to her, very nearly reducing her to tears. She shivers before the majesty of the law, and promises she'll never, never, *never,* shoplift again. She is like a wet kitten—tiny, shivering, pathetic.

I finally relent, and tell her she is free to go. "But before you do," I say. "Maybe I can give you a little advice."

"I know. Don't be a shoplifter."

"Yes. Exactly. But that's not all." I take a deep breath, and give her a piece of my mind. I hold nothing back. Because I have standards. There are some things I simply cannot stand aside and watch.

These are my days: wake, work, sleep, wake, work, sleep, wake, work, sleep.

I hardly even have time to eat—and still haven't lost any weight. In fact, I worry that I'm transforming into a picture-perfect Super 9 customer. A bovine chunk of downscale consumerist urges stuffed like a sausage into a leisure suit. I don't mind being programmed to buy, buy, buy, if at least I'm left the dignity of buying gorgeous little items. But there is nothing gorgeous about Super 9. Plus, I am beginning to hum along to the in-store music.

I return home on Wednesday, or possibly Tuesday (all blending together), to find the dial tone merrily buzzing on my phone. Voice mail! I collapse in my soiled chair, kick off my shoes and rub my feet as I check my messages.

The first is Carlos, my sexy-voiced Latin admirer. He says he'll try again. I consider staying home to wait for his call, but decide a sick day would not be wise during my second week.

The second is Maya. Going through Elle-withdrawal, I suspect.

The third message is Sheila, from Superior Employment. I forgot to tell her I found a job. She says not to worry, dear, she's still looking. She sounds thoroughly pessimistic.

Fourth message is Spenser telling me to stop by the office on my way to work tomorrow. Don't know if I should be worried or pleased. Dare I hope I'm needed for another assignment? Would prefer posing as a cage-cleaner at a hellhole kennel, in search of prizewinning bitch, to another day at Super 9.

I defrost dinner and ring Maya. She thinks I'm angry about the bartending job, but I don't have the energy to work myself into a snit. Eight hours wrestling shopping carts in discount hell is too exhausting. Why can't Saks need help with shoplifters?

We have a nice chat, then I wash the discount grease out of my hair and collapse into bed.

It's still dark when I wake to alarming scrambling sounds outside the trolley. After full-panic mode is engaged, I decide the noise is merely the pugs doing their business. Check the clock, it's only nine-thirty—I must have fallen asleep around eight.

I hear a human cough. The noise is footsteps. Eddie Munster.

Fully awake, I tiptoe to my stack of water-condoms which are squatting by the front door like round rubber ducks in a row.

I grab an armful, and like an avenging fury, heave open the door. The little bastard is hunched at the end of the trolley, turned away from me, clearly doing something nefarious.

I shriek like a banshee and slam him with rubbers.

My aim is true. The first one catches him in the back of the neck. He flails and bellows and the next two condoms burst on his shoulders and ass. He trips and falls, the feeble runt, and the barrage continues. I am high on vengeance, I am retribution personified, I am unloading a week-and-a-half of Super 9 angst on Eddie's sodden and supine form.

I stand over him, the coup de grace in my hand—an aqua Trojan with a reservoir tip—and let him have it at short range.

The instant the rubber leaves my hand, my brain registers, with a flicker of surprise, that this is not, in fact, Eddie Munster.

I've just bombed the living hell out of a seventy-year-old man.

"You aren't—you aren't—" I say. "Who *are* you?"

He wipes water from his eyes and pulls bits of burst condom from his hair. "Your landlord," he says. "Mr. Petrie."

chapter 16

"So," Spenser says, tapping a pack of cigarettes on the Formica table.

"So!" I say brightly. Judging from his expression, I'm not here for good news.

"You watched the videos, right?"

"They were far out," I say. "Man." Trying to keep things light.

He doesn't crack a smile. "And what do you do when you spot a perp?"

"Be certain they have committed a crime, discreetly follow them out of the store and apprehend them."

"Do you warn them off, if you decide that's all that is required?"

I shake my head. "That's Phil's decision."

He can't possibly know about the dentally-challenged wet-kitten woman, can he?

"Phil's decision? Not yours?"

"I just round 'em up and shoot 'em down," I say.

"Very good." He swivels in his chair and fiddles with the VCR. "Now watch what you *don't* do."

"Not another shoplifting video," I complain.

"No," he says.

No.

It's me. In living color on Super 9 closed-circuit TV.

There's me playing electronic darts in the toy department. There's me, ensconced in a beanbag chair reading *US Weekly* magazine. (Note to self: never sit in beanbag chairs—very unflattering.) Me learning to play piano in the electronics department, and me twirling troll-head pencils for longer than is right. Me putting coats of silver polish on my fingernails and toes, and me watching *One Life to Live.*

I'm considering telling Spenser that the camera really does add ten pounds, when we get to the finale: me, catching-and-releasing the wet-kitten. And then me, giving her fashion advice—an obscenely long eleven minutes on fast-forward, as a blurry, jerky Elle pirouettes the woman from rack to rack, offering sage advice and fashion tips.

It finally ends. Spenser resumes tapping his cigarettes.

"Yes, but, honestly," I say, desperate to end the silence. "Honestly, she picked the ugliest things in the department. I mean, she would have looked horrible. The skirts? The shirts? For someone with her coloring? And the laces and bows were—" I shudder, unable to think of an accurate description "—not good."

"*When* do we approach the shoplifter?"

"Once they've left the store."

"And *who* decides if they should be charged?"

"Phillip."

"So *what the hell* did you think you were doing?"

I feebly try to defend myself. "It was my, my professional opinion that this was purely an isolated incident. I know that's wrong. I should have called Phil. But I talked to her. I'm sure she'll never do it again."

"Well, if you're absolutely certain," he says.

"Definitely," I say firmly. "No question."

He hits fast-forward. As I head for Housewares, the wet-kitten immediately shoplifts every single item I've recommended.

There's a long dense silence.

"I'm fired, aren't I?" I say. He can't fire me. I just lost my home. You can't fire someone who just lost their home, can you?

"If there were any justice in the world, you would be." He flicks open his silver lighter, then flicks it closed again. "But I like you, Medina. So I'm putting you on...what's it called? When you've been warned? Starts with a *P*."

"Probation?"

"Parole."

For two days, contrite over my monumental, mouth-breathing, videotaped fuck-up, I spend eight hours a day at Super 9 actually pretending to shop. And watching for shoplifters, of course.

Day three, I decide to be mother of five. There's a sale on diapers, so I dump four packs of Huggies into my cart. What else does a mother of five need? Valium? Liquor? Birth control, obviously—but I'm not in the mood for condoms, for some reason.

By three o'clock, I'm beat. I finished shopping hours ago, but continue to rattle around with my cart full of products for children ages sixteen months to eighteen years.

I'm soul-numbingly bored. I trudge into the tool department and stare at a pegged wall of wrenches. That's a lot of wrenches.

I'm not the only one who's impressed. There's a man fiddling with a ratchet-thingie, and I turn my hawklike Sherlock Holmes gaze upon him. He smiles and knocks the wind out of me. He's gorgeous. Heart-achingly gorgeous. Underwear model, TV star, young-Mel-Gibson beautiful.

He's a trim six-foot-something, with dark wavy hair I want to run my fingers though and tanned skin I want to rub up against. Emerald eyes I want to fall into, and wide beautiful lips and flashing white teeth—and I realize I'm describing the guy on the cover of a romance novel, but I can't help myself.

I twist a curl and say: "Ga."

He smiles wider.

I try again: "Hi."

He says hello. He sounds smooth and creamy.

"Shopping for a wench? A *wrench*. A wrench." Kill me now.

He laughs. "Not really. You know men and tools—I can resist anything except a display of hardware I'll never use."

I consider saying "Ga" again, when a voice calls my name. I turn, expecting Phillip, who's been harassing me since the wet-kitten incident. It is not Phillip. It's ZZ from the Goleta garage, with his stick legs and enormous belly.

"Yo there," ZZ says. "Ever find a place?"

I shoot a desperate look at Gorgeous. He winks, slips the ratchet-thingie into his pocket, and walks off, leaving me drooling.

"Excuse me?" I say to ZZ, who is still talking.

"Never said you have kids," he says, with a gesture at my cart. "No carpet-crawlers allowed. Might wreck the place."

Wreck the garage? What is he...wait, wait. Back up. The ratchet-thingie? His pocket? He shoplifted! It's true he is Gorgeous—beyond gorgeous, he is Ga-Ga Gorgeous—but he just blatantly shoplifted in front of Elle Medina, professional Retail Loss Reduction Associate. That was a mistake. I will wait until he has left the building and then...except, of course, he's already gone.

Fortunately, when I was a kid, my friend Janey and I spent untold hours targeting cute guys and tailing them through stores, giggling. Years of preparation finally pay off. I direct

ZZ to the beard-trimmers, grab a bink and diaper-rash ointment from the cart—figuring if Ga-Ga spots me, he'll think I'm just getting a few things—and locate the suspect in Aisle 16. Home and Garden.

He's subtle, I'll give him that. Only the trained eye can discern the clues. But by the time I follow him outside, I figure he's lifted eight or ten items. Mostly from Electronics, but he also stopped at the jewelry counter to look at watches. Every time the salesgirl showed another watch, the neckline on her top got lower. I couldn't blame her.

Finally, we're outside. I haven't fucked up. I can make my first collar. I dismiss an errant lady-cop-with-handcuffs fantasy, and authoritatively say: "Um, excuse me?"

He turns, a half smile on his face. Not nervous at all. "You caught me," he says.

"Yes. Yes. I saw—inside, at the, in Electronics—"

"I should know better than to lie to a woman." He looks me over. "It's not only displays of hardware I can't resist."

I blush. "I work for the store. I was, I saw you—putting the wrench—in your pocket and…I'm afraid I have to call security?"

"By all means," he says politely, and waits.

Fuck. Now what do I do? What if I tell him to come inside, and he walks away? I'd enjoy watching him walk away, but I cannot lose my job when I need to find a new apartment in a couple weeks.

"Follow me, please," I say, and to my great surprise, he does.

"I'm Joshua Franklin," he says. Why is he introducing himself? Shouldn't he want to keep quiet?

"Elle. Elle Medina."

"Elle Medina. That's a musical name. Listen, Elle. I didn't steal anything."

I apologize, but am impressively firm, and insist we speak with Phil.

He apologizes too, for some reason, and says, "I hope you don't get in any trouble."

It all goes by the book. I'm professional, competent, and efficient. There is only one snag: when Phillip asks Ga-Ga to empty his pockets, he cannot.

Because they are already empty. No illicit wrenches, no contraband watch.

"Miss Medina?" Phillip says.

"But I *saw* him!" I say.

"I'm sorry," Ga-Ga says.

"You're fired," Phillip says.

Back at the green Formica table, I hang my head and stare at my lap.

"Franklin's lawyer already contacted Super 9," Spenser says. "He's gonna sue."

"Yeah. I heard him mention that."

"Super 9, in turn, is talking about suing me."

I continue to look at my lap.

"For negligence. Hiring unqualified and incapable employees."

"I'm really sorry," I say again. Spenser is a chain-smoking freak, but he shouldn't be sued for my fuck-up.

"So I'm gonna sue you, Medina."

I finally look up.

"I'm kidding," he says. "But I've gotta let you go."

I nod. Of course he does.

"Hey. Don't take it so hard. Coulda happened to the best of us."

"I saw him shoplifting. Honestly. I really did."

"I looked at the tapes," he says. "And the guy might not be a pro, but he's a talented amateur. Old scam. He marks the store detective. That's you. Then pretends to shoplift, without actually pocketing anything. You catch him, he sues the company for defamation. Doesn't actually sue, of course. They'll settle out of court. But he'll pick up five or six grand, minus his attorney's fees, for an afternoon's work."

"Five or six thousand dollars? For pretend shoplifting?" Hmmm.

"Don't get any ideas, Medina," Spenser says. "I like you. I really do. But you try a scam like this, you'll end up doing seven to nine at a women's prison. I like you—" he blows smoke through his nose "—but you're an idiot."

chapter 17

A new list.

Income: Paycheck from Señor Spenser: $479.84

Outcome: BCBG's broken while in Nordstrom: $188-ish.

Private Investigator-type lipstick—Chanel: $25

Private Investigator-type sunglasses—Armani: $150, more or less.

Thus, from my week-and-a-half of employment, discounting valuable experience gained at very first job, I am ahead by roughly…$100?

That's not so bad, considering I was not only fired, but was instrumental in initiating a lawsuit. Impressive first effort, I'd say.

But I still need a job. Perhaps Sheila called. Perhaps *any-*

one called. I pick up my phone to check the dial tone, because it's possible the phone rang silently. The tone is straight and even. No voice mail. Not even from Carlos.

I know I should count my money to see precisely how much I don't have, but am deeply afraid. I had $500, and then made $100, and haven't been spending much due to constant bargain shopping at Super 9. Of course, there's gas and orchids and the bottle of twelve-year-old port and the cartons of Godiva Chocolate Raspberry Truffle ice cream. But theoretically, I still have $500-ish.

I take a deep breath, and count—$312.

I take a hit of port, and a faceful of chocolate raspberry truffle, and something goes *gurgle, guzz, gurg* from the vicinity of the toilet, and I realize it is a sign. I am flushing my money down the toilet. I am tossing my life in the shitter. I am circling the drain. Out of money. Fired from job. Evicted from trolley. Flung condoms at ginger freak-head. Lust for Ga-Ga Gorgeous grifter. Am generally pathetic, ridiculous and slightly drunk.

But now is the time. It is time to grow up. I open my fridge-type unit, seeking some nutritious, grown-up food. There is none. I shopped far healthier for Louis than I do for myself. Granted, I spent a small fortune every time I entered a gourmet food store. But still, if I did it for him, I can do it for me...and on the cheap, too. I should have nationalized booty from Super 9—there was no other store detective to stop me. Sure, and I could dress in outfits from the Li'l Dowdy department.

At least I still have my car. It may look like Halloween, but I love my orange freak-car. I slide behind the wheel and turn the key. The engine purrs.

First stop is Super Ralph's, Santa Barbara's solution to hacienda-style grocery shopping. I will buy sensible, nutritious, low-fat food in bulk.

But inside, temptation surrounds me. Truffle oil calls my name in Aisle 3. Pickled asparagus ambushes me in Aisle 12.

I am on the verge of kicking my good intentions in the teeth when I spot a forty-pound bag of rice on a bottom shelf. Price? $11.95. I am overwhelmed by a surge of sheer economy. Twelve bucks for forty el-bees of rice. My cupboard will never be empty again. Nourishment is only a cup of water away, and I'm sure to lose weight.

I wrestle the bag into my arms. Economical, but ungainly. I drag it to a checkout line. I inspect magazines while I wait, the rice growing steadily heavier in my arms. Definitely room for another *O*-type magazine. Maybe *L* should have a Frugality column. First month? Rice.

I really should have grabbed a cart. My arms are going dead and my shoulder screams in agony. I finally heave the bag onto the conveyor belt, feeling quite superior to the woman in front of me, who is buying frozen pizza, two packs of American cheese and a head of iceberg.

I pay my twelve bits, and heft the bag over a shoulder. It prickles my neck. It's made of that brittle plastic-burlap that cattle feed comes in, and as I heft it a few grains of rice trickle from a slight gash. Must be careful not to spill rice all over my beautiful car.

I stumble towards the exit, hoping to find a cart. No cart. Doesn't matter—I'm parked right out front.

As if unwilling to leave home, the bag attempts to wiggle from my arms the moment I am in the parking lot. I claw frantically at it, but gravity is the enemy, and I feel it eeling from my grasp as I shuffle forward.

I clutch anew, and for a lovely moment think I'm going to make it.

I don't. The bag slips and smashes to the asphalt like an overripe melon. The gash widens and rice flows like water from the hole. Fucking ducky. I tussle with the burlap, trying to force the hole upward to stanch the flow. In a flash, I rip a larger opening.

"Shit!" Rice surrounds me in a two foot radius. I'm tempted to flee, but goddamn it I'm an adult now, and I don't abandon sacks of rice in parking lots. Plus, I'm hungry. I grab the sack in a death-grip and heave. It flops and emits a new rivulet of rice. "Fuck you!" I shove the bag, earning dirty looks from several passersby. "I'll kick your burlap ass."

"Here, let me," a man says. "Before someone reports a rice-beater."

Louis Merrick. Merrick of the Coffee Condom Catastrophe. Way to make a good second impression. Third impression. Whatever. I'm just lucky that I'm not on my hands and knees, picking up individual grains.

"Merrick," I say.

He effortlessly lifts the sack and starts toward my car. The bundle in his arms looks like an injured child he's rescued from a burning building. He's no Ga-Ga Gorgeous, but he can really manhandle a bag of recalcitrant grain. I am far more giddily gratified than I should be about rescued rice.

I open the trunk, and he lays his salvaged armload gently down.

"Safe and sound," he says.

I consider saying, "My hero!" but ask him what he's doing here instead. It comes out ungrateful.

"Uh—" he points to Ralph's Super Hacienda. "Grocery shopping? I live down the street."

"Oh, right. Right." I look at him. His hair is still freaky, but it's sort of mussed, and he looks a little tired, and I am definitely warm for him. "Thanks," I say. "Really."

"That's a lot of rice."

"I like rice. A lot." Then I blurt the truth: "Plus it's cheap. I lost my—I haven't found a job."

He looks politely embarrassed, before saying he's glad he ran into me. "I wanted to apologize. About the other morning, with the, um…"

"The frolicking condoms."

He laughs. "Somehow I feel responsible."

I wave away his apology. "Nothing you could do. Turns out I'm the reincarnation of Calamity Jane. But thank you."

"I did wonder, of course," he says. "Why you carry enough rubbers to accommodate a regiment of sailors on shore leave."

"They weren't for accommodating sailors. Or *anyone.* Remember the crank calls? The kid was playing pranks on my apartment, too. Like tossing dead squirrels at me. So I got the condoms for water balloons, to peg the little juvie."

His eyes widen in what could be amazement, amusement or abhorrence.

"What?" I say. I haven't even told him the part about bombing Mr. Petrie.

He shakes his head.

"Well...Merrick..." It's time to slink off with my rice. "It was nice—"

"Why do you call me Merrick?"

"I like it. Merrick. It's a solid name."

He doesn't believe me, but I refuse to explain.

"What's your last name?" he asks.

"Medina."

"Should I call you that?"

"No, that would be weird."

His eyes crinkle. "Then will you have dinner with me, Elle?"

I am not quite sure if he's laughing at me. "When?" I ask suspiciously. "I'm sort of busy the next few weeks."

"Tomorrow night?"

"Okay."

He smiles. "Okay. I'll pick you up at seven? Where do you live?"

"No!" Must not let him see where I live.

"No to seven?" he asks, "Or—"

"Why don't we meet at the restaurant?"

"Because you'll be late. How about we meet at Shika at six-thirty?"

I tell him okay.

"And is Italian good? I was thinking Bucatini's, but they do more pasta than rice."

chapter 18

I don't know why Merrick said I'd be late if we met at the restaurant. As it happens, I begin preparing at two-thirty, and arrive at Shika twenty minutes early.

"Hi, sweetie," Maya says.

"I lost my job," I say, sliding onto a stool. I tell the sad story, and she is appropriately sympathetic, though she goes hard on Ga-Ga. I try to explain that he cannot be judged by mortal standards, but she scoffs.

"So why are you all spiffed up?" she asks.

"A date," I say.

"With the new Louis?"

I nod, although the reminder of his name takes a slice out of my joy.

"Well, you look beautiful."

"Don't I?" I say. "And guess who hasn't eaten a bite since this morning!"

"Elle—you won't look any skinnier from missing one meal."

Actually, I would. But that's not the point. "It's not that. It's economic strategy. I'm gonna overorder tonight, so I can take food home in doggie bags, and eat it for days. But I figured I should be hungry, too—so I can pack it in."

"You get that from *Cosmo?*"

"No, that's my own," I say, proudly.

"And I suppose going Dutch is out of the question."

"If I want Dutch, I'll go to Denmark."

"Holland."

"Anyway, it's not like I haven't invested in this date. Think about it—my outfit costs $500, my makeup another $200. Hair is $150. I'm not counting accessories and hair products and diets and skincare and all that. It takes me three hours to achieve this level of perfection, not including the months and years spent in training and experimentation. And shopping. He'll roll up wearing whatever he found crumpled on the floor of his closet this morning, with his weird hair and maybe ten minutes of worry, anticipation and deviant sexual fantasy invested in the date. I've put in eleven hours on him specifically, and like three weeks on men in general. I read four articles about cellulite and two about stalkers. I am bathed, shaved, scented, colored, curled, peeled, painted and sartorially fucking splendid. I ought to charge his architect ass by the hour."

Maya applauds. She is joined by second pair of hands, which entered during my tirade. You get no points for guessing to whom the second pair belongs.

"I am early," I tell him.

"You are sartorially splendid," he says. "And from here, the cellulite is hardly noticeable."

I giggle, because I know he is teasing, but I won't be laughing if he ever catches me naked. I stand, afraid barstool has similar effect as beanbag chair, and stride towards him.

Oh, God, now what? What am I supposed to do? Shake his hand? I haven't been on a real date since the summer after high school. My college dates, before moving in with Louis, weren't even real dates—we wouldn't *go* out, we'd *hang* out.

Merrick meets me halfway and busses me on the cheek. It's very sweet, and my instinct is to gush, but I clamp down.

"Do you want to have a drink first?" he asks. "Or are you ready to eat?"

"I'm ready," I say, quickly. Don't want Maya monitoring my date. Plus, I am officially starving.

We walk down State to Bucatini's. It's a semi-outdoor Italian café, with white-cloth tables lining the brick patio, and a Santa Barbara-green awning above. When I was in high school, this was a greasy BBQ place, but no traces remain. A hostess lights the candles as Merrick and I sit, and I'm suddenly shy. This is a real date. It's not a morning coffee meet. It's the kind of romantic date that is supposed to end naked and sweaty, and I feel a pang of guilt about being disloyal to Louis. Like I'm cheating on him.

He didn't even bother ending our engagement before marrying another woman, and *I* feel disloyal. Well, fuck Louis. Maybe I wasn't the perfect wife-to-be, maybe I spent too much and maybe I was aimlessly coasting, but I was loyal and I was honest and I loved him as well as I could.

"Elle?" Merrick says.

"Sorry. I was thinking."

He quietly waits.

"This used to be a barbecue place, when I was in high school," I say.

He doesn't say anything.

I glance at him over my menu. He's in a linen shirt again—this one a soft blue that makes his gray eyes stand out. Despite the red hair, he's handsome. He has a strong face. There's nothing beautiful about it, but it's masculine and really present. On the walk from Shika, I noticed he smells of lavender soap and shaving cream, and I touched his arm and then touched it again.

But I don't know what to say. My dating skills haven't just rusted, they've entirely disintegrated. And I'm worried about what he's going to think when I order two meals. The waiter arrives with a bottle of Chianti, thank God. I have a reason to remain silent as he pours, Merrick tastes and we all approve.

I take a huge gulp of wine and ask about his day. I am already wearing sexy underwear. If I give him time "in his cave," then he'll know I'm really serious.

He tells me his day was pretty good. He's amusing and light, and seems happy to carry the conversation. He asks about me, and despite my plan I tell the abbreviated Super 9 story.

He says, "Elle." He says, "You got fired?" He says, "Couldn't you talk to them?" He says, "I don't understand how you could get fired."

And I'm put off completely. He sounds so much like Louis—like *my* Louis—being the stern adult, that when the waiter returns to take our orders, I'm ready.

"I'll have the Shrimp Renato," I say. "And the Prosciutto and Melon to start." I dare myself to order the penne as well, but lose my nerve. Instead, I say: "We could use more bread. And I'll have a cup of the soup."

Merrick orders, and asks: "How do you get fired?"

"It doesn't take much," I say, in an airy fashion. "Poor performance at job skills generally does the trick."

"And that was the case with you? You performed poorly?"

I'm suddenly quite proud. Not just anyone, within two weeks at her first real job, could be responsible for the start of a lawsuit against a major corporation. I tell him the whole sordid tale, including being accused of shoplifting at Nordstrom and the suit against Spenser.

He is appalled. "Don't you feel bad for the private detective?"

Of course I do. "His insurance will cover it," I say, hopefully.

"Insurance? He wouldn't need insurance if you'd been doing your job. Elle, your whole reason for being there—the reason he was paying you to leaf through magazines in the changing room—was to prevent theft. Did you ever think—"

I finish my soup and third glass of wine before Merrick finally winds down. I feel like shit.

"That's a nice shirt," I say, to change the subject.

"What?"

"Your shirt. It matches your eyes."

"And you've never had a job before?"

That worked well. "Not exactly. I mean, I have. But not exactly."

"Do you have any skills?"

"I have skills," I say, too loud. "I just don't have *job* skills, that's all. Do I wish I could type? Do I wish I could run spreadsheets? Yeah, especially when I have to pay the rent. But people waste their lives working—I've wasted enough time. I wasted six years." I stop to swig more wine. "You remind me of him."

"Who?"

"My fiancé. My ex-fiancé." I pour myself another glass. "He was always lecturing me, too."

"Is that why you left him?"

"No, that's why he left me."

He gently unclasps my hand from the wine bottle and pours himself another glass. "I'm sorry. I didn't mean to lecture."

"Doesn't matter." Now that he's sorry, I feel like crying. "Maya does it, too. But she's shorter than me, so I can slap her around."

"You can slap me around later," he says, and asks how long Maya and I have been friends.

We drink and talk, and the rest of the food comes. I nibble a shrimp. The bread basket is empty. Nuts. I'm still hungry, but if I stop now I'll have a complete meal to take home.

"Is it not good?" Merrick asks, watching my birdlike pecking.

"It's delicious. I'm just...resting."

"You're resting."

"Uh-huh." I take another sip of wine. "Can I have a bite of yours?"

He pushes his plate toward me, and I forklift a massive bite of linguini and a plump olive. Delicious. I spear and spin with my fork, and he asks if he can have a bite of mine.

I grudgingly fork the smallest shrimp and pass it over.

"When I was a kid," he says, "I thought shrimp tasted like baby fingers."

"Which explains why your little brother is called Lefty," I say.

We both think this is funny and the tension between us eases. I ask about his family, and he tells me as we eat—both of us from his plate. I tell him about mine while trying to defend tomorrow's meal from his forking incursions.

The waiter eventually comes to clear the table, and I ask to have my still heaping plates put into a doggie bag. If he asks, I'll pretend to have the perfect purebred Chesapeake Bay retriever. He doesn't ask. So I tell him to throw in a little bread for my Shih Tzu and to bring the dessert menu.

"You hardly ate," Merrick says. "How can you want dessert?"

"My dessert compartment is free," I say. "I'll have the tiramisu."

"Just a decaf for me," Merrick says.

"And he'll have the crème brûlée."

Merrick pays the bill and we stand awkwardly outside the restaurant. Not sure what happens now. It's been too long since I dated. I'm a little drunk and ready to go home.

"That was lovely." I transfer my bulging doggie bag to my left hand, and stick out my right to shake. "Thanks so much."

Instead of shaking, he takes my hand and holds it. "Is your drink compartment full?"

"Umm..."

"Come and have a drink," he says. "I'm even willing to go back to Maya's."

"Shika's not that bad," I say, and to back up this outrageous lie I agree to join him.

As we enter the gloom of Shika, Merrick heads for the privacy of a booth. I head for the safety of the bar. In a moment, he joins me.

"Maya, you know Merrick," I say, as if we weren't here two hours ago.

"I know him well enough to call him Louis," she says. She looks like a fresh-faced and beautiful sprite. I haven't checked my makeup in hours. I am a bloated manatee.

"Elle insists on calling me by my last name," Merrick says, clearly hoping Maya will tell him why.

"Does she?" Maya says. "That's curious."

"What are you going to have to drink?" I ask, to change the subject. "I'm thinking maybe schome schnapps." I eye the selection behind the bar.

"Sounds like you've had enough already," Maya says.

"I *ate* dinner," I protest.

Merrick snorts and Maya moves down the bar to pour us beers. Monty's stool is vacant, for once.

"How do you know Monty?" I ask Merrick. Because I live in terror that conversation will peter out.

"Everyone knows Monty. He owns half of Santa Barbara. My office is in one of his buildings. I've done some work for him."

"He owns half of Santa Barbara and spends his days here?"

Merrick shrugs. "He's a character. Once challenged Fess Parker to a fistfight." He tells me the story, but I'm not really listening. I finish my beer and grab at his, but he pulls it out of my reach. I'm not proud; I pout until he buys me another.

By the time I finish my second, I'm slightly cross-eyed. Still vivacious and charming, though. I pause for breath, and Maya makes Merrick promise to drive me home.

"I'm not that drunk," I say. And I'm not, really. Just nervous. "Walk me to my car. I'm parked two blocks away. By the time we get there, I'll be fine."

"Elle..." Maya warns.

"If I'm not okay by then, Merrick can drive me home." Sheesh, the way I've been acting you'd think she'd be ready to see me die a fiery death.

Walking to the car, Merrick says something about Maya and me being good friends.

"Best friends. Ever since I beat up Ricky Parker in the seventh grade for calling her fat." I trip on a crack in the sidewalk. Merrick catches me and holds me and I turn my face towards his neck. "You smell good."

"You sure it's not pizza you're smelling?" he says with a smile, as we pass a pizza parlor.

"Oh, my food!" I pull away, panicked.

"It's right here." In his other hand. He really is lovely. An architect, too. And good with rice.

"I like you," I declare, and nestle closer. He kisses me. A sweet light kiss. Delicious. We kiss some more and touch and walk and I'm dizzy when I say, "The car's right there."

Should I ask him to come home with me? I miss being held. I look up at him, try to block the glare from his freak-hair, and he says, "In that lot? With the locked gate?"

I turn. A chain is strung across the exit. "It was open when I parked there."

He brushes his lips across my temple and whispers into my ear. "Let me take you home."

"Yes, please."

★ ★ ★

"You're sure your house is back here?" he asks as we stumble through the garden.

"Of course I'm sure," I snap. My ardor has cooled at the thought of his expression when he catches sight of the trolley.

He looks dubious. Then he sees it. "Is that a trolley?"

"A *converted* trolley."

"I've never seen a trolley made into a home before." He sounds more intrigued than disgusted. "It suits you."

"Suits me how?"

He presses against me and kisses a trail down my neck. "It's unique." More kissing. "I like it."

We're going to have sex. Louis Merrick, architect and ginger freak-head, is the first other man I'll have sex with in six years. Is this a bad idea? It could be pitiful rebound sex. It's not like we're moving into a relationship, but if we start with pitiful rebound sex, that'll be the end for sure. On the other hand, I *want* sex.

"I don't know," I say.

"What don't you know?" He runs his hand along my back, nibbles my earlobe.

"Um…" I say. "Mmmmm."

He unzips my dress and pulls it away from my shoulders. I'm flushed with pleasure—part Merrick, part Chianti and part the knowledge that I'm wearing a La Perla bra. Matching panties, too. He twists one of my corkscrew curls around his finger. "How do you get it to curl like this?"

"It's natural," I whisper. Do I have clean sheets on the bed?

His hand glides over my breasts. My nipples harden. "Are these natural too?"

I arch my back in response, and my arms are around him, and I'm touching him everywhere, his arms, his back, his shoulders, his ass.

"Inside," he says. "The key?"

Who cares about clean sheets? I fumble, lust-fogged,

for my key, and hand it over. He fiddles with the lock as I keep touching him. He shoves the door open and flicks the light.

"There's shit all over the floor," he says.

"It's not that messy," I say, working my way toward his zipper.

He grabs my exploratory hand. "No. Literally."

I pull away and step inside. "If that little juvie let the pugs—"

But that ain't dog shit, Toto. I guess the *gurgle, guzz, gurgle* coming from the toilet, was, in fact, sending a message.

"Looks like your toilet overflowed," Merrick says helpfully, from the safety of the doorstep.

There's an inch of bilgey-water in the kitchen and bathroom areas. My first post-Louis date ends with me standing in a shit-trolley with my tits hanging out. All I need now is to slip and fall into the sewage—that will make my humiliation complete. The moment I think this, I clutch at the wall, to prevent the nightmare from happening.

"Whoa," Merrick says. "Careful there."

I suspect he's trying not to laugh. "It's not funny! My toilet—my toilet backed up."

"No shit, Sherlock," he says, and his lips tremble.

"Get out!" I shriek.

"Sorry." He looks contrite. "Let me give you a hand cleaning up."

"Go." I say, clutching the wall, while trying to hunch back into my dress.

"Are you sure? I can—"

"Go!"

He goes. I stand frozen, stunned, surveying the horror. He returns a moment later, and I do *not* slip and fall in surprise.

"Doggie bag," he explains, putting it on a counter. "I'll call you."

Sure. Who wouldn't call a girl who lives in a septic tank?

★ ★ ★

Mr. Petrie answers my frantic knocking at 6:55 the next morning. He fixes the toilet as I sit outside and nibble at a carton of melon and ham.

He emerges an hour later. I fall over myself thanking and praising him, in the hopes that I'll convince him to let me stay. I mean, the trolley is officially a shit-hole now, right? Who else will want to live here?

"So…no hard feelings?" I say, after ten minutes of gushing gratitude. "Over the water, um, the water balloony thing?" I explain that it was Eddie Munster's fault, and Mr. Petrie ought to speak to his parents. "Though I haven't seen the little bastard around in days."

"The little bastard was here visiting his grandparents," Mr. Petrie says. "He's back in Bakersfield now, with his parents."

"So no hard feelings?"

"Of course not," he says.

I attempt, by sheer force of will, to make him say that, as far as that goes, I'm welcome to stay.

"As far as that goes," he says. "With the plumbing and damage to the floor, you can kiss your security deposit goodbye."

I gape.

"And I'll tell my grandson you send your regards."

chapter 19

Call Sheila at Superior every morning for almost two weeks. By the third day, she stopped calling me "dear."

I miss yet another handful of Carlos's calls. I do not hear from Merrick, and am disappointed. Not only have I run out of non-rice food, but I'd been hoping he'd offer me the job as his assistant, if only out of pity. Maybe he's worried I'll stink up the office. Who wants Pig Pen as a receptionist?

Twelve days before I am evicted from trolley. Have not found a new apartment. Spent $75 to get my car out of the parking lot. Spent $120 on towels, to replace the ones I used to clean the Great Poop Debacle. In retrospect, should not have bought Egyptian cotton. The aqua is pretty, though, and cheap colors always fade and disappoint. I'll have these towels forever.

In addition to new towels, I have $183.

I owe roughly $4,000 on credit cards, plus $1,500 on the IKEA card.

I ask Maya if I can stay with her and Brad when I get kicked out. She is nice about it, but not pleased.

I call my father. He doesn't call back. I sometimes wonder if I moved in with Louis just so I'd have a male authority figure around the house.

I call my mother. She does call back. She mentions the busboy job at the café next door again. I actually consider taking it, but I don't, on the grounds that things cannot get worse. I have hit an all-time low. There is only one direction.

And, as if the universe is conspiring to prove me right, the phone rings.

"Eleanor Medina," the sexy Latin voice says.

"This is she," I say, breathlessly.

"This is Carlos Neruda."

"Carlos," I say.

"I saved all your messages," he says. "Very charming—half the men in my office are in love with you."

I felt bad that I kept missing him, so I'd left a few voice mails for him. Just because, you know. Just because. He'd usually call back to find me gone, so I'd leave a new one. Well, it wasn't a big thing. Just three messages. Maybe four.

"Oh, well..." I say. "You're a friend of Brad's?"

"I'm sorry, Elle," he says. "I'm not a friend of Brad's. I am your worst nightmare."

"Are you calling from Iowa?"

He laughs. "Can't say that I am."

"Then you're my second-worst nightmare, at best."

"You're making this very difficult for me," he says. "If you could be ruder, so I'd dislike you, that would help a good deal."

"Ruder?"

He sighs. "Your credit is in the shits, Elle. Three credit card companies, which for some reason I can't understand extended you credit in the first place, have given up hope of ever being paid. They turned you over to a collection agency. That means me."

"Collection agency?" I squeak. "How'd you—how did you find me?"

"VW dealer. Where you applied for even more credit.'

"Oh, no."

"Oh, yes. From here on out, it's you and me and a debt in the amount of $6,497.43."

"Oh, no."

"Oh, yes."

"Would you stop saying that? What do I have to do?"

"Do you have a job?" he asks.

"No."

"Savings?"

"No."

He asks a few more questions, and I keep saying "no."

"Jesus, Elle," he finally says. "What were you thinking?"

"I don't know. My fiancé was going to pay the debts, once we got married, but—" And I tell him the whole story.

He's a good listener. When I finish, he commiserates and says: "Well, I'm gonna need a good-faith payment. It's that or the repo man, for your clothes and car. How much can you send?"

I calculate. "Twenty-five dollars?"

He chuckles in an entirely seductive Latin fashion, and even though I'm the butt of the joke, I'm thinking maybe I do want a Latino boyfriend. One who doesn't know I wallow in sludge.

"At least four hundred," he says.

"Four hundred! But I—"

"Let me tell you where to send the check."

"No, no, Carlos, I can't—"

He ignores me. I dutifully write the address and payment schedule on the back of a Rusty's Pizza menu. He tells me how much he enjoyed speaking with me, and we hang up.

I stare out the window at Mrs. Petrie's garden. Disappointing that Latin admirer is credit police. I perk up—at least he said nothing about my IKEA card.

chapter 20

There's a knock on the trolley door. Must be Maya, come to roust me from my latest crisis. I mentioned Carlos's call to her last night, and for some reason, she considers this a problem. Actually, I agree. I hit an all-time low, and immediately go lower. The universe is conspiring, all right.

I shuffle to the door, my partially braided hair unraveling, my flying pig pajamas sagging. Maya, of course will be her usual, adorable, blond self. I open the door and a bouquet of white cala lilies floats in front of me. It swishes to the side, and Ga-Ga Gorgeous is there. Not Maya, but Joshua Franklin, the faux shoplifter. Mr. I-Get-Five-Grand-For-An-Afternoon-And-You-Get-Fired.

"Hey!" I say, my wrath making me articulate. "Hey!"

He smiles sheepishly, and looks—incredibly—even more attractive. "I suppose that means you remember me from Super 9?"

"Ga," is all I manage. I pull up my pajama bottoms and smooth down my top. Why couldn't I at least be in my cute kimono, my hair twisted back in chopsticks?

"You're probably wondering what I'm doing here. I got your address from Ross Investigations," he says. "Well, my lawyer got it. He wanted to subpoena you, get a signed statement. I told him it was ridiculous to pester you…I'm so sorry about what happened."

His hair is gorgeous. His nose is gorgeous. "I…well, that's okay. I mean, I did get fired, but…that's okay."

He gestures with the flowers. "Well, that's why I stopped by. To apologize and drop these off."

"Oh! They're gorgeous."

"Honeysuckle," he says, and all I want in life is to hear him say that word one more time.

"What?"

His forehead is gorgeous. His lips are gorgeous. "I got them at Honeysuckle. It's this garden place downtown. It's like your garden here—" he gestures behind himself, and all I want in life is to see him gesture like that one more time "—but in a shop."

I blush and stammer, as he says goodbye, smiles gorgeously and leaves. The door shuts, and I am cut off from all the *gorgeous* in the world.

I rush to the mirror, to determine precisely how much of an awful mess I look. I look a tremendous earthquake of an awful mess. There's a knock on the door.

It's Ga-Ga, again, and all the *gorgeous* comes rushing back.

"I know this is—well, you have every right to be incredibly angry with me. And I know flowers hardly make it up to you. I don't know if I *can* make it up—but I wondered…would you have dinner with me?"

I emit a noise not unlike a peep.

"No?" He shakes his head. "Of course not. I just—well, I wanted to ask." He smiles bravely, his gorgeous eyes sad, and steps away.

"Wait," I say.

He turns, hope radiating from his perfect features. "Tonight? At eight? Would that be okay?"

I glance at the alarm clock beside my bed. There are roughly six hours between now and the dinner hour. A little short on preparation time, but I can manage.

"Yes," I say. "Tonight."

We're in his car—a brand new Audi—cruising along the shoreline toward the restaurant. Ga-Ga oozes sexuality. I ooze wild terror that I will fuck this up.

When I opened the trolley door for the date, he said how beautiful I was. Then he looked at my shoes and said: "Prada?"

I fell in love. They *were* Prada. It took me forty minutes to choose them. And he knew. He knew they were Prada. He is gorgeous man, inside and out.

Shoes come up again as we pass Shoreline Park, where we see a mother chasing her toddler through the park. She is young and chunky and wearing stiletto pumps.

"That's a good way to break an ankle," Ga-Ga says.

"Or at least snap a heel."

"Is that what happened to those BCBGs on your counter?" he asks.

Be still my heart. He knows a pair of BCBGs. "The heel," I say. "It broke. While I was running. In Nordstrom's."

He raises a gorgeous eyebrow, and the whole story comes tumbling out.

"You fell?" he says. "And they charged you a hundred and eighty-eight bucks for a pair of broken shoes?"

I nod, aware that he is disappointed in me, and am relieved when he pulls into a lot a half block from the beach.

The restaurant we are going to? Citronelle.

I didn't even know there was a Citronelle in Santa Barbara. It must have opened while I was away. It's located on the second floor of a hotel on Cabrillo Boulevard, with a view of East Beach and the ocean. I almost tell him I can't eat there, memories of breakup with Louis will turn stomach, but instead say, "Oh, Josh—I love Citronelle."

"It's Joshua, actually. Not Josh."

I cringe and apologize. How pretentious for him to go by Joshua instead of Josh. It would be fine if he were gay, of course. But then he tells me the restaurant is owned by Meeshell Reesharrrd, in the same cheesy French accent I use, and I realize I've found my soul mate.

He orders champagne. He orders oysters. I love champagne and oysters, except for the bubbly and slimy bits.

"So, what do you do?" I ask. "I mean, other than—whatever." Recalling the lawsuit, I flush a bright red.

He waves away my embarrassment. "I didn't shoplift, Elle."

"I know," I say, too quickly.

"Do I look like I need the wrenches?"

He doesn't. He looks like he needs nothing but me. "Well…"

"I know it must seem like I—"

"Set the whole thing up? To start a lawsuit?"

"It was my lawyer who insisted I sue. I'm in business. Honestly, if I needed the money, I'd have approached venture capitalists, not Super 9."

Well, that sounds perfectly reasonable. "But I saw you."

"You didn't. You couldn't have. Because I didn't take anything. Are you sure you saw what you think you saw?"

And actually, I'm not. I mean, I was blinded by his beauty. I was saying "Ga-Ga." Clearly, I was not in my right mind. I laughingly admit that I'm not entirely sure, and with that bit of awkwardness out of the way, we small-talk until dinner comes.

We have a lot in common. He recently moved to Santa Barbara. I recently returned to Santa Barbara. We both like long walks on the beach, sunsets, afternoon movies in the rain and…well, all sorts of things.

He gazes longingly into my eyes, swallows an oyster, and says, "Joshua loves oysters."

"Pardon?"

"Oysters—I love them."

"Oh! Yeah, me too."

We finish the oysters and both order cobb salads. Then we both order strawberries and cream for dessert. Lots and lots in common.

Including the fact that neither of us can pay the bill.

When it arrives, Joshua pulls out his wallet. He flips through it with increasing concern, and turns to me. "This is so embarrassing, Elle—I just got new credit cards, and I forgot to put them in my wallet. Do you have a card? I'll pay you back tomorrow."

Tomorrow! "Of course!" I look through my miniscule purse, but I know there's no card. I don't even own a card anymore. I stuck a twenty in there for emergencies, though, and I suppose this qualifies. "Oh, no. No card. I've got twenty dollars. How much is the bill?"

"Ninety-eight, before tip."

"Um, how much have you got?"

"Fourteen and change."

"What are we gonna do?"

"Give me yours," he says. I do, and he tosses it on the table. "There's the tip. Now we leave before the waiter gets back."

"What?" I look furtively around the restaurant. "We're in Citronelle!"

"Not for long."

"What if the waiter sees?" I bleat in panic as we stand.

"Shhh. Act natural. I'll come back tomorrow to pay."

"Promise?"

"I promise. Now kiss me—we can pretend we were too caught up to notice we shorted the bill."

He kisses me. It's gorgeous. We kiss our way downstairs and out the restaurant. We kiss on the sidewalk and are still kissing when we hear someone yelling: "Hey!"

"Run," Joshua whispers in my ear.

And you know what? I *can* run in heels.

* * *

We catch our breath two blocks later, leaning against each other, laughing and kissing. God, this is fun. My heart is hammering and I'm wired from running and being kissed by Joshua. Louis—either Louis—would flip if he knew I'd skipped out on Citronelle.

I am mesmerized by the gorgeous exciting thrill that is Joshua. So when he suggests that we take the party back to the trolley, I enthusiastically agree.

We have sex. And once I stop worrying about how I look naked, it's fantastic. Strange to be with a man who isn't Louis, of course. And whose body I don't know. Well, strange to be with a man who I don't know at all, really. I mean, he doesn't know what rings my bell, and vice versa. So it's mostly just strange.

Still, we go through three (!) of my leftover Planned Parenthood condoms. I think I'm falling in love. Can't help but wonder, though, as I bask in afterglow, if I should ask him not to yell "Joshua is coming!" when he climaxes.

The phone rings. At first, I hope it is Merrick. Then I remember, and hope it is Joshua. I pick up and hear: "Elle Medina."

"Carlos! Hi. How are you? Beautiful day here, in Santa Barbara."

"Elle...do you want to hear the bad news, or the bad news?"

"I'm in love, Carlos."

"Since last week? Congratulations. Who's the lucky man?"

"Just the most gorgeous man ever. We had dinner. Then we, um, had breakfast, too. At Cajun Kitchen, for under fourteen dollars, so don't worry. And then..."

"What?" Carlos sounds genuinely interested.

"Well, you *know* how men are."

"I consider myself an expert."

"And do you call women after you—" I realize I'm making an assumption. "You're not gay, are you?"

"I'm straight," he says. "Thanks for asking."

"So, do you call women after you, you know. The day after?"

"Depends."

"You dog, Carlos," I say. "Joshua called the next afternoon. And again yesterday. And Thursday we have another date! He has a surprise for me."

"A surprise? Like he's married?"

"No-no-no! Nothing like that." I checked his ring finger while he slept. No marks, no tan line.

But I guess Carlos hears uncertainty in my voice. He says, "You want me to run a credit report on this guy?"

"Don't be ridiculous. The surprise will be flowers or something. I'm just so…happy."

"Why do you do this to me? You know I have a job, here. If you start miserable, it makes my life easier. Okay?"

"Sorry."

"I never got that check, Elle."

"No, I never actually sent it, because I only have $102. But I'm gonna sell my—" I look desperately around the trolley; I must not mention IKEA furniture "—Tahari dress."

"For four hundred dollars?"

"And my shearling coat." Too warm to wear it in Santa Barbara anyway.

I swear I can hear him shaking his head over the phone. "Four hundred dollars, Elle."

"I'll get it to you. I promise."

"And then we're gonna put you on monthly payments."

"I'm looking forward to that."

"Liar." He laughs. "And, Elle—an IKEA card? That was a big mistake."

chapter 21

Life is a blur of Joshua. Granted, we only had one date and two phone calls, but I have spun a gossamer web of daydream and fantasy. We have been to Bali and Paris, and to Venice twice. Our wedding was spectacular, despite the paparazzi. Our children have his eyes and hair and features, and they have me for…well, the uterus and womby stuff. Hadn't really thought what they'd have from me. Possibly my ability to fill out forms with remarkable speed.

But reality encroaches. Joshua daydreams have fully occupied days, as I've unsuccessfully searched for new job and apartment. "Man," however is on my list. So I haven't failed my duties completely.

Tomorrow is big date. I read in *Glamour* that the second date is the most important, as we have passed Stage One and are now in serious territory. (Was slightly concerned to discover that sleeping together is actually Stage Four.) I am frantic with anticipation and anxiety. What if he realizes he doesn't like me? What if my toilet explodes, or condoms or dead squirrels erupt from my tote, or if he realizes what a pathetic and unlovable person I am? Far easier to date carroty freak-heads. Carroty freak-heads who do not call after trolley shitwater incident.

I want to buy something new and gorgeous to wear, so Joshua will know we are meant for each other, but my monster stack is officially in the double digits. In effort to end cash-flow woes, I dream about moving in with Joshua, and never having to apply for another low-pay, no-status, not-hiring-me-anyway job in my life.

Maya thinks my love—she cruelly calls it infatuation—for Joshua is cute, in a giggly, elementary-school way. She also thinks I'm a total loss, and will soon be living in a van. She will be less amused when I convince PB to loan me money.

So, this morning, I fling open my closet to wrestle my money problems into submission. I am ruthless. This pile to keep, this pile to sell.

Four hours later: sell pile is miniscule, but there are a few items that have always added ten pounds. I drive my poor unwanteds to a shop on upper State which sells preowned designer clothes.

Utterly horrible, watching the beady-eyed woman run her bony fingers over my lovelies. I almost snap, but do not. I stand, smile pasted firmly on my bloodless face, and await judgment.

"One hundred and twenty dollars," she says, folding a DKNY skirt.

Shit. I was hoping for one-fifty. The New Elle, however, haggles: "That's less than I expected. How much for the faux crocodile boots?"

She eyes me queerly. "That's one hundred and twenty for the lot."

"*What?* I paid that for the belt alone! One hundred and

twenty is a crime. This is runway robbery." I whine and cajole until she agrees to look over the clothes again.

"The Theory blouse is stained," she says, when finished. "One hundred even."

Joshua and I have dinner at Downey's, which is sort of staid and stately and *très* expensive. I brought my $100, just in case. The food smells delicious. I don't know how it tastes, as, despite being ravenous, I only order salad. To make a good impression. Maya scoffed when I told her my plan. She said this only works on other women, and even they hate you for it. But she's in a relationship, she doesn't know what it's like.

Best part of dinner? He *pays!*

I am aglow with pleasure.

Then it gets better. He slides me an envelope. "What's this?" I ask.

"Open it."

I do, and it's full of money.

"Count it," he says.

"One hundred and seventy-three dollars. For what?"

"Count it again," he says. "This time without eyeing the dessert cart."

"I have a thing for dessert carts." I say, and remember I am the New Thinner Elle. "I wouldn't touch the desserts, of course, but they're always so well-presented, aren't they? Anyway. Twenty, forty, sixty, eighty, one." I flip through the bills. "One hundred ninety-eight."

"Two-eighteen," he says. "And it's yours."

"Mine?"

"From Nordstrom's. The BCBGs. I spoke to the manager about your fall, and the store's liability. He thought refunding the purchase was the wisest course."

I squeal and tell Joshua exactly how wonderfully perfectly gorgeous he is. I ask for details about the Nordy's triumph, but he humbly says there was nothing to it. "But to celebrate," he says. "Let's go for a drink, shall we?"

"Drinks are on me," I say grandly. "Let's go to Shika. I know the—"

He laughs in disbelief. "Shika? You mean—Shika? You're kidding, right?"

"Of course! Not Shika. Ha ha." I feel sick for betraying Maya.

"I know the guy who owns The Gothic," Joshua says. "We'll go there."

See? We even have *that* in common—we both know bar owners. And once I know Joshua better, I'll insist we go to Maya's.

The Gothic is a tragically hip bar that specializes in expensive martinis and quasi-pornographic art. The place is packed at ten on a Wednesday. Shika doesn't even get this busy during Fiesta or Solstice.

We sit at the bar with the owner, drinking twenty-year-old Armagnac. He's almost as good-looking as Joshua—except that his face is florid from drinking too much. They're discussing whether the Bahamas or Mexico is more fun. I've never been to either, so I keep quiet. Which is probably a good thing—I don't want to fuck up in front of the beautiful people.

Joshua keeps rubbing my back and running his fingers through my hair, so evidently I'm doing fine. Until a pair of feminine hands covers his eyes. A brunette stands behind him. She leans close enough to lick his ear, and whispers, "Guess who?"

She is my nightmare. She's in a bar, so she must be twenty-one, but she looks nineteen. She's five-two. Wearing a black deeply cut unitard which showcases her spectacular figure and caramel-colored skin. A red sweaterette is tied around her middle—a false attempt at modesty which only serves to make her waist look even smaller. She manages to be both tiny and voluptuous at the same time, like Salma Hayek.

"Joshua thinks it's Jenna," Joshua says.

I am too busy staring at Jenna's buoyant breasts, straining

for release from the unitard, to be horrified at Joshua's referring to himself in the third person again. She has such sweet cleavage it makes me want to convert.

"Oh, Joshua!" Jenna pouts. "How did you know it was me?"

"Your scent. Obsession, right?"

I hate Obsession. I've always hated Obsession.

"Of course, darling." She kisses him.

"How are you?" he asks.

"Exhausted. I worked two shifts at the café yesterday, and one today. I just want to relax and have a good time." She eyes Joshua at this last bit, which makes me want to humiliate her for being a waitress. I may be unemployed, but if I *did* have a job, it'd be better than that.

"Where do you work?" I innocently ask.

"Café Lustre."

"Never heard of it—is it new? I've been away, in D.C."

"The *strip* club," she says.

"You wait tables at the strip club?" Yuck. "Are the tips any good?"

She laughs, beautifully. "I don't wait tables. And yes, the tips are excellent."

I hate her. I want to punch her sex-kitten little face.

"Jenna's a dancer, Elle," Joshua says.

"Oh. I've considered doing that." I close my eyes, tightly. What am I saying?

"Right," Jenna says. "Men line up to see *you* naked."

That's it. I might as well go home right now. There's no way I'm going to win a sexpot contest with a girl who belongs on the cover of *Maxim*. But Joshua leans into me and kisses me, long and hard. "I'd pay to see you strip."

My heart bursts through my chest and does a victory lap around the bar. Joshua pulls me to my feet, and puts his arm around me. "In fact, I'm ready for a private showing. We'll see you guys later."

I'm officially in love.

chapter 22

I'm quite gratified that skills learned from "Stripping for Your Virtual Boy-Toy" article pay off. Joshua is so overwhelmed by my wanton-harem-girl-in-a-trolley erotic display, that he interrupts the dance routine for main course. Am happy to serve it up.

The sex is even better than last time. Wonderfully gorgeous. Extremely nice. At least the "Joshua is coming" doesn't bother me so much.

Joshua leaves during the night. I suspect I'm supposed to be offended, but am only pleased. Now I don't have to worry about my morning face, hair, breath and personality.

Stage Two is officially successful. Cannot remember Stage Three, but suspect it's clear sailing from here.

The next morning, in celebration of utter good fortune, I decide to treat myself to a latte and a blueberry muffin. The sun is shining, the day is warm. I buy a paper and bring it with me to the Brown Pelican, the restaurant at Hendry's Beach, and sit at one of the tables overlooking the ocean.

I can see the nooks and crannies on the Channel Islands, several miles off the coast. Can't believe I ever lived in D.C. Did it for Louis, of course, and at the time it seemed right. He was in his third year of law school when we met. I'd just finished my sophomore year. He took care of me, and I of him. Felt natural to move in together when he finished school, and got hired at S, M & B. His apartment was much nicer than the dorms.

I'd considered graduate school when I'd finished my B.A. in Psychology, and had even been accepted into the master's program at American University. But by the time registration rolled around I'd lost interest. Was too busy playing wife to Louis. Besides, at twenty-two, I had plenty of time. But now, four years later, all I have to show for it is a way with silk throw pillows and the ability to pick the best dish on a lunch menu.

Sitting at Hendry's, the ocean sparkling at me, aching pleasantly from sex, I realize I don't miss Louis at all. Six years, and I don't miss him. Should I feel empty, or free?

I finish my breakfast and force myself to look at the classifieds, hoping to find a job that requires competence with silk pillows and lunch menus.

The ad stands out like a beacon:

> Earn $200/night
> Exotic Dancing
> Stop by Café Lustre
> 2-4 p.m. weekdays

$200 per night! I can't believe Jenna is making so much money. Why can't I make 200 bucks a night?

Because I don't have that good a body. I have cellulite and a thick waist.

Well, sure. But Joshua said he'd pay to see me naked. If someone who looks and fucks like he does wants to see me strip why wouldn't other men? And $200 a night, just for taking my clothes off, well that's easy enough. I'll just close my eyes and think of… Money.

Sure I will. There's no way I'd ever strip in public. I get embarrassed dancing with my clothes *on.* And how old is too old to strip? I called a number for information about selling my eggs, and when I told them I was over twenty-four, they said thanks but no thanks. So stripping seems out of the question.

Then the check comes. The latte and the muffin and the omelette and the mimosa comes to $23. Plus I had to fill the Beemer with gas today—and have a new muffler put on. I pay the bill, and leave four dollars tip, and I have seventeen dollars left.

Not on me. Not in my wallet. My total, overall, complete, entire and absolute wealth is: seventeen dollars. Carlos will be furious.

That's it. No choice. Today. Café Lustre.

Not sure what to wear to stripping interview. I check my wardrobe, and the only thing remotely appropriate is a Vivienne Tam see-through net dress in red with embroidered flowers, that goes over a red satin slip. Convinced Louis to buy it for last year's office Christmas party. Of course, if I get the job, I'll have to lose the slip.

The café is a windowless box of a building. I open the door and nervously step inside. Dark. Stuffy. And there's a naked blond girl writhing on the stage to an old Foreigner song. Those can't be real tits. How does she get them to stick up like that? Oh my God, she's putting one of them in her mouth. I can't do that. Am I suppose to be able to do that? I thought only dogs could do that.

There are waitresses in skimpy porn-costumes and a topless girl is rubbing her tits in a seated guy's face. He's sitting on his hands, like he's afraid to touch her, which seems odd. She turns and presses her "down there" (as my mother calls it) against his obvious hard-on (as my mother does not call it). Is that part of the job? I thought you only had to get naked, swing around the pole and you were done. This is all wrong. The little Jenna sexpot was right. I cannot do this.

Must get out. Get out now. I turn to flee and—Jenna.

"Oh hi, Jenna! I was just—" I want to say *leaving,* but cannot in the face of her superior expression "—here to apply for a job."

She's wearing only a g-string. Well, this is awkward. I try to keep from looking at her breasts, but my only options are the dog-woman on stage and a couple of lap mushers.

"You're here for a job?" she asks.

No! No! "Yes. Yes!"

"You know what? Good for you." She hooks her arm through mine and smiles. "A lot of women are all snotty and superior when they hear you dance, but they don't have the courage to even try it."

We walk side by side, arms clasped, and my elbow knocks her bare tit as she leads me towards the bar. Doesn't seem to bother her, so I pretend it's not happening.

"Maybe we can even work on an act together. Joshua loves girl-girl shows."

"I, um...Joshua what?"

"Wesley—the owner—he doesn't come 'til later," she says. "Tony usually takes the first look."

At the bar, she introduces me to Tony, the white version of Mike Tyson. He's wearing a summer seersucker suit with black dress shoes. Not a good look.

"Elle's looking for a job," Jenna says.

"I can see that," he growls. "Get back to work." He talks like he's way too fond of *The Sopranos.*

"Don't mind him," she says. "His bark's bad, but his bite's worse." She kisses me on the cheek. "Good luck."

"Thanks," I stammer, as she disappears into the greasy gloom.

"Step back. Let me take a look at you," Tony says.

In a daze, I step back. Because that's what I always do—what I'm told. What if I hurt Tony's feelings by saying there's been a mistake, I don't really want a job?

"Turn around."

I obediently turn. But I will not remove any clothing. This is *not* Planned Parenthood. I'll tell him, when he's finished gawking, that I've changed my mind. Worse comes to worse, I take the job and never show up. I'm sure it happens all the time.

"All the way around," he says. "Okay."

I stop turning, desperate to invent an excuse to be gone. I'm here doing a research project? I'm actually a man? I have two wooden legs?

"You're way too old for this," he says.

"What?"

"You are too old, baby."

"I am *not*. I'm only twenty...one."

"Sure you are. You oughta try the Screen Actor's Guild."

"The what?"

"Screen Actor's Guild. The S.A.G."

Is he telling me I ought to be in pictures? "Why?"

He eyes my breasts disdainfully. "Because they SAG, baby."

The greasy gloom turns red as my rage rises. I humiliate myself, and he insults me?

A topless wonder passes by with a tray.

A glass of cranberry juice. A splash and a bellow, and I start running.

Heels, don't fail me now.

SC-100

SANTA BARBARA SMALL CLAIMS CASE NO.:12-45978

—NOTICE TO DEFENDANT— YOU ARE BEING SUED BY PLAINTIFF	***—AVISO AL DEMANDADO— A USTED LO ESTAN DEMANDANDO***
To protect your rights, you must appear in this court on the trial date shown in the table below. You may lose the case if you do not appear. The court may award the plaintiff the amount of the claim and the costs. Your wages, money, and property may be taken without further warning from the court.	*Para proteger sus derechos, usted debe presentarse ante de esta corte en la fecha del juicio indicada en el cuadro que aparece a continuación. Si no se presenta, usted puede perder el caso. La corte puede decidir en favor del demandante por la cantidad del reclamo y los costos. A usted le pueden quitar su salario, su dinero, y otras cosas de su propiedad, sin aviso adicional por parte de esta corte.*

PLANTIFF/DEMANDANTE:	DEFENDANT/DEMANDADO:
Anthony Dingle	*Elle Medina*

PLAINTIFF'S CLAIM

1. ☒ Defendant owes me the sum of: $ *700.00* , not including court costs because (describe claim):

   She threw cranberry juice at my suit.

2. This claim is against a government agency, and I filed a claim with the agency. My claim was denied by the agency, or the agency did not act on my claim before the legal deadline. (See form SC-150.)

3. I have asked defendant to pay this money, but it has not been paid.
   ☒ I have NOT asked defendant to pay this money because (explain):

   Seemed like I'd get more money if I sued.

4. I understand that
   a. I must appear at the time and place of trial and bring all witnesses, books, receipts, and other papers or things to prove my case.
   b. I may talk to an attorney about this claim, but I cannot be represented by an attorney at the trial in the small claims court.
   c. I have no right of appeal on my claim, but I may appeal a claim filed by the defendant in this case.
   d. If I cannot afford to pay the fees for filing or service by a sheriff, marshal, or constable, I may ask that the fees be waived.

5. I have received and read the information sheet explaining some important rights of plaintiffs in the small claims court.

6. No defendant is in the military service except (name):

I declare under penalty of perjury under the laws of the State of California that the foregoing is true and correct.

Anthony Dingle
(SIGNATURE OF PLAINTIFF)

* * *

I haven't left the trolley for three days. Hair in knots. Eyes puffy. Pajamas beginning to stink. Am reminded of country-western song I once heard on AM radio—*She Walks Like a Woman, But Smells Like a Man*.

I've spent a total of nine hours, give or take a few, standing in front of the mirror with my pajama top raised, wondering if my tits *do* sag. I turn this way, and that way. Maybe. Definitely not. A little. No way. Still haven't decided.

Joshua has not called. Has not returned my calls. Is he with Jenna, who is unafraid to appear in public in all her gynecological glory?

Merrick hasn't called, either. I almost feel worse about that. I mean, sure I had a trolley full of crapwater, and I threw condoms at him and he disapproves of my getting fired from Super 9, but he…I don't know. I thought he'd call.

Even Maya hasn't called. Her desertion hurts the most. She knows I'm falling apart. But I'm afraid to call her, because she hates me. We got along great in high school, then for years when we didn't live in the same town. I know she loves me, but a couple months of the real Elle, up close and personal, is enough to turn anyone against me. I don't know what to do. It's not going to be much fun moving back in with them if they hate me.

It's finally time to admit I'm beaten. No money. No job. Bad credit. No man. Possible sagging tits. Pending lawsuit. And due out of the trolley in five days.

I call my mother.

"Mom, it's me."

"Who?"

"Elle. Your daughter."

"Oh, hi, honey. How are you? Did you get a job?"

"No." I can't tell her the truth. She'll just tell me it's all my fault. And she's right. "No job, no apartment…"

"Well, keep trying. I'm sure you'll find something. I saw on *Oprah* the other day a woman who'd made a career organizing other people's closets. You know how much you love closets. I remember saying, when you were still in grade school…"

For once I'm able to tune her out because there's a clicking on the phone. "Do you hear that?" I interrupt.

"What?"

There's silence on the line. "Oh. Nothing. Um, Mom, I was thinking about your offer? To let me come and stay? And, well—" The clicking starts again. "There! That clicking."

"Your call-waiting, you mean? You really ought to get Caller ID. I saw a segment on *Maury,* and this woman was being stalked by an ex-boyfriend, who was a cop, she said if she didn't—"

Call waiting! In a burst of optimism I'd ordered it along with my voice mail. I forgot I had it. "Hold on, Mom. Back in a sec."

It's Sheila from Superior.

"Sheila, hello! Sorry it took so long to pick up. I was just doing a little ten-key practice."

"Of course you were. I'm calling because I think I've got the job for you."

"A job? For me?"

"The pay isn't great, ten an hour, but it's fun work."

"Well, I *was* hoping for more."

"Don't push it, dear."

"No, I'm sorry. What's the job."

"You're going to work as a telephonic metaphysical counselor."

"Um—a what?"

"A phone psychic, dear!"

"A phone psychic," I say, reverently. My future flashes before me: the humble beginnings, the slow rise, and finally the nation-wide infomercial which makes me a household name. "You are a genius, Sheila. I won't—I won't let you down."

"Please don't, dear. Oh, but I must ask you one question before I send you to them—do you feel you have been blessed with the Gift? The correct answer is 'yes.'"

"Since I was a child," I say. "My mother always insisted I was an intuitive. She's a counselor herself—in Sedona. The red rock country, you know. It's a nexus. I come from a…a long line of psychics."

"And…?"

"Um, what? Oh! And the answer is, yes."

"Very good, dear." She spends five minutes giving me the job information. I'm about to hang up when I remember my mother's on the other line.

I hit the button, and hear: "…Cub Scout leader! Well, Dr. Laura had a thing or two to say about that, believe you me. She told her to—"

"Mom? Mom!"

"Yes, dear?"

I don't have the heart to tell her I've been on the other line this whole time. "The reason I called, Mom, is that—"

"I heard, you want to come live with me."

"No. I got a job."

"You just said you didn't have a job."

When did she suddenly start paying attention? How can she talk for ten minutes without knowing I wasn't there, but have heard everything I said before that?

"I've got one now," I say. "And I wanted you to be the first to hear. I'm going to be a phone psychic."

"A phone psychic? That's wonderful! Latoya or Dionne?"

"Neither, Mom."

"Not Cleo?" she says with awe. "I heard she was shut down."

I laugh. "I don't really know, Mother."

I am so pleased, I let her tell me about the advice her customers have gotten from various phone psychics over the years, as I go through my wardrobe. I wonder what the other psychics will be wearing.

chapter 23

Morning. First day of new job—no, new *career.* Have planned the definitive phone psychic outfit. My ankle-length, Indian print skirt, bought cheap last year at import store in Virginia, with a linen peasant blouse. I tie a purple silk scarf around my head like a gypsy. My curls hang loosely from underneath the scarf. I check the mirror. Is it too much? Maybe a few less bangles. I remove half the silver clanging bracelets and look again. Perfect.

Psychic Connexion is located in Goleta—not far from ZZ's place. Inauspicious, but somehow comforting. I picture a ramshackle-yet-healing place: high ceilings with dusty skylights, pale-wood floors slightly scratched, the smell of incense and herbal tea, white walls covered with violet tapestries.

Or not.

The lobby of DRM Incorporated—which is the name

of the company that owns Psychic Connexion—has all the charm of an airport lounge. It's gray and bland and professional. The receptionist waves me to the back. I walk through a midsize cubicle farm, featuring institutional colors, furniture and even scent.

DRM is into more than psychic counseling. I pass signs for other departments: Business Advice, Sports Line, Bear Buddies, Threesomes and More, Cross-Dressing and so on. The sex stuff makes me feel I'm back at Café Lustre. I half expect to see a naked woman writhing on one of the desks. But there are only dreary people talking on phones.

I spot the Psychic sign, check out my compatriots and realize I've worn absolutely the wrong thing. Everyone else is in jeans and T-shirts. Not even cute T-shirts—they all have slogans. I despise slogans.

I pull up the shoulder of my blouse in an attempt to make it look less peasantlike. I hate feeling fashionably out of place. I don't even like if I'm wearing a sweater and everyone else is in short sleeves.

I hover near a middle-aged guy's desk. He's balding, with a blond bushy beard. A bright pink expanse of stomach bulges out between his Chuck Norris T-shirt and his blue jeans.

He says thanks for calling, hangs up and looks at me.

"Hi," I say. "I'm new today, from Superior. I'm suppose to be working here."

"You sure you're in the right place?" he asks. "Look's like you're ready for a costume party, Madame Zelda."

I snatch the bandana from my head. "At least my chub of a stomach isn't hanging out my shirt."

He laughs and pulls down his shirt. His bright blue eyes almost disappear when he smiles up at me. "What's your name?"

"Elle." I grin at him, oddly pleased I've made him laugh. "Elle Medina."

"I'm Darwin. Good to meetcha. C. Burke's not in, he's out for—"

"C. Burke?"

"Christopher C. Burke. Our manager. He's overfond of his middle initial. He's on paternity leave, I don't know who's supposed to train you…." He shrugs. "It'll have to be on-the-job training. Sit there. I'll call the switchboard and tell them you're accepting calls."

"With no training?" I squeak.

"What do you need to know?"

"Um…*everything?*"

This stumps him for a moment. "Well. Most of the network are call-ins, people who work from home, but they like to have some people in the office, and temps can't telecommute. So you're stuck here. The switchboard knows when you've hung up, and automatically sends you more calls. The phone's easy to work. Headset. Accepting, not accepting." He prattles on about the phone, and the sheet of emergency numbers, and what sort of place it is to work.

"But, um…what about being psychic? Aren't there exercises, or meditations, or something?"

He grins. "Didn't they ask if you have the Gift?"

"Well, yeah, but—"

He pulls a pack of tarot cards from his desk. "Use these to start."

I have no idea how to read tarot. "Um…tarot's not really my strength."

"No? Well, palm reading's not gonna cut it, Zelda." He laughs again, and his phone rings.

"But what if I tell someone's future wrong?"

"Psychic Connexion," he says. "Why am I laughing? Because your grandfather knew you'd be calling, and he gave me a joke to tell you." He pauses to listen to the caller. "That's right, Grandpa Brenner."

Darwin motions me toward my desk. "Grandpa Brenner says he misses you and is glad you've called Psychic Connexion for advice and guidance." He mimes that I should open the desk drawer, and I do, and there's a cheat sheet of sorts. "Oh, you want to hear his joke? Um…yeah. Let me see if I can recall. It was so funny how Grandpa Brenner told it."

My phone rings. Darwin raises his eyebrows expectantly, so I turn the other way, pretending I don't see him. The woman at the desk on my other side is the only other person not wearing jeans. She's an Earth Mama, wearing a shapeless magenta tunic and blue leggings. An amethyst pendant hangs from her neck, and her long gray hair is twined into a braid in back. She should color her hair—she'd look much younger.

She hangs up, and looks at me and my still-ringing phone.

"Aren't you going to get that?"

"Oh. Is that mine?" I babble, hoping it'll stop ringing. "I didn't realize—"

"Yes. Answer it."

Fuck. "Hello?"

"Is this the Psychic Connexion?" It's a man's voice.

"Uh-huh."

"Are you a real psychic?"

"Um—" Probably shouldn't say no. I glance at the cheat sheet. "Thank you…for calling…the Psychic Connexion." It's kind of hard to read—looks like a copy of a copy of a copy. "Can…I have…your name…and birthdate please?"

"My name is James. Birthdate—ten-twenty-sixty-seven."

"Oh, mine's the twenty-first. What a coincidence." Wait a minute, I can use this to good effect. "I mean, see, we already have a connection."

"What year?"

I giggle. "Wouldn't you like to know?"

He chuckles. "What's your name?"

"Elle," I tell him, then wonder whether it's okay to use my real name. Or is phone psyching like stripping, and I need a stage name? Something exotic. Like Mathilde or Seraphina.

"So what's my horoscope, Elle?"

"Um…" I'm suppose to give him his horoscope? I flip my cheat sheet over. Blank. "Well, let me get some other information from you. Then we'll get back to that." I continue reading from the crib. "Can I…have your…home address…so I can…send you our free psychic…newsletter?"

"I already get that. What's my horoscope?"

"I have no idea," I admit. "Horoscope isn't really my area of expertise."

"Oh? What is?"

"Tarot reading," I say, brightly. "How does that sound?"

"Fine. Here's my question: I'm thinking of sleeping with my brother's wife. Will I get caught?"

"James! Shame on you." I hate infidelity. How hard is it to keep your dick in your pants? I'd pretended it was no big deal Louis slept with another woman, but that was only because I wanted my wedding. On the other hand, it *is* only sex, not necessarily the melding of souls. Well, unless you're me and Joshua. Of course he hasn't called recently, so I guess his soul wasn't melded. "I think there's a better question than 'will I get caught?'"

"Yeah. I wouldn't normally…I mean, but she's really sexy."

I spread the cards into a mess onto the desk. There's a picture of a dark-haired lass on one of them. "Brunette, is she?"

"Yeah," he says, impressed.

"Um…" I strain at the cards. Nothing pops out. There are a lot of wands or rods or staffs showing, though. Quite phallic. "And you're very…warm for her. I'm getting a sense of a really electric, um, sexuality."

"Oh, yeah." He sounds as if I'm telling him to go ahead and boink her.

I scan the jumbled cards for something negative. And find Death, a skeleton in a cape, holding a sickle in its right claw. "Death is in the cards," I intone.

"He's going to kill me," James says.

"Your brother," I say.

"So he will find out?"

"Definitely. And—ouch—are you sure you want to hear this?"

"Yes—yes—what does it say?"

"The progression is from the nine of staffs to the one of staffs. Nine is a powerful number. It's, um, powerful. And staffs, of course, refer to male sexual energy. So if you *do* sleep with her...well, I'm afraid it will have an adverse effect on your sex life. Sort of reverse Viagra."

He praises me for helping him avoid the close call, and I mentally thank my mother for all the nonsense she's spewed over the years.

"Wow, Elle," James finishes saying. "That was really helpful. A lot of readers don't get that specific."

I preen. I've actually helped someone, and it was easy. "Don't thank me, James, thank the cards. But you know what you should do? Ask your sister-in-law if she's got a friend for you."

"Well, she has been trying to set me up with one of the women from our church."

These people are church-goers? And he was going to tup his brother's wife on the side? "Well, that sounds very... lovely. Someone who shares the same values."

I do another tarot spread—more like 52-pickup—and sure enough, the cards recommend a date with the church lady.

"Thanks for your help, Elle."

It's the first time I remember hearing those words attached to my name.

"You're very welcome. Give me a call if you have any other dilemmas you need help with."

A nice touch, I think—asking for the repeat call. I'm a natural.

We say goodbye and I swing around in my seat to check if Darwin and Earth Mama have witnessed my first success.

"Do you have any idea how to use those?" Earth Mama asks.

"The tarot cards? Of course I do," I say.

"How?"

I finger the cards as I settle back in seat. "I divine inspiration from the pictures."

"There are serious consequences," Earth Mama says, "to using the cards improperly. If you don't know what you're doing, I recommend you look into another line of work." She gestures toward the Naughty Schoolgirls sign across the corridor.

I look at the picture on the card in my hand. It's a white-haired lady. "For example," I say, as if she hadn't spoken, "from this card I divine that an old crone will become an obstacle in my life."

"If you are going to work as a counselor," she says sharply, "I suggest you educate yourself. Real people call with real problems, and the last thing they need is an ignorant girl offering bad advice. The cards are temperamental and subtle, and—"

"Give her a break, Adele," Darwin cuts in. "It's her first call."

"I just don't understand how they're hiring people these days. She makes a mockery of the whole profession."

"We're phone psychics, Adele." Darwin looks at her with sympathy. "I think she did really well, considering she has no training…I mean, other than her innate Gift."

This quiets Adele down. "No training? Well, as long as she's not just in it for the money."

"Me?" I scoff. "If I were in it for the money, I think I could find something that pays a lot better than this."

My phone rings, and instead of nerves I feel excitement. "Thank you for calling the Psychic Connexion."

I field nine calls—not including a bunch of hang-ups and try-outs—and my mean time logged is twenty-four minutes, which is above average. Most beginners get a lot of tens and elevens. Darwin tells me it was a good first day—he says C. Burke will look over the numbers at home, and be impressed. I decide to like C. Burke, not only because he is a responsible father on paternity leave, but because I will be his new star psychic.

It was mostly easy, too. A lot of love questions: Is this man right for me? When am I going to meet Mr. Right? Is my boyfriend cheating? That sort of thing. I did get one lady who wanted to know if her dishwasher was broken. I asked what it was doing, and she described the noises and shudders. We talked about appliances and warrantees and stuff, then the cards told her to call Sears and ask them. The cards are wise.

Adele was at me all day, trying to teach me about tarot. She's annoying, but nice. She's like my mother, except she believes in all the New Age stuff instead of talk shows. And I'm fairly sure she could recognize my voice on the phone. But the more she talked about the cards, the less I understood; I tried it on a caller, but stumbled over the word "Hierophant," and decided I was doing better my own way. Darwin suggested I try numerology—getting all the dates and numbers apparently increases your log-in time.

On the way home, I stop at Shika to tell Maya about my beautiful career. She's not there. Instead, a guy in his early twenties, with unevenly shorn hair and a ring through his eyebrow is pouring beer for the four customers at the booth. The argument group—I sort of coincidentally knew it was their day. Neil, the teddy bear, is there. Merrick is not.

"—never said blind people don't deserve access," Neil is grumbling. "But Braille keypads on drive-up ATMs is ridiculous. It's like convertibles. You know how they make convertibles? They build the whole car, then chop off the top."

"Bullshit, Neil," one of the other men says.

"Chop off the top," Neil repeats. "What I want to know is, what the hell do they do with the extra tops? Probably sell 'em to the military-industrial complex for ninety grand a pop—like those toilet seats, your tax money at work. The whole two-party system is a joke."

"Going at it again, huh?" I say to the eyebrow-ring bartender.

"It's an argument group. They come in once a week to vent."

"Yeah. I had no idea today's their day," I lie. "And that's, um, the whole group?"

"More or less."

He's probably in his cave. Not that I care. "Maya around?"

Eyebrow-ring shakes his head.

"Oh, well, I'm her friend Elle...."

"With the blender, right? She mentioned you. I'm Kid."

"Kid?"

"As in 'Billy the.' My mom had a thing for westerns."

"Ah." This is the guy Maya hired instead of me? "So why didn't she name you Billy?"

He looks at me. "Can I get you anything?"

"Well..." No fun to sit here without Maya. "I don't—"

"I'm buying," Monty says, sliding onto his stool.

"Hi, Monty." I give him the once-over. "Looking sharp as ever."

Kid flips his head in greeting. "Gin and tonic?"

Monty nods. "And you, Elle?"

"Same."

Kid fiddles with bottles and I ask Monty how he's doing.

"Sold a property today. Made a tidy little sum."

"Is that why you're buying?" I grab a handful of pretzels. Stern lecture of Maya on stale Fritos has resulted in plethora of fresh bar snacks.

"Well, the three dollars hurts even less today. How's Spenser for Hire?"

"Spenser? Turns out Spenser is for 'fire.'" I tell him the story as we sip our G&Ts.

"So you didn't get fired for *not* arresting the shoplifter, you got fired for arresting the *non*-shoplifter?"

This strikes us as funnier than it is—but we're lubricated by gin and our mutual amusement at the nickname "Spenser." On a roll, I tell him I'm now working as a phone psychic, and loving every minute of it. He congratulates me with another G&T, and says, "Maya tells me you're living in a trolley? I didn't think that was legal. I should invest in a bunch of used trolleys, start a trolley-park in Goleta."

"I'll be your first tenant. My landlord kicked me out."

He asks why, of course, and I tell him the water-balloon story. He puts his glass on the bar and his skinny shoulders shake with laughter. "Pegged him until he fell down? I ought to set you on Fess Parker. So where are you moving?"

"Back with Maya, I guess."

"I've got a place, if you're interested—it's only a studio."

"Monty, I've been living in a trolley. A studio can only be viewed as a step up. How much?"

"Six hundred."

My heart stops. "A week?"

"A month. You interested?"

"How bad is it? Brown carpeting and a microwave instead of a stove?"

Monty looks offended. "It's a nice apartment."

"Then I want it."

"Then it's yours."

I beam. He beams. I know I should ask about first, last and security. Instead, I say, "Can I have dog?"

"Anything but a cat." He takes another sip of his drink. "Can't stand cats."

"And, um…you'll want $1800 to move in?"

He gives me a look that makes me wonder exactly how much Maya told him. "Place is empty anyway. You move in when you want, and keep your job, and give me the six hundred on the first of next month."

The first is like two weeks away. Ten dollars an hour times eight hours a day, times ten days…$800! Minus taxes and stuff, and ignoring Carlos and every shopping instinct I have…and I can do this. I *will* do this. A regular job, a real apartment…the New Elle has finally arrived.

"So," Monty asks. "How are things in the man department?"

Get home from drinks with Monty and check voice mail. Zero messages. I take a hot shower, spend thirty minutes conditioning my hair, and when I step out, hallelujah, the dial tone is buzzing.

Four messages. Please, God, let them be Joshua, Joshua, Joshua and Joshua. They are:

1) Strange voice, asking for Angie. Very important.

2) Louis: Blah blah blah. Stamp collection. Blah blah. The ASPCA. Blah blah blah.

3) Merrick: Called to say hello. Hello. Hope all is well.

4) Strange voice, telling Angie to forget it. No longer important.

No Joshua. I replay every minute of last date, and still think I did okay. No obvious gaffes. No terrible debacles. Maybe he doesn't like salad-eaters. Maybe he's with Jenna. Maybe I'm not exciting/attractive/wild enough for him. If I were him, would *I* date me? No. I'd date Halle Berry.

At least Merrick called, and Carlos didn't. But neither did Maya. Suspect she is truly sick of me. So I've been sulking and not calling her, either. See how *she* likes it. Although I guess she probably does like it. Anyway, I should be the adult, and call with both bits of good news: have a job, and a place to stay.

Perfect Brad answers with an anxious "Hello?"

"Brad, it's Elle."

"Oh. I thought you were Maya."

"Wish I was. Where is she? She's not at the bar."

"Still at the doctor."

"The doctor? What for?"

"She miscarried."

Oh, no. "I didn't even know she was pregnant."

"Neither did we. She's getting checked up right now."

"When did it happen?"

"Day before yesterday."

No wonder I hadn't heard from her. And good friend that I am, I've been sulking. I ask what happened, and if she's all right, and he tells me the whole story.

"It wasn't like we wanted a baby," he says. "But it's still somehow sad."

"Can I come see her?" I ask. "What can I do? I'll bring ice cream."

He sort of chuckles. "Come tomorrow. And just…bring yourself. You always make her laugh."

chapter 24

Stayed up late, mentally designing gift basket for Maya. Am resolved not to spend money, even when presented with this valid and convincing opportunity. Will have to make my own raffia, chocolate éclairs, violet bath oil and handwoven basket—which is slightly daunting.

Surprisingly, I'm happy to be back at work. It's just talking on the phone, isn't it? People call *me,* asking for help. I'm much better giving advice than taking it. And although I didn't have time last night to check into numerology, this morning I caught sight of the cover of *Marie Claire.* A special horoscope issue. Talk about fate.

I read it while waiting for my next call. It's a relief to know that if someone asks for their horoscope I'll be prepared. Of course, I've had three calls already, and no one's asked. Most people who want a horoscope call the horoscope line.

I'm at a different desk today, in the corner next to Straight Sex. Which is odd, because the majority of the phone-workers are men. Wouldn't have thought women called for this sort of thing.

I glance up from my magazine as a guy plants himself at the next desk. He's young, wearing an orange velvet shirt that clashes mercilessly with his blue hair.

"Good morning," I say.

"Phone sex?" he asks.

"No thanks."

He laughs. "I meant are you *working* phone sex?"

I smile and shake my head. "Psychic Connexion."

"I did Psychic for a while. This pays better—and it's more straightforward. Nobody wants to talk, just moan." His phone rings, and he picks up and says, "Hi, this is Gina," in a soft, husky voice. He listens a moment. "A red lace teddy, with black thigh-high stockings attached to my garters and black heels and my bottom is just aching to be spanked…."

Must be cross-dressing. I check the sign. Still says Straight Sex. It dawns on me that all the men are pretending to be women.

"I'm so wet," Blue Hair says. "How many fingers? There's one…oooh…there's two…and there's three…oh, baby…" Blue Hair notices me watching and winks. "There's another girl here with me, her name is Jasmine. You want to talk to her?"

I wave my hands in a horrified rebuff, and he winks again. "Oh—Jasmine can't talk, both her hands are busy at the moment. What does she look like? Angelina Jolie, with bigger tits—she's got a high, bubble-ass and her long, long legs are spread and can you guess what she's doing to herself?"

My phone rings, thank God. I launch into my spiel, desperately blocking out Blue Hair's sex talk, but the woman doesn't want to get the free newsletter, which is a bummer because I get a buck for every mailing address. I take her name, anyway. It's Janet Taluga—takes me three tries to get the spelling right.

"I want to know what to do about my husband," she says. She has a soft, pretty accent.

"What's wrong with your husband?" I ask.

"I thought you'd tell me." Oh—she's one of those. There are two types of Psychic Connexion callers. Those who don't care about metaphysics, as long as you give good advice, and those determined to prove you can't foresee your way out of a paper bag.

"I can tell you, of course…but why waste the Gift on information you already know?" She doesn't respond, so I say, "Ah! Wait, I'm getting something…" and flip through the pages of *Marie Claire.* "You sure you don't want your horoscope?"

"If I wanted my horoscope, I'd have called the horoscope line."

Her accent is definitely Southern. "He's from the South, isn't he?"

"Yes," she admits. "But with my accent, that's not so big a stretch."

"Mmm." She isn't going to give me anything. What can I tell her? My eyes land on the headline Don't Get Sucked into His Sucky Mood. "I'm getting that his temper isn't always even. He's a little moody."

"Oh, no. He's not moody at all."

She lies just like I do—utterly unconvincingly. "Janet. The cards don't lie. I'm pretty sure he's moody."

"Only sometimes."

"And is that what makes you wonder what to do about him?"

She doesn't say anything.

"Is he mean, Janet?"

"No," she says softly.

"He has a temper."

"I—I…" Sounds like she's crying.

"He yells at you," I say.

"Sometimes."

"You know, Janet, sometimes we end up staying with a man far longer than we should. I know what that's like."

"You do?"

"Six years."

"Did yours hit the bottle hard?"

"Your husband drinks?"

"Most nights."

"And that's when he loses his temper?"

"Sometimes. Usually. Yes."

"And you're wondering if you should leave him?"

"Is that what you see me doing?" There's both hope and fear in her voice.

"Well..." I hesitate. What if they had just had a spat? On the other hand, what if he's beating her? I search my desk for the sheet with the crisis intervention hotlines on it. "Have you tried counseling?"

"He would never—oh my God, I gotta go. He'll *kill* me when he gets the bill."

"No, Janet, wait! Just let me—"

The line goes dead. I'm left holding the hot-sheet, a sick feeling in my stomach. I should have been quicker. But how much responsibility do I have? She's calling a psychic hotline—what does she expect? This makes me feel no better. I should have been quicker.

Blue Hair is talking about where he wants to put his tongue, and I can't get over the stomachache. Maybe Janet only called in a fit of pique, and I've overreacted by imagining she's abused. Maybe I'll go mad from listening to eight hours of phone sex. This is a twisted job. It's like being a pretend therapist, for people who don't have money or are afraid of therapy. It's great when it's entertainment—chatting about men and love—but this serious stuff scares me. I'm not sure I'm gonna make it.

My phone rings before I'm ready. It's James again—my

first repeat caller! He met the woman from his church for donuts this morning, and now he wants to know what their chances are.

"But first," he says, "I want my horoscope."

I feel abruptly better. "Now *that* I can do."

Maya's gift basket contains: A thermos full of Cosmopolitans (Kid helped); a beach rock in the shape of a heart, if you squint your eyes; two dozen gorgeous roses; a dog-eared copy of *Pride and Prejudice* that Maya lent me seven years ago; a lavishly hand-illustrated card, signed E.M. and a butter-ring from Anderson's.

"And it cost nothing!" I tell Maya triumphantly.

"The roses? Sixty dollars at Honeysuckle."

I grin. "Free, at the rose garden." The city garden, across the street from the Mission.

"Elle—you stole these from the rose garden?"

"Six o'clock in the morning, in my bathrobe, with a pair of cuticle scissors. Now *that* is love, Maya."

She laughs. "And the butter-ring? You broke into the bakery? Mrs. Anderson will not be happy."

"I sold my BCBGs."

"Your broken BCBGs?"

"I super-glued them."

She laughs again, and Brad shoots me a look of such gratitude I feel quite like Mother Theresa, washing lepers' feet. Only younger and taller, and with better skin.

"And the card?"

"Hand-drawn," I say proudly.

"I'd never have guessed," she says with a straight face. "But what did you pay the kindergartner who drew it?"

chapter 25

On Sunday, I call Joshua twice. Leave one message.

On Monday, I call Joshua twice. Leave one message.

Tuesday, for a change, I call five times, and leave no messages.

I also work. Have not met C. Burke yet, but my log-in times are creeping up nicely. I found a training manual. Read five pages, and threw it away. It was all about keeping people on the phone and squeezing them for as much money as possible. Made me feel almost like Adele; I know it's not a noble calling, but there's no reason we can't be helpful and nice and funny, instead of greedy, grasping frauds.

Turns out the customer doesn't have to pay any disputed charges. That's the other reason they tell us to push the free psychic newsletter—so they can prove people called. So I only ask for addresses when I remember. It's only a buck extra, anyway. And if you just listen, and ask questions, people like to talk. There's nothing to it.

Wednesday, I get another call from a woman complaining about her boyfriend. Her name is Nyla. She's from Chicago. Her voice is husky and she talks in a flat Midwestern accent.

"I think he's sleeping around on me," she says. "Am I right?"

Always best to avoid yes and no questions, so I ask if she trusts her intuition, and if her suspicions and hunches usually prove true. We talk for a while about that, then I ask what makes her think he's sleeping around.

"He's been distant. Kind of cold—well, even colder than usual. And not much interested in sex."

She doesn't have the abused-animal feel that Janet conveyed. "How long have you been together?"

"Four years."

"And he's never been distant before?"

"Not like this. He's always been sorta…contained. Well, but now it's like he doesn't care about me at all. I mean, like I'm a convenience, a dishwasher, or cup-holder or something."

She explains, and he does sound cold. Not cruel—just like he doesn't care about Nyla either way. "You sure you want to stay together?" I ask.

"God, yes! I can't leave him."

"Why not?"

"Well. He pays for everything."

"But he's not there for you, emotionally. Right?"

"He's a doctor. And he works really hard," she says. "He's a, um, a good provider. I mean, I couldn't leave him. He, you know…"

"Pays for everything?"

"*Everything.* Last week I got a Vivienne Westwood. And a Fendi bag that cost like sixteen hundred. *Vogue*'s pick of the year."

My chair starts to feel a little uncomfortable. "So?"

"*So,* if I left him I couldn't afford an apartment on the lake, or wear Gucci, or shop at Whole Foods, or eat at the Pump Room, or—"

"The cards say you're lost," I tell her.

"Lost?"

"You've forgotten who you are. The cards say you have to—well, here's the Juggler." Adele hisses something to me about there not being a Juggler, but I can't stop now. "You've been juggling your life around him, like moons in an orbit." What the hell does that mean? I am becoming my mother. "You need to be your own planet."

"But...the Pump Room is on *his* planet. Prada is on his planet. His planet has all the good stuff."

"Your planet has plenty of good stuff," I say. "You just have to look."

"I don't know. This isn't what I—I just wanted to hear if he's sleeping around."

"You better start looking for a job, Nyla. Because the cards say splitting up is definitely an option."

"No," she says firmly. "Forget it. I'm calling another psychic."

"Until you find one who says he's not sleeping around? The problem isn't him. It's you."

She says something impolite and gives me a dial tone.

An older woman calls. Her name is Valentine, which I love. I get her address...and she lives in Montecito! I ask if she lives next to Oprah. She says no. But I still gushingly question her about her house, her garden, her furniture, shopping habits and life. She's seventy-four, has outlived three husbands, and is on the prowl for the fourth. She was born on a dirt farm in Georgia. She is vibrant and happy and prefers cotton and wool fabrics in bright colors. She doesn't like antiques much, and I think I break some sort of record, because the call is sixty-two minutes long.

Darwin is amazed. Adele is jealous—she says, "You didn't even offer her a reading!" C. Burke will promote me. Sheila will be proud. Monty will be paid. Even Carlos will get his money.

I am buzzed, eager for the next call. It's a woman who wants to go off the pill without telling her boyfriend. Her numerology (she is a 7 or maybe 4—couldn't quite get the math right) informs us that she should rescue a dog from the pound instead.

And I'm on a roll. Everyone should rescue a dog. Except the allergic man. He, it turns out, should take up ballroom dancing.

Thursday is a good day. I have two skeptics, who I'm really starting to like. You can joke with them. They want to believe, but know it's ridiculous. So my goal is to give them a good reading—well, good advice—despite themselves. And if you sorta halfway admit that no, there's nothing psychic about it, but you're happy to listen to them talk, it's all peachy.

I have ten or eleven normal calls. Bread-and-butter, Darwin calls them. About love and money and sex. I've discovered that women's magazines are far better fortune-telling devices than tarot cards, though I still read off the names of cards occasionally, for verisimilitude.

Adele isn't entirely convinced that this is proper for a psychic reading. I tell her my personal Gift is synched with the contemporary moment, with the cultural mood—not with ancient cards or runes or zodiacal signs. She's still pondering that, I think—but we get along pretty well, now. Except that I'm a little jealous of her. She, oddly, seems to have a reputation among Texans—a lot of them call and ask for her by name for their bread-and-butter questions. I am eager to develop my own list. I'm getting a few repeat calls already, which Darwin says is unusual. The rumpled and paternal C. Burke will love me.

I have three crisis calls on Thursday, too. Women in trouble—I am faster with the hot-sheet this time. I give them the crisis numbers, and tell them very sternly that the cards say they should *not* be calling 900 numbers, but absolutely must call the hotline numbers. I give them the regular number for the office, too, in case they need to talk. That's sort of against policy, but we're allowed personal calls, and who's gonna know if they're friends or ex-clients?

And on Friday, I get a paycheck. Superior pays every week, and I'm halfway done with the money I need for first month's rent. I'm moving in today, and I'll pay Monty next week.

I attempted to cry myself to sleep last night because Joshua has not returned my calls, but the truth is I only miss the attention, and the sex, and the contact high from his beauty. Hmm. That's quite a lot, actually.

I'm with Perfect Brad, now. I'd stopped by to give Maya get-well cupcakes and borrow PB to help me move. Goodbye, trolley and hello, studio. It's a converted attic in an old Victorian, located between State Street and, well, the Department of Motor Vehicles. Not the most beautiful neighborhood, but a pretty good one—and I won't need my car much anymore, because I'll be able to walk everywhere downtown.

The building is a project of Monty's—he bought it last year and is having it restored. It's almost finished, and it's lovely. Arched ceilings, painted creamy white. Soft buttery yellow walls, and muted olive carpets. Through the old bay window, I feel like I'm hovering above downtown. It has a kitchen and a bathroom, and they are each in their own place, with absolutely no overlap. I love it.

"It's perfect, isn't it?" I tell PB.

He grunts under the strain of my bureau and tells me it's great. "Maya's dad," he says.

"Huh?"

He puts the bureau down. "Maya's dad. He talked to Monty about it."

"What it?"

"You. Needing a place."

"Mr. Goldman! I had no idea. What a sweetie." Perhaps Mr. Goldman needs an orchid. "Oh, would you move that just over here, Brad? Thanks."

When we finally get all the furniture upstairs, I walk Brad to his car and head back to the trolley. Mrs. Petrie said that if I get out today, they'll refund me a hundred dollars of my security.

Good thing the trolley is so small there aren't many surfaces to clean. Still, I am a dirty bird—sweaty, malodorous and thoroughly disheveled—when Joshua walks in the door. He is clean, well-dressed and thoroughly gorgeous.

"Moving out?" he asks.

"Moving up!"

"New job and new apartment." He smiles, and the sun shines a bit brighter. "You've got it going on."

"New job? How did you hear about that?"

"Your message. Well, one of your messages."

"Oh! I…well, I was calling because I thought you, um, left your wallet here, but it turns out it wasn't your wallet. Not that it was anyone else's wallet. It was mine. An old one. Maya's, actually. A friend. She—"

He stops the babble with a kiss. When I regain my breath, he asks about work like a real boyfriend would. "Work is amazing!" I say. "Mostly I just talk on the phone, which is a personal strength of mine and—"

"You work the phones, not the office?"

I tell all, and he listens with attentive gorgeousness and says: "Are you free for dinner tonight?"

"I'm a bit of a mess," I say, so he'll tell me how beautiful I am.

"You look okay."

"Um, but I can clean up. Where shall we go?"

"My house. In Montecito."

"You have a house in Montecito?" Notice how often

Montecito is coming up, recently? Oprah, then Valentine and now Joshua. And it's not just because it's the next town over. It's fate. It's in the cards.

"I'll make dinner," he says. Then asks, a little doubtfully, if I can be there by seven.

I wipe cobwebs from my forehead. "No problem."

chapter 26

Montecito makes me feel like Lisa Simpson at a runway show. Glamour everywhere, perfect clothing on perfect bodies with perfect hair, and I clomp around cowlike with my Velcro hair and Target clothing. It doesn't matter that I'm wearing Celine over Calvin Klein heels—I am a bovine clumping intruder, and Montecito knows it.

At night, Montecito is in permanent blackout mode. Mansions, estates, chateaux and modest little seventeen-room haciendas are shrouded by foreboding, custom-wrought gates and impenetrable, perfectly-manicured hedges. There are no streetlamps or road signs. It is impossible to arrive in Montecito unless you're intimately familiar with your destination.

It takes me forty-five minutes to find Joshua's house. It's a mansion. I cannot be this lucky. Despite the presence of Joshua's car, I'm sure I have the wrong place. I ring the bell anyway. At least I can get directions, and possibly I'll meet Oprah, Jeff Bridges or Rob Lowe.

The door opens and, in a glow of honey-colored light, Joshua appears. He's wearing a black ribbed sweater and jeans, and his feet are bare. Even his toes are sexy.

"You look gorgeous," he says. "Prada?"

"What?" Is *Prada* his standard greeting? Because there's no way this dress can be mistaken for Prada. I almost correct him with a stern "Celine," but kiss him instead; I had a caller yesterday whose husband thinks she's a nag, and I told her, would you rather be right, or happy? So I figure I should take my own advice.

The kiss is nice, but not hot. He leads me into the house, and I follow, worried about the absence of heat. Does he need time in his cave? Maybe I should have worn something sexier, like Saran Wrap or Jenna's body.

"Did you have any trouble finding the place?" he asks.

I am almost too stunned by the immensity of the living room to respond. It must be two thousand square feet. A half-dozen logs are burning in the fireplace, with enough room left to roast a mastodon. Around the hearth, and it's definitely a *hearth,* is a phalanx of couches, a battalion of tables, a regiment of chairs. With, um, assorted other military-metaphors of carpets, lamps, bookshelves, artwork. It's a showroom. I have to restrain myself from looking for price tags.

He asks if I'll have some wine, and I nod, afraid to ruin the moment by speaking. I follow him into an *Architectural Digest* kitchen and perch at one of the stools around the center island. But it's bigger than an island. It's a continent. Joshua pulls the cork from a bottle of Pinot Grigio and pours two glasses.

"To us," he says.

There is an *us!* He thinks we're an us!

I beam and clink glasses—nothing breaks, nothing sloshes out of my glass. He tells me he's making salmon, and starts chopping an onion on the butcher block. He is a gorgeous chopper.

"Can I help?" I ask.

"No, thanks. Joshua likes to cook."

Elle doesn't know what *that's* about. Elle thinks referring to yourself in the third person is bizarre. But if that's the price Elle has to pay for gorgeous man in gorgeous Montecito mansion who cooks salmon and gives Elle envelopes full of cash, Elle will think it is the cutest thing ever.

"How long have you lived here?" I ask. What I mean is, how do you afford this place?

"About a month, now."

"You rent?"

He laughs, gorgeously. "Not quite."

"You don't *own* it?"

"Not quite that, either."

He lives with his parents. His wife owns it. "Well, um…it must cost a fortune," I say.

"Oh, no. It's free."

I almost spill my wine. "What? How?"

"The owners are only here a couple months a year, so when they're not using it, I do."

"Oh! A house-sitter. You really scored."

He looks up from the cutting board, slightly perplexed. "Yeah, I guess you could call me a house-sitter. Anyway, I wanted to ask your advice."

"Me?" There is an *us,* and he wants *my* advice! A good thing I do this professionally. "Well, um…have you ever considered adopting a dog from the shelter?"

"No. Anyway, how does the phone gig work?"

"Oh. The phone gig? Um…" I watch him pull fresh salmon steaks from the fridge and put them under the broiler. "It's actually pretty good. I'm really able to help people. Like, two days ago this woman called who hasn't spoken to her mom in a year. And they live in the same house. So I told her—"

"No, I mean—how does it *work?* Is it an 800 number and you take credit cards, or a 900 number and they get charged by the minute?"

"900." Why doesn't he want to hear my estranged-daughter story?

But then he asks a bunch of questions about behind-the-scenes Psychic Connexion, and it's like we're having a real conversation about my career. I'm quite proud.

"Three ninety-nine a minute," he laughs. "And they get *you* on the other end?"

"Why is that funny?"

"Oh, Elle." He reaches across the island and cups my cheek in his hand. "You're adorable."

I press my face against his hand, like a dog begging for treats. I want so much for him to like me.

Over a candlelit dinner, I tell him about the parent company, and the divisions and laws and equipment and all that. He's so attentive and absorbed in me and my life that when he asks if I can get him some paperwork from C. Burke's office, so he can really understand how the business operates, I agree. I guess it is pretty interesting.

Dessert is raspberry tarts he picked up at a bakery in the village. I am afraid of mine; it will inevitably become an unsightly and embarrassing stain on my Celine. So I regale him with work-related stories, and ignore the luscious tart. I mean the pastry.

"Straight Sex is one of the categories?" he says. He feeds me a bite of raspberry tart. "Tell me more."

I do better. I show him.

The king-size bed has real linen sheets. They need ironing, but still, real linen! The good-morning squeak is delightful. A little difficult to truly relax while terrified he'll spot cellulite, but still pretty delightful. Am so blissed out during the drive home, that I almost forget I've moved, and have to cut off a trucker to get to my exit.

It's drizzling rain, and my new house is slightly spooky, with its Victorian turrets in the gray light. I don't even know who else lives here. It's mixed residential/commercial, but I didn't have time yesterday to pry into the question of fellow tenants. Haven't been in the front door yet—used the back all day yesterday, for moving. I'm glad it's morning. The house must appear sinister, at night.

I step inside the front door and a man looms over me. I yelp.

"Elle?" It's Merrick. In the foyer of my building. "What are you doing here?"

"You scared me," I say.

"That was not my intent."

"That was not my intent? Who talks like that? You sound like Spock." There's a plaque on the open door behind Merrick. It reads: *Louis Merrick, Architect.* "You *work* here? You don't work here. You work here?"

He gestures inside. The room is dominated by a large drafting table, beyond which are a couch and two antique Chinese wooden chairs. "Front room's my office. There's a bedroom in back."

"You live here? You don't *live* here."

"Would you stop that? I do work here, and I do live here. At least I sleep here. I'm building a house, and I'm running into problems. I'm staying here until I get it sorted out." He looks fresh and showered and coffeed, and smells of lavender bath gel. I am stale and rumpled, with a raspberry stain on my left tit. My hair is in knots, and I smell of Joshua. "Were you looking for me?" he asks.

"I live here."

He frowns. "Monty rented you one of the spaces?"

"Why shouldn't he?"

There's a glint of evil amusement in his eyes, but he just says, "No reason. Except no one else has moved in yet. Which one do you have?"

"The studio at the top." I eye his lair through the doorway. "Mine has a view." His looks out on the parking lot.

"I know. I did the plans for the renovation."

"You did?" Feels oddly intimate, living in a place he designed. "That's weird."

"Thanks. Those are words every architect hopes to hear." He gives me a once-over, eyeing my disheveled dress and snarled hair. "What happened to your trolley?"

"What do you mean, what happened? It's not like they had to destroy it. Oh, the demolition crew came the next day. A little TNT, and it was okay. I mean, c'mon. It was only a backed-up toilet. Like you've never had a backed-up toilet. I suppose when your toilet backs up, it doesn't stink. No, when you—"

"I mean," he says, "why did you decide to move here?"

"Oh. I got kicked out."

"For what?"

"The water bombs, mostly."

"What? The water what?"

I mumble, "Bombs."

"The water bombs," he says in a flat tone, like he can't be hearing me right.

Why won't he let it go? "The water bombs," I say, loud and clear. "You can't have forgotten the condoms. I told you I had them to peg the juvie next door, didn't I? Well, it got out of hand."

He shakes his head, unable to comprehend this new disaster. "Do you want some coffee?"

I hesitate. I do want coffee. But I don't want to talk to him. I suppose I can't order it "to go," though. I follow him into his lair, and he pours two cups—no sugar, lots of half and half. The Chinese chairs look like genuine antiques. The coffee is wonderful. Merrick's wearing a slate-blue T-shirt and jeans. And I think his hair is a slightly different color red. Seriously. It could be the light, but I think it's gone from flaming-carrot to dull cherry. It is, if anything, even worse.

"So, you made water balloons out of all those rubbers?"

I sip my life-giving coffee and nod.

"How'd the ribbed one hold up?"

I grudgingly laugh. "Couldn't tell the difference. Though that may be the one that that stuck to Mr. Petrie's hair."

"Mr. Petrie?"

"My landlord."

He chokes. Looks like coffee's about to spurt out his nose.

"Old guy," I explain. "I'd never met him. I thought he was the little juvie."

He says, in a strained voice: "How old?"

"Like seventy." I can't tell if he's amused or horrified, but what do I care? "Spry, though. You shoulda seen him dodge. Until the one that knocked him over, I mean. Then he just flailed, while I bombarded him."

Merrick has a nice laugh. I know, because I listen to it for maybe three minutes.

"It's not that funny," I say. "He kicked me out and kept my security deposit."

"Sounds fair."

"Yeah, can't say I blame him."

"And now you have a new place, and are apparently—" He inspects the signs of my ravishment and dissipation "—enjoying yourself."

I bridle. "What does that mean? Enjoying myself? I am *not* enjoying myself. I'm having a…I had a sleep-over. At Maya's. And forgot a change of clothes. Thanks for the coffee."

I head for the door, but he's not done with me. "How about work? You find a job?"

"Yes."

"Doing what?"

"Consulting."

"What kind of consulting?"

I stop at his drafting table. It holds sketches of something large and grand. "Just—you know, consulting."

He flips the sketches closed. "No, I don't know. What exact—"

"Did you ever hire an assistant?" I look around the room. There is not a stray pencil, blueprint, invoice, or phone message out of place. Only the empty coffee cup I've left on the side table. "Because you've really got a mess going here."

"Yeah. She starts next week."

"Good," I say.

"Good," he says.

We stand there. Looking at each other. I remember kissing him outside the trolley. I like his voice, and I like his eyes. But he has red hair, and I have Joshua. I step back.

He says, "Elle…"

"What?"

"If you want—" he hesitates, and I think changes his mind about what he's going to say "—if you have trouble with the place, upstairs? Talk to me, not Monty. He's already had one hip replaced."

I scowl and leave. But I put a little swing in my backyard as I walk upstairs, just because. When I glance back, at the first landing, his door is closed. Ah, well. Me and Merrick, alone together. I'll be lucky if he doesn't scold me every time I walk past his office. He's so much like the original Louis—stiff and formal and moralistic. He wouldn't even let me see his sketches, like Louis and his legal briefs.

Not like Joshua. He likes when I get into his briefs.

chapter 27

The next morning, after a day spent settling into my new home and ignoring Merrick's presence downstairs, I sneak out. I'm worried he'll corner me for interrogation re: my "consulting." It is consulting, of course, but he'll insist I'm a fraud, just because I'm not really psychic. Perhaps every man named Louis is the same.

At work, I'm greeted with excellent news. Today, my desk is at a safe distance from Girls with Toys.

"How's the numerology coming?" Darwin asks as I settle in.

"Great," I say. I picked up a copy of my namesake magazine, *Elle,* which always offers a horoscope-type numerology section. "I'm learning a lot."

He nods thoughtfully. "You ought to pick up a *Details,* for when you get men."

"Sports Illustrated," I say. "I start asking about their favorite

teams, I'll never get them to shut up. Hmm. That's not a bad idea."

I am about to expand upon this when Adele appears in a cloud of patchouli. She's in full New Age regalia today: a lavender smock over a violet *Crystallize the Earth* T-shirt, with fuchsia leggings and raspberry wool socks. And, of course, Birkenstocks. "Your technique may be unorthodox, Elle," Adele says, having caught the end of our conversation. "But there's no denying that you're doing well. It just goes to show."

She says that a lot. It just goes to show. But she won't tell you what, specifically, it goes to show, unless you ask.

"What, um, does it show?" Darwin asks.

"The path between the crown chakra and the heart chakra detours the mind." She draws a line from the top of her head to between her breasts. "Though not, of course, the mind *chakra*."

Darwin and I agree: "Of course not. Heavens, no. It doesn't detour around *that*."

"Still, I do wish you'd educate yourself, Elle."

I nod. She's right. I really should. Despite her appalling fashion senselessness, she's good on the phone. Sensitive and thoughtful, sometimes wise. And good with Texans.

I am about to agree—yet again—to do the research, and the meditation, and the workshops and healing circles, etc., when the phone rings.

It's Valentine, the Montecito matron. I greet her enthusiastically, and tell her I was in Montecito just the other day. I manage not to boast about Joshua's gorgeous setup—don't want her feeling inferior.

Fortunately, she's not listening. She's too upset, because Rowdy, her Pomeranian, was hit by a cyclist on Coast Village Road, and hasn't recovered the use of one of his back legs.

"That's terrible," I say. "Poor little Rowdy. I hope you got the biker's license plate."

"A cyclist, Elle—not a biker," she says. "That's what they call them. Cyclists. With their egg-shaped helmets and black stretch knickers."

"A cyclist, of course. And don't tell me—I'm getting a flash—did the accident happen on Coast Village Road?" I don't do that a lot, honest. But every now and then, to keep the caller impressed.

"Why, yes!" she says. "That's exactly where it happened! I'm calling because I want you to tell me, with no sugar-coating, what are his chances for recovery?"

"Well…I'm feeling that the vet told you his chances are not good," I say. Otherwise, she wouldn't be asking.

"Not good, not good," she says, clearly overwrought.

She loves this dog. What do I tell her? Get one of those little doggie-carts? I flip hurriedly through *Elle,* but it's no help. I make psychic-on-the-verge noises, and dig through my stack of magazines. Ah! There it is. *Prevention*. They often have articles about pet care.

I open to a column about acupuncture for dogs and cats. Weird. But so are phone psychics. "I'm getting something, Valentine…I'm sensing…it's quite clear…Rowdy would benefit from acupuncture. I can't say if he'd regain *all* the mobility in his leg, but it would at least help with the discomfort."

"Acupuncture? My vet didn't suggest acupuncture."

"I'm not surprised. You know how stodgy and thick-calved vets can be."

"Thick-what?"

"It's untraditional, Valentine. A bold move. I can't be sure, but I think Rowdy has a blockage of the, er, paw chakra, which should be directly connected to the crown chakra, but—" A wad of paper bounces off my forehead. Darwin motions for me to shut up, because Adele will overhear. "—well, best to let the acupuncturist do her job. I think that's the thing for Rowdy, though."

She thanks me profusely, and promises to call back when Rowdy recovers.

"Nothing in life is guaranteed," I tell her. "It's all process. It's all flow. Have you run into Oprah yet?"

The switchboard tells me I have a request, which means a repeat caller.

"Psychic Connexion," I say. I'm convinced, by the way, that connexion is pronounced differently than connection. I spend a good deal of time trying to say it right.

"This is Nyla?" the woman says. "I don't know if you remember me..."

"Of course I remember you!" You hung up on me after calling me names. "I'm pleased you called back."

She apologizes for being rude, and I pretend to be far too highly evolved to worry about such things, though in truth I'm tremendously jealous of her Fendi satchel. "You're the only person I called who wasn't just saying what I wanted to hear."

I nobly refrain from saying I told you so.

She gives me the story about her remote but wealthy boyfriend again. She just wants someone to talk to, maybe.

"Um...have you ever considered therapy?" I ask. "I mean real therapy?"

"I go twice a week. But I don't want Susan to think I'm all messed up. I tell her my relationship with Peter is great. I'm sort of competitive with her."

"You lie to your therapist? Nyla—that's a bad idea."

There's a pause. "She's sort of a year younger than me. And happily married. And a size two."

"Size *two?*" I say. "Sounds like she needs therapy for anorexia. Lay it on me. You still think he's unfaithful?"

"Oh. Actually, he is. I mean, I know he is."

"And?"

"And I don't want to leave him. So I don't know what to do."

"Have you spoken with him about it?"

"I'm afraid to. I'd sort of rather pretend, and stay together, you know?"

"Nyla," I say.

She cries a little.

"Nyla, let me tell you how I see you spending your days. You sleep too much, maybe twelve hours a day. And you shop the rest of the time—for clothes or food or gorgeous little *things.*"

"Most days. Not twelve hours. Not usually. I do other things. I go to art galleries, sometimes—"

"You shop enough to know which days Bloomies and Nieman Marcus receive new merchandise. In fact, you have regular salesgirl who holds your size for you when new Chloe and Gucci stuff arrives. Her name is what? Cathy… Karen—?"

"It's Carrie," she says. "How did you know?"

Salesgirls always have *K* or *C* names. "That's not all I know, Nyla. I know that when you get home with your new Prada, or Calvin Klein, or Roberto Cavalli…you think you'll be happy, but you're not. You immediately try it on in front of the mirror in your closet, or your bathroom—you know the one, the only mirror you can trust to give you an accurate reading, not like the skinny mirrors at the store. Twice a week you decide you like something, and you remove the tags and hang it in the closet with all the other stuff you once decided you really like, but you've never worn because you didn't have the right occasion. But most days, you find what you bought makes you look bloated, or squat, or crooked, or flat, or puffy, and you fold it back into the bag and leave it on the closet floor, hoping one day you'll have enough energy to return it."

"I've never told anyone—"

"How many bags are in the bottom of your closet, Nyla?"

"I don't know. A few?" Her voice breaks. "Six?"

"More than six."

"A dozen?"

"Are you happy, Nyla?"

She sniffles. "No."

"I wasn't eith— I'm not happy knowing you're unhappy. There are two things you can do right now. One is forget about it, keep doing what you're doing and stay unhappy. The other is to try something new, something radical."

"Stop shopping?"

I laugh. "That's *way* too drastic, don't you think?"

"Oh, thank God!"

"I'm going to give you an assignment. When we hang up, you sit down with a pad of paper and think of five jobs you'd like to have. Don't worry about how much money you'd make, just write down five things you'd like to do, and we'll go over your list tomorrow. And keep them reasonable—apparently careers like architects and veterinarians require a lot of education."

"But I'm not good at anything."

"You're not the only one—uh, I mean a lot people aren't good at anything, and they do it anyway, and they feel better than they ever had before."

"Five jobs?"

"Five jobs."

"I'll do it," she says. "I'll call tomorrow. And, Elle… thanks."

By the end of the day, I'm exhausted. I zone through the freeway traffic, my mind still at the office. I like the silly calls. I like the chatty calls and I like the good calls. I even like the crisis calls, giving the hotline numbers to people who need them, and feeling like I'm really helping. I like Darwin and Adele. And I like C. Burke, though I've never met him.

This afternoon, I slipped into his office to get the info Joshua wants. It's not important stuff, just things like the carrier we use, equipment leasing, purchase orders, scripts, manuals. C. Burke's office is a glorified cubicle, but it has a door. I closed it behind me, terrified I'd get caught and lose my job. Still, if I don't take the stuff I might lose Joshua. But before I could rifle through drawers, I heard someone pause outside. I panicked, certain I'd be fired, humiliated and impoverished. But they walked past. I waited until they were gone, opened the door and fled. Empty-handed.

I pull into the lot next to Merrick's Volvo. My Beemer, even with the square taillights, looks worse than usual squatting next to his silver, late-model Volvo. But you know what? I don't care. I like being a psychic—even if it's a fake one. I like my apartment—even if Merrick designed it. I like my boyfriend—even if I'd never actually call Joshua that within his hearing, for fear he'd deny it.

I've paid Monty his $600—virtually on time!—and still have a couple hundred left. The apartment is truly mine, although I'm blowing through Chanel No. 5 like it's water. I spritz some every time I pass Merrick's door so he doesn't think I smell like sewage.

My little list is not looking so stupid anymore. I have crossed off apartment, car and job. Man I've scored through in pencil.

The phone's ringing when I unlock my front door. I happily answer—ready to talk to anyone.

"Eleanor Medina."

Anyone other than Carlos. Shit.

"Thought you could get rid of me by moving, did you?"

"No, Carlos, I wouldn't do that. I just—the trolley was awful, so I moved. And I've been meaning to call you, but I've been busy."

"The new place costs more, or less?"

"The same," I lie. "Basically the same. And guess what? I got a job."

"I need a check, Elle."

"I sent one! You didn't get it?"

"Twelve dollars?"

"It's a start. It's the New Elle. I know it's not much, but that's because I don't have much. And now that I have a job, I'll be able to send more."

"Don't mess with me, Elle."

"I won't. Promise."

"Where are you working? I've got it listed here you have no previous employment, and—"

"That is so not true. I was a, um, character reenactment technician, in a historical, um…"

"I don't even want to know. What are you doing now?"

I tell him the story, and we're friends again. He does demand the phone number for Superior, but he's laughing as I tell him.

"A phone psychic," he says again, disbelief clear in his voice.

"I'm very good at it."

"Can you tell what I'm thinking now?" Thank God, the Latin seduction is back in his voice.

I giggle out a "no."

"I'm thinking you better send five hundred bucks, Elle, or I'm gonna have to garnishee your wages."

¡Ay caramba!

chapter 28

I'm thinking I'll get a King Charles spaniel, a chocolate lab or maybe a borzoi. I don't really know what the King Charles or the borzoi look like, but I've always liked the names: one regal, the other exotic.

I'd interrupted Maya during breakfast to drag her to the Humane Society. The idea being to cheer her up, take her mind off the miscarriage. When I showed up, she was untidily sipping coffee in her robe and slippers. I helped myself to the coffeepot as she reluctantly shuffled to the bedroom. She reappeared in five minutes looking pert and perky, in a navy blue sweater I recognized from high school. I hate her.

"This isn't cheering me up," Maya says when we reach the kennels. It's a blustery day for Santa Barbara, gray and cold. The cast-off dogs shiver in their cages, barking and cringing.

"Me, either. The only thing I can still fit in from high school is earrings."

"That's not true," she says. "There's always socks."

I roll my eyes and kneel in front of a fluffy red dog with a spotted tongue. "Priscilla. Chow Chow mix. Four years old. Family was too busy to care for her. They had her four years, then became too busy?"

"You do know they *sell* puppies, don't you? Purebreds. For like, hundreds of dollars."

I pat the Chow goodbye and move to the next cage: Tadpole, a fat tube of a dog, with a shiny coat and an eager face. "Yeah, but I read a thing in *Vogue* or *Glamour* about puppy mills. Plus, they said that there are plenty of purebreds in shelters. I can probably find a perfect Afghan."

"Since when did you decide you need a dog?" Maya asks.

"Since forever. My dad refused to let me have one as a kid, and once he left, my mom maintained the ruling like it had been grandfathered in. When I tried to get Louis interested he complained about his sinuses."

We stop in front of a pit bull mix with a brown-and-white coat and a scar on his muzzle. He's probably the fifth pit bull mix we've seen.

"Those pit bulls are horndogs, aren't they?" Maya says.

Which reminds me: "I've got a court date on Monday."

"You're not trying racquetball again, are you?"

"Different kind of court." As we finish the circuit of dog cages, I admit to the Café Lustre incident.

"Cranberry juice?" Maya is agog. "How *do* you do it, Elle?"

"It's a gift."

We finish our tour in front of the cage of an oversize male Dalmatian named Hoser. He's large, glossy, purebred and beautiful. Plus, he'll match my furniture. But there's a little note on his cage saying that he's already been adopted. So I return to Priscilla. She's very nearly purebred Chow Chow. And she was tossed aside after four years. I was tossed aside after six, so I know how she feels.

I fill out an application in record time, and hand it to the woman in the office. I scan the fliers on the wall as she looks it over. Dog walkers and trainers. Someone selling an Invisible Fence. A poster about that missing puppy, Holly-Go-Lightly, who still hasn't been found. She's become a local celebrity, with increasingly dire warnings about her health and medicine. A stack of business cards for someone who sells handcrafted collars and leashes: I take one of those. I already have the food and water bowls, of course.

"This won't work." The woman behind the counter looks up from my application. "You don't have a yard."

"Well, I'll walk her." I say. "Downtown, and at Hendry's and the Wilcox. She'll get better exercise that way, anyway."

"You need to have a fenced-in yard. And the fence has to be at least five feet, with a sealed perimeter."

"A perimeter? What is this? Fortay Knox, or the Humane Society?"

"I'm sorry, ma'am, that's our policy."

I hate, I hate, I *hate* being called ma'am. "Why? What does it matter where she walks, as long as I walk her?"

"But what if you don't walk her?"

"But I *will*."

Maya fidgets with a brochure about spaying and neutering, as I feel my jaw clamp. "So you're saying I can't adopt Priscilla."

"No, I'm sorry."

"Is there *any* dog I can have?"

"Policy is, you have to have a yard to adopt a dog."

"What if someone drops off a dog without any legs—will I *still* need a five-foot fence?"

The woman stares at me. "We don't often get legless dogs."

"You know, it might *behoove* you to put up a sign, telling people they can't adopt a dog without a yard." Can't believe I just said behoove. "It's not very humane to let people bond with one of these poor dogs, then casually rip their heart out because of some mania for perimeter security. You think they're better-served living in those kennels? How many dogs will die because you insist on yards? Because walks on the beach aren't good enough? Huh? Huh? When is this madness going to end?"

I pause for breath, glowing with self-righteous fury, and the woman says, "This is a no-kill shelter. We place one hundred percent of our dogs. To homes with yards."

"You know," Maya says, after I slink away. "You were right. That did cheer me up."

I work Sunday. I am dogless, but unbowed. It's slow, though. In the first hour, I have a half-dozen people who won't commit to a reading, then nothing for the next hour and a half.

In the afternoon, I get a handful of twenties and twenty-fives, all the same: yeah, you'll find a man, but you have to work on yourself first. Prince Charming doesn't ride up and marry just anyone, he marries the princess. The princess is *not* needy and desperate. She is not disrespected, she is not helpless and she sure as hell will climb on that horse herself if need be. And remember: you gotta kiss a lot of frogs.

Well, it sounds good when I say it. I got it from an article in *Mademoiselle.* Or *O.* Or somewhere.

I'm in another slow period, doing the crossword, when James calls. He's the guy who was hot for his sister-in-law. I'm relieved to be interrupted. I only have two words, and they're both celebrity names. I suck at crosswords—maybe *L* should have a crossword for the wordly disinclined.

"Hey James," I say. "What's a six-letter word for bee yard?"

"Apiary."

I count the letters. "It fits! How did you know that?"

"I'm that kind of guy, Elle. I know all about the birds and bees."

I laugh. "What can I do for you? You want your horoscope?"

"Nah. I just wanted to tell you, I'm thinking of asking Sandy to marry me."

Sandy's the church lady his sister-in-law set him up with. "Married? This is pretty quick."

"But we've seen each other every day since our first date. We've got a lot in common. Same church, and we both like NASCAR and McDonald's."

"Oh. Well. Um."

"What do the cards say, Elle?"

The cards say Louis and I lived together for six years before we decided to get married, and then we didn't. "Well…NASCAR and McDonald's are a good start, James. But it's only been what?—almost two weeks?—since you started seeing her. Maybe you ought to get to know each other a little better. It's a big step."

"Well, the thing is, um…" He hems and haws for five minutes before I pry it from him: "She doesn't believe in sex before marriage."

"Ohhhh." Understanding dawns. "And, um…no sex sex, or no sex at all?"

He doesn't understand.

"I mean, I understand she wants no actual, main-course, meat-and-potatoes type sex. But is she also against the, erm, side dishes? The not-quite-sex sex?"

He still doesn't get it.

I consider having him call Blue Hair—whose name is Ian, actually, an International Relations major at UCSB. He's wearing his orange velvet again, and is at the desk next to mine, on the Straight Sex line. But James is my client through thick and thin, and I have a sudden flash of intuition: he's a virgin.

"You know," I say. "Hands, mouths…" Every third day, more or less, I spend eight hours listening to the most explicit aural sex possible. It is all I can do not to bring James up to speed with an X-rated, moan-heavy, monologue.

"Oh! You mean…not going all the way to home base."

Home base? "Yeah. The cards here say that marrying her for sex isn't such a great idea. You ought to get to know each other first. And there's plenty of things you can do that aren't, uh…the home run."

"Her father is the pastor," he says. "I couldn't ask her to do that sort of thing…."

I spend twenty minutes informing him that some women actually enjoy that sort of thing. "And masturbation is always an option, James, if you need to take the edge off."

He insists that he doesn't jerk off.

I insist he does. He's a man. Men do.

He insists he doesn't. And I believe him. This man is considering marriage, and he doesn't even know how to bring himself off. He doesn't need a psychic, he needs a Chicken Ranch. I waggle my fingers to get Ian's attention. He looks up with a grin; he's been eavesdropping on the call, like I thought.

"Listen," I tell James. "I've got a friend here, another psychic. Her name is Jasmine."

The phone is ringing when I get home. It's Joshua.

"My sweet little psychic," he says. "Did you get the stuff from work?"

"Well…not exactly."

"Why not?"

"There hasn't been quite the right moment. Why do you want it, anyway? I'm afraid if I take anything I'll get in trouble."

"I'm interested in everything about you, Elle."

I melt.

"And why would you get in trouble wanting to know more about the company? You should get promoted for that kind of behavior."

He does have a point. "Okay. I'll try again tomorrow. Do you want to come for dinner tonight?"

He doesn't. He'll call in a few days. Once I get that information we can get a room at the Harbor Inn, have dinner and drinks. Then we can laze around the pool together the whole next day. Once I get that information.

I am in bed by 8:30. The darkness is heavy, its weight compresses me. I wish it were heavier. I wish I could sleep. I lay in bed for hours, and look at the clock: 8:52. I turn. I fidget. I tuck and untuck. I wish everything were easier. Finally, I sleep.

I wake the next morning past ten. I know I'm sick about something, but can't remember what. Then I sit up, remembering: I have to go to court.

I dress as conservatively as possible. A pale pink cashmere sweater set and gray flannel pants. Even a pair of pearl earrings left over from the eighties. I walk the half mile to the courthouse.

If the Santa Barbara airport is a hacienda, the courthouse is a Spanish-Moorish palace. Its white ceramic facade is surrounded by lawns and a sunken tropical garden. I, however, do not rate the grand courtroom with the polished wood pews and Spanish murals. I rate a dinky room with not even a pulpit for the judge to sit behind. Very downscale and disappointing.

There are twenty-five or so people in the room and I spot Tony the bouncer immediately upon entering. Still looks like a white Mike Tyson, and I am cheered, sure no one will believe him over me. He sees me, and makes a rude gesture with his stained suit in my direction. I sit on the other side of the room.

Judge Miller presides. Only she may be Magistrate Miller. I wasn't listening. In any case, she's neatly efficient and not nearly as intimidating as Judge Judy or similar. Well, maybe *nearly.* But at least this isn't being televised. If it was, I'd never have worn pink.

In twenty minutes, Tony and I stand before her.

"Did you or did you not, Ms. Medina, throw—" she consults a piece of paper "—cranberry juice at Mr. Anthony Dingle?"

I giggled when I heard his name was Dingle. I almost laugh now, but the judge's stern expression stops me.

I swallow. "Well, you see, um, Your Honor, I sort of did, but..."

"Yes or no?" the judge asks.

"Your honor, as you can see, I did him a favor." I gesture toward Dingle, currently wearing an atrocious brick-red suit. "Look what he wears. That color does nothing for him. And the cut is criminal."

"You got a friggin' problem with my suit?" the Dingle says.

The judge says, "Ms. Medina. Did you or did you not throw the juice?"

"It was self-defense, your honor. He told me my breasts were sagging."

Twenty-five pairs of eyes, including the judge's, beam to my breasts. But I'm prepared: I've got a Wonderbra under my cashmere—no one's gonna accuse these babies of sagging.

"The juice," she says, and I think I detect a bit of sympathy. "Did you throw the juice?"

"I don't know if I threw it, exactly. I sort of spilled it, maybe? But those are fighting words, aren't they? I mean about my—"

"Ms. Medina! You are ordered to pay Mr. Dingle for the replacement of his suit, in the amount of..." She consults her paper again, and turns to Dingle. "Seven hundred dollars for *that* suit?"

I snort.

"Seven hundred twenty," Dingle says. "I'm rounding down."

"But you have no receipt and no credit card slip?"

He shrugs a Tyson-esque shoulder. "Don't keep that stuff."

"Your Honor," I say, arching my back slightly. "I would

like to state, erm, for the record, that the suit in question is heinous, that my breasts do not sag and that if he paid a cent more than thirty-nine ninety-five, he got reamed. For seven hundred dollars, he could have bought—"

"Yes, yes," she says. "Ms. Medina, you are hereby ordered to take possession of Mr. Dingle's…admittedly offensive garment. You will repair the damage, or have it repaired and return the suit to him no later than three weeks from today's date. Is that understood?"

"Yes, Your Honor." Wooo! Down from seven hundred bucks to a dry-cleaning bill! I won my very first case. And here I thought Louis's job was so difficult and technical.

We sign this and that, and the Dingle glowers at me, and mutters, "Bitch."

I smile, as we exit to the hall, and say under my breath: "Fuck you, you white Tyson wannabe."

His Neanderthal brow creases in confusion, but he follows me down the hall with: "Bitch."

I stop to confront him. He's really quite large. And wide. Very wide. But I will not back down. "You're an ear-biter, Dingle. If you paid seven hundred bucks for that crap suit, you—"

"Bitch! You bitch!"

"That's it? That's all you can say? You slope-browed, off-the-rack, overgrown jelly vendor—"my volume creeps upward "—*Sopranos*-watching—"

Merrick says: "Hey. What's up?"

Merrick again!? Always catching me at my best. He looks at Dingle. Looks at me.

"Nothing," I say, petulantly, and take Merrick's arm for moral support.

"Fuckin' bitch."

"What did you say?" Merrick says to the Dingle, all masculine aggression, and he's my hero.

"Fix my suit or I'll sue your saggy tits," Dingle tells me. "And not small claims, next time." He walks massively away.

"What?" Merrick asks, watching the departing hulk. "Was that?"

I shake my head. "That was Dingle. Will you beat him up for me?"

"Were you in court?" He obviously can't believe it.

"Yep! It was kind of fun, actually. I won!" I notice Dingle's suit in my hand. "Sort of. Anyway, what're you doing here?"

"Planning permits. But what—how—?"

Incoming scold. I make sure Dingle's gone, and disengage my arm. "I won't keep you, then."

"Are you going home?" he asks, taking a breath. "I'll walk with you. Or did you drive?"

"No. I mean, yes. I'm going home. I walked." I don't know why he makes me so nervous. Possibly a reaction to his Chernobyl haircolor. Or because I can't tell if he finds me attractive, absurd or appalling. Or all of the above. But I do not want to tell him the Dingle story. "Don't you have to get your permits?"

He taps his portfolio as we head for the street. "All done. So tell me about court."

"Not much to say. There wasn't even a pulpit."

"You were hoping for powdered wigs?"

"She never used her gavel, either. It's not at all like you see on TV."

"No," he says, and I suspect he's laughing at me. "What's it like then?"

We cross Anacapa Street and walk past the library and through La Arcada, an outdoor shopping arcade. "There used to be a shoe store here," I tell Merrick, in an obvious attempt to change the subject. "Footnote. It was a great little store."

"Was it about Super 9?"

"It was mostly about shoes. But they sold accessories, too."

"Super 9 thinks you're involved with the shoplifting? Or is this about your employee theft?"

"I told you I didn't do that! And it wasn't about Super 9, anyway. I don't want to talk about it."

We wait silently for the light to turn, then cross State.

"So, that's why you're dressed that way," he says.

"What way?"

"You know. Less...elaborate than usual. You look like a sorority girl or something. Like you work in a bank."

I smile at the idea. Those two institutions would eat pigeon pie before accepting me into their folds.

"Well..." He cocks his head at my ensemble, definitely checking out my breasts. "Did it work?"

Momentarily thinking he means my Wonderbra, I say, "Yes." Then realize he means the whole outfit. "I mean, yes."

He nods. "That's what I thought you meant."

I pause outside Saks. The male mannequins in the window are wearing Hugo Boss suits. Lovely clothes, but why bother? As if men ever look in shop windows.

"What do you think of that one?" Merrick points to a sage three-button.

I look at him. At the suit. At him. At the suit. It would look great on Joshua. It would look good on Merrick.

"I don't think so," I say.

"I think it'd look good."

"Since when do you wear suits? I've seen you dressed up—you wear mandarin collar linen shirts."

"Well, Santa Barbara," he says. "When do you see anyone in a suit?"

"Other than Monty, never."

"But for New York, I need suits."

I suspect he's trying to impress me. *Oooh,* he goes to New York on business. Actually, I am kind of impressed.

"You should play up the Santa Barbara thing," I tell him. "I mean, when you're in New York. Go sub-casual. They'll be amazed how confident and cool you are."

"You think?"

"Well, not *sub*-casual. But you know...go like you are."

He's wearing a charcoal-gray long-sleeve tight-fitting sweater, and gray wool pants. Sort of a Ben Stiller look—but with freak-red hair. "You live in Santa Barbara, you ought to remind them you're a visitor from a faraway, and far better, place."

He appears to be considering this as we continue walking. "That actually makes sense. What do I owe you?"

"Hmm?"

"For the consultation. You never told me what kind of consultant you are."

"Eclectic," I say, as we stop at another light.

"Spare any change?" a homeless guy asks me. He's fidgety and wiry, with curly gold hair and intense blue eyes, and I love him for interrupting.

Merrick and the other people at the light watch to see what I'll do. I want to give him money. But I don't want to give him money with an audience of light-waiters. Still, I am a princess, and do what I please. I open my wallet, and it's empty. I'm trying not to carry too much cash, so I don't waste it on trivial items such as food and drink.

"Oh, Jeez," I tell the guy. "I'm sorry. I have maybe—" I check the coin-pocket "—almost a dollar in change."

I try to give it to him, but he won't take it. "Even I have ten bucks," he says, and we laugh.

Merrick gives him a five and the light changes and we cross. I expect him to say something about the guy. He doesn't. The original Louis always bragged about how generous he was to "charity cases."

"Thanks for that." I gesture behind us. "My money's in my other wallet."

He gives me an indecipherable look. "No problem. I see him downtown sometimes. He's one of my favorites. One time I was eating lunch in that little park, outside the *News-Press,* and saw him asking people to pick up after their dog. Respectful, but firm. I liked that."

I like that he likes that. I like that he has a favorite homeless person. I end up telling him my own personal dog story, including the punch line about it being a no-kill shelter.

He has a nice laugh. He tells me about his childhood dog, Bounder, who was afraid of awnings and wheelbarrows. I tell him about my childhood imaginary friend Pebbles, who was afraid of nothing.

We stop outside our house, sorry the excuse for conversation has ended. Well, at least *I'm* sorry. I don't know what he's thinking, except he says, "You're so calm about having gone to court."

"I had an imaginary gerbil, too," I say.

"I'll probably never go to court in my life."

"You were just *at* the courthouse."

"I mean in court. A *lawsuit*."

"What about jury duty?"

"That's not a *lawsuit*."

I shake my head. "It was just small claims."

"But...how do you do it? Get yourself into trouble all the time?"

"I'm not in trouble," I say. I got off easy at court. Of course, there's no denying I do attract a certain amount of contention.

"Elle, I heard that guy threatening you."

"He's just mad because he thinks the suit looked better before I decorated it." I show Merrick the purple stain.

He shakes his head in disbelief as we enter the foyer.

"Anyway, the Dingle's mostly harmless." I hope.

"Sure, that's why you were so happy to see me. What's a jelly-vendor?"

"A what?"

"A jelly-vendor. You called him a jelly-vendor."

"I did?" I shrug. "I dunno. It just slipped out."

"Slipped out? Jelly-vendor." He runs his fingers over his forehead like he's got a headache. "Let me get this straight. You have a job as an eclectic consultant. You were taken to small claims court for ruining a weightlifter's suit. You're a fake bartender, a wannabe loser-Oprah, and a shoplifting store detective. You go on dates for the doggie bags." His eyebrows move upward. "You waterbomb your landlord. Is there anything you *won't* do?"

"Settle," I say. I give him the swing in the backyard again, on my way upstairs. This time, when I turn on the landing, he's still watching.

chapter 29

"Hello?"

"Is this Janet? Janet Taluga?"

"Yes."

"This is Elle Medina. From Psychic Connexion. You called a while back."

"Yes, I—I did. But how—how did you get my number?"

"I'm a psychic, Janet." Plus, Perfect Brad searched online for her name. "But the question isn't how, it's why. I have a feeling you need to talk to someone."

"But you called…I mean, how much is this costing?"

"Don't worry about the phone bill. I'm calling from work. Oh, costing *you?* It's free, Janet—except I'm asking you to speak with me."

A long pause. "About my husband?"

"About whatever's on your mind."

Another pause. "He doesn't mean to hurt me. He's always awfully sorry. It's the drink makes him do it."

"Janet."

"Don't yell at me."

"I won't yell at you. I just want you to talk to the right people about this. I have a few numbers. You have a pen and paper?"

"Yes."

I can hear that she's lying. "Go get a pen and paper, Janet."

Rustling. She returns. "I love him, though. I really do."

"That's okay. That doesn't matter. I'm not telling you what you should do, or feel, anything like that, except call and chat with these people who understand what it's like, going through what you're going through. They won't make you do anything. They'll just listen, which I think is what you need. You don't like what they say, hang up."

Another pause. "Okay. What are the numbers?"

Am next to Ian Blue Hair again this afternoon. Trying to read *Vogue,* but the sex talk distracts me. I shift in my seat. Might be getting slightly turned on. How can this be? He's a man I'm not interested in, pretending to be a woman I'm *really* not interested in, talking to a man who thinks he really is a woman. Hence, I cannot be turned on. I must be ovulating.

Possibly just missing Joshua. I left three messages with him, and was finally rewarded with a message of my own: "Hey, Elle—I miss you, too. I've been swamped, but we'll get together soon."

And I *should* make it soon. Because Ian Blue Hair, without interrupting his description about how hard he wants it, and where, gives me a knowing grin. Like he can tell I'm getting turned on. He can't tell, can he? God knows what sort of extra-sexual-perception you get, talking filth on the phone eight hours a day.

Darwin spots me and hurries over from his cubicle, sipping from a venti Starbuck's cup. "Adele," he calls. "Break time?"

She pops up from two aisles over, runes in her hands. Looks from him to me, and nods. They crowd over my desk for a whispered conference.

"They check the outgoing calls, Elle," Darwin says.

"Who does? What outgoing calls?"

"Like a twenty-seven minuter to someone in Georgia this morning?" Adele says.

"Ohmigod. They check those?"

"They check *everything.* It was a client?"

"Well, yeah. I mean—she called here, first."

"Shit, Elle," Darwin says. "That's grounds for termination."

"Don't be a worrywart," Adele tells him. "We caught it."

"What do you mean, caught it?" I ask. My phone rings, but we all ignore it.

"The comptroller thought it was my account," Adele says. "I told her it was a private call, and I thought it was yours, but I didn't know. Worst they'll do for a private call is subtract it from your paycheck. They won't fire you, like they will for poaching."

"Poaching? What the hell? Did I sneak into the king's forest and kill a fucking deer?"

"Don't tell us," Darwin says. "We're on your side. But management…it's policy to shitcan poachers."

"Policy," I hiss. "Policy is just another word for—"

Adele straightens as a man from another department walks past. "So that's how the crop circles work," she says loudly. "Is that your phone ringing?"

I pick up, and it's Nyla.

She says, "I'm thinking of going off the pill."

I take a deep breath, willing myself to be calm. Fired for poaching. I can't get fired. I need this job. I like this job. God bless Adele and Darwin.

"You're thinking of what?" I say.

"If I'm pregnant, he *has* to marry me."

"Nyla, did you make your list of careers? Your five careers?"

"I was going to, but this pill thing..."

"No excuses. We can't talk until you make your list. Call me after you've done it. I'll be here all day tomorrow."

"But—"

"And don't go off the pill. Think how you'd look in Roberto Cavalli with a bloated hippo body." I hang up.

Darwin and Adele stare at me. Adele's mouth is open wide enough for me to see her back teeth are capped.

"What?" I ask. "I won't call anyone again, I promise."

"You hung up on a client," Darwin says.

"Oh, that. It's part of my plan."

"You're not suppose to hang up on clients, Elle," Adele says.

"Well, I've been thinking. Just talking isn't enough. Talking gets you nowhere. Task Orientation, that's where it's at. Give them a list of tasks to perform, and when they're done they call in to report."

"Despite what you've heard," Darwin says, "talk isn't cheap. Not at four bucks a minute. Talk pays the bills, Elle."

I turn to Adele. "Are we in the bill-paying business, or the intuitive consulting business?"

"That's a good question." Adele straightens her rainbow-colored crocheted vest, and I avert my eyes in horror. "And the truth lies within. We are both a service industry, with, um—" She pretends she can hear her phone ringing, two aisles away, and holds a finger up like she'd rather talk to me, but has to answer the call. As if I don't recognize that ploy.

I don't care what they think. I know I'm right. I'll be the star of Psychic Connexion. They'll put a picture of me next to the front door. C. Burke will shower me with praise and bonuses.

And speaking of tasks and C. Burke...

Five minutes later. I am in the inner sanctum. C. Burke's office. I am aware that the ghost of Calamity Jane haunts me, so am incredibly careful. I close the door silently behind me. My stomach aches. I flip through his files.

* * *

Merrick's in the hall when I get home. Neil, the enraged teddy bear, is with him, wearing a tool belt and hammering at a doorway. Maya told me he's a carpenter, and does a lot of work for Monty. And is Merrick's best friend.

What is it with men and their best friends? Even the most normal guy in the world will have this utterly bizarre best friend. It doesn't matter that they're from different planets. They don't even notice. You see it all the time. A fairly regular guy whose best friend is a Wall Street sleazebag, or a partially homeless juggler, or a depressive night clerk, or something. It's plain weird.

Of course, Maya's best friend is me.

Anyway. Merrick sits on the stairs, a bottle of beer between his legs, wearing a green cotton button-down and jeans.

"I'll hide them behind the palms," Neil is saying. "You'll never know they're there."

"Never know what's where?" I ask.

"Beehives," Merrick says. "At my place."

"Here?"

"My other place."

"They're great for pollination," Neil says. "And all the honey you can eat."

"The hives are ugly, Neil. They'll ruin the view."

"I believe they're called apiaries," I say

Merrick ignores me. "And I'm allergic to bee stings."

"You are not," Neil says.

"Not usually. But if your bees are anything like you, they're killer bees."

"Africanized. Africanized bees. Not killer bees. That's a media creation—and not only is it incorrect, it's stupid. Think about it! African varieties interbreed with local varieties, right? Right?"

"Neil. We're not at Shika."

"Sorry." He takes a deep breath. "I'd like some variety in the honey is all. I put them at your place, I'll call it Honey from the Sea."

"You live at the beach?" I ask.

"You haven't shown her your house?" Neil says, oddly surprised.

"And if you really do have a house, why don't you live there?" I ask.

Merrick gives Neil a look. "It isn't finished. I told you I'm having problems."

Neil chuckles and starts hammering again.

"What's so funny?" I ask.

"Nothing," Merrick says. "Nothing's funny. How was your day? How's the consulting business?"

"Fine." It's like I've been taking lessons from that nurse at Planned Parenthood. Any shorter a *fine,* and I would've said nothing.

He gives me a once-over. I'm in jeans, an oatmeal sweater and flip-flops. I look chubbier in jeans than any other item of clothing. I'm becoming a real slob, working at Psychic Connexion.

"No dress code at the consulting thing, huh?"

He thinks I look fat. At least I have normal hair. "No."

Neil stops hammering. "What kind of consulting?"

"Eclectic," Merrick says. "Like you and carpentry. No job too large or small."

"Yeah?" Neil says. "What do you specialize in?"

"Is that my phone?" I say. "I think that's my phone."

I race upstairs. I think I hear one of them say *mmm-hmmm* at my huge ass. But it's an *mmm-hmmm* like you say to a chocolate milk shake, so it's all good.

chapter 30

"How about him, instead?" I let a black-and-white Australian shepherd mutt lick my fingers through the fence. I'm at the County Animal Shelter; a more permissive organization than the Humane Society, they don't have a perimeter-security policy. They do, however, insist upon matching you with an appropriate dog. The volunteer, a nice-looking woman in her early sixties, asks about my life and house, and directs me toward what she considers the best match. Sort of like a personal shopper. But I'm more interested in this shepherd than in her pick.

"Too much working dog in him," she says. "He needs someone who'll really spend the time—not just loving him, but working him."

Well, that makes sense. "This lab here, then. What's her name? Pixie! There's a sweetie…oooh, who's my sweetie?"

Pixie is a hyperactive ball of kinetic energy, ricocheting in her cage like a pinball.

"Not Pixie. I really think the first dog we saw would be—"

"How about this little guy?" I say, eyeing a cute tan and white dog. "He's darling!"

"He's a rat terrier." The way she says it clearly means *no.*

I sigh. "So it's the first one or nothing?"

"She's the staff's favorite. She's a doll." We make our way back to the first dog, who watches with sad brown eyes. "Look at that face," the volunteer says. "How can you not love that face?"

She's a purebred boxer. And if you ignore the three-inch string of drool escaping one of her jowls, she does have a dear black-masked face. The problem is her fur. She has none, from the back of her ears to the base of her tiny stub-tail. Her skin is black and scaly, and you can count her ribs at a distance of twenty feet. I can't decide if she looks more like a lizard or a rat—either way, she appears to be three days from being buried in the backyard. "Scab" is written at the top of her information card.

"You call her Scab?" I ask.

"When she came in, we picked a cup and a half of scabs off her. Frank started calling her Scab, and it stuck. You can name her anything you want, though." She smiles at me. "This little girl wants to go home with you. Should I start the paperwork?"

I'm sorry. I know I should say yes. I know that's the right thing to do. But adopting a depressed, hairless, scaly, drooling dog is not wise. Not for me. I'm surface-y, and this dog's surface is truly wretched. Plus, there are definitely plenty of boxer lovers who will adopt her.

"No," I say, and I swear the dog's eyes grow sadder. "No."

Back at home, I call Joshua. We should be able to talk about these things, right? Feeling like a bad person for rejecting a scaly dog, I mean. And about other things, too, like not wanting to steal papers from the office.

I get his machine. "Hi, Joshua! It's me. You're never in. Well, I was about to get those papers and stuff, but actually, when I think about it, I'm kind of uncomfortable taking them, actually. If you see what I mean. Anyway, I went to the pound again, but didn't adopt a dog yet. I thought maybe we could go together, and you could help me pick one. Umm…so give me a call? Love you."

He didn't call back that day. Or the next day. Or the day after that.

He is not going to call.

I attempt to drown my sorrows in work. Task-Oriented Reading has taken root, and is bearing fruit. Flowering, blossoming, flourishing, etc. Assorted one-time callers being converted to repeaters, bread-and-butter calls now result in more than watered-down New Ageism and sympathy.

The cards tell Ann from Sacramento to ask her shy, handsome co-worker out herself. She calls back in two days—he said no. He's got a girlfriend. But he also has a buddy….

The auric shift informs Steph from Dubuque to keep her knees together until Stage Four. She lasts until Stage Two. It's a start.

The numbers and the signs, the runes and crystals and the Gift—they have tasks for just about everyone: walk to work, buy yourself flowers, go to a movie alone, tell him how you feel, *don't* tell him how you feel, put aside fifty bucks a week, ask her which she prefers, stop calling a 900-line, there's a lovely dress in the Shapely Woman's department at Super 9 for only $49, wear the garter belt if it'll make him so happy, join a bird-watching club.

I lose some casual callers, but such is life. Can't please everyone all the time. I know, because I told Darlene from Baton Rouge that very thing.

When not on the phone, I spread the Task-Oriented

word among my co-workers. They look dazed, and try to avoid me. I don't care. This works. I write a pamphlet. Darwin starts calling me "comrade." I am having a fairly fantastic time. At work, at least.

The phone rings. A man's voice: "Elle… Can your psychic powers divine who this is?"

The voice is familiar. Not a repeat caller, though. Not Carlos, thank God. "Joshua? I'm so glad you called!"

"Joshua? No. It's Louis."

"Louis? How the hell did you get this number? If this is about your fucking stamp collection—"

"Merrick. It's Merrick."

"Oh. Merrick. Oh. Hi. What do you want? How did you get this number?"

"Maya gave it to me."

Must kill Maya.

"So are you going to give me a reading?" he asks.

"Sure. Let me lay out the cards." I flip through my magazine. "Hmmm…I see trouble. Trouble at home. It appears your apartment will be flooded when the person upstairs plugs her bathtub and leaves the water running all day."

"No—for real, Elle. Pretend I'm a regular client. What would you tell me?"

"First, I'd get your address for our free psychic newsletter."

"You know my address."

"Let me fill this out…" I'm done in a jiffy, because I'm good with forms. Don't know if I've mentioned it. "Done."

"Now what?"

"Whatever you want. You're the client."

"Well…shouldn't you tell me something about myself?"

"I can't," I say. "I know you. It only works with people I don't know."

He laughs. "You don't know me *that* well."

"Well, ask a question," I say. "We'll see what I can do."

"Okay. Will you have dinner with me this Friday?"

"Oh. Wow. You know, I'm actually kinda seeing someone." I am, too. Maybe Joshua's machine is broken. Or he's out of town on business—whatever that may be. Or cavorting with Jenna. No. No, he's *not* with Jenna.

"Seeing someone for real, or seeing someone like you're consulting?"

"I am consulting," I snap. "In fact, I've developed a whole new theory for the business. It's called Task-Oriented Readings." I tell him how it works. "The only problem is people are making fun of me for writing a manifesto."

"Like *Das Kapital.*" He laughs again. "Das Krystallball?"

I grunt at him. It annoys me, for some reason, that he's being charming.

"So what's my personal task?" he asks.

"I don't know," I grumble.

"I think it's to persuade Elle Medina to have dinner with me."

"I told you, I'm seeing someone." Why won't he believe me? Is it so hard to believe that I have a boyfriend? And I do. Have a boyfriend. He's just busy. "His name is Joshua. He lives in Montecito."

"You call him that? Joshua?"

"I know, I know. It's lame he doesn't go by Josh. But he's not gay. *That* I know for sure."

"I meant," he says a little stiffly, "do you call him Joshua, or by his last name?"

"Oh. Yes. Joshua."

"So how'd you meet?"

"At work," I say, all innocence.

"He's a phone psychic, too?"

"Not here. I met him at Super 9."

"He works at Super 9 and lives in Montecito?" There's a slight pause. "Elle, please tell me you're not dating the shoplifter who got you fired."

"Well, technically…yes. But he didn't actually shoplift—" I stop speaking because I don't want to interrupt Merrick's unattractive whoops of laughter. "I don't see what's so funny—"

"You…you're…"

"He's *gorgeous.* And he knows all about Prada." Sort of. "And he's a great cook, and he's spontaneous—"

"Spontaneous how?"

"Spontaneous like I never know when he'll call, or stop by or, er…"

"Yeah?"

"And we went to Citronelle for dinner, and neither of us had enough money, so we stiffed the bill and ran out! And he lives in this huge mansion, and we're thinking of, um, living in Montecito and…and we're going to Venice."

There's a long pause as I catch my breath.

"Uh-huh," he says.

"What?"

"I don't know, Elle. You—" He sounds tired and disappointed. "I never know what's the truth with you. Well, this has been enlightening. You do a great job. You really answered my question."

"Merrick…"

"I've gotta go," he says.

"Go where?"

He hangs up. My face hurts. I stare at the phone.

Five minutes later, it rings again.

"Psychic Connexion. This is Elle."

It's Nyla. Doing really well. "You were right about being a magazine editor," she says. "But you know what? Bookstore clerk sounds pretty good. I know they don't make any money, but I don't need money—not if we stay together. And we will, too, if I get out of the house and start doing something. And I like books—I mean, I spend almost as much time in Barnes and Noble—are you crying?"

"N-no."

"What's wrong, Elle?"

"Nothing. I just—I saw a sick dog at the pound, and I

have my period, and I...I'm sorry. I shouldn't be unloading on you."

"No, that's okay."

But it's not. She's paying, I'm the professional. I take a deep breath: "Just needed a little weep. Better now. Listen, Nyla, I have one last task for you. It's a biggie. Are you ready for it?"

I can hear the smile in her voice when she says: "I'm ready for anything."

"You have to stop calling."

"What?"

"It's expensive, and it's his money. And more important, you don't need me anymore. You can do it yourself. You can *only* do it yourself. We both know it. You're a...you're really great, Nyla. I like you a lot. If you lived here, I think we'd be friends. But you have to do the rest by yourself. Most of all, you have to know you *can* do it yourself. I believe in you. Your next task is this—believe in yourself."

I hang up, breathless and light-headed. I take my headset off for a brief break, and feel someone standing behind me. I swing in my chair, and a harried-looking guy in a mediocre suit is standing there.

"Elle," Darwin says from his desk. "This is Christopher Burke. Back from paternity leave."

"Christopher C. Burke," Burke says.

"Oh!" I pop out of my chair and offer my hand. "It's great to finally meet you."

"You hung up on a client."

Ouch. Well, nothing to do but explain: "It's all part of my plan. Task-Oriented Readings. Clients have to complete a task before calling back—I don't know if you've had a chance to read my pamphlet?"

He nods in understanding, and I thrill with possibility of my first convert to the cause. He smiles softly, and says: "You're fired."

★★★

Spend twenty minutes weeping in the Psychic Connexion parking lot, too upset to drive. This is far worse than being fired from Super 9 shoplifting patrol. I was good at this. I liked it.

Now I'm afraid to go home. How will I face Merrick? What will I tell Maya? And Sheila, and Monty, and Carlos and my mom…

What should I do? Where should I go?

Only one thing occurs to me: picking up the Dingle's dry cleaning. Am already humiliated and defeated, there's no reason not to complete my disgrace.

I drag my tear-stained face into the dry cleaner's. The pretty, forty-something Asian woman behind the counter wants $28.95.

"What?" I say. "That's a little high. The suit itself wasn't worth forty." I should've bought one of those home dry-cleaning kits. Could have saved twenty dollars—which, now that I'm unemployed again, I desperately need.

"The stain was cranberry," she says. "On seersucker. And look now—not a shadow."

She's right. The stain is absolutely gone.

"Twenty-eight ninety-five, then," I say, with an attempt at a smile.

"Tell your boyfriend, be more careful—it'll save a lot of money in the long run."

My boyfriend. I fork over the cash, and look away while she counts the change, afraid I'm going to start crying again. A framed article on the wall says *Local Dry Cleaner Awarded Environmental Award,* and the picture shows the woman holding a wedding dress while smiling into the camera. I may be unemployed and unwed, but at least I'm not killing the earth.

"Bag or no bag?" she asks.

"Is that how you got the environmental award?"

"Partly." She smiles.

"Then no bag, I guess."

I take the suit and am about to leave when she says, "Oh, wait. This was in the pocket." She hands me a matchbook, three lollipops and a bunch of receipts. The matchbook says Café Lustre, and features three topless girls in lurid poses. "Tell your boyfriend," the woman says, "he doesn't need that sort of place. He has a pretty girlfriend, and she picks up his dry cleaning, too." She pauses a moment, and I think she's going to ask if I cook and wear sexy underthings and give the Dingle time in his cave. "But the one in the middle?" She means the picture on the matchbox. "She's cute. Almost makes me want a lap-dance."

I look closer. The one in the middle is Jenna.

Saturday morning. Haven't left the apartment in two days. I wake to knocking at my door. Roll out of bed wearing the red Daryl K pants and white T-shirt I had on yesterday. Fell asleep watching Conan O'Brien interview supermodel Giselle Bundchen. She was complaining about how hard it is to be Giselle Bundchen. She must die.

I open the door, and it's Joshua. He looks extra Ga-Ga Gorgeous, there's a nimbus of heavenly light around him. Plus, he's bearing a bag of bagels and an egg-crate tray that holds two cups of coffee.

Love is rekindled in my heart. "Joshua!" I say. "I didn't expect—the place is a mess."

He's supposed to say that it doesn't matter. He says: "What happened to your hair?"

Aack! It's in braids. I look like Swamp Thing. I loosen the braids and twist my hair into a knot. "It's um…for conditioning. You brought me coffee!"

"And cinnamon raisin bagels."

Always wondered who ate raisin bagels. "My favorite."

"There's something I want from you," he says over his coffee cup. "I think we should go into business together."

Ga-Ga wants to go into business with me. We'll be *Time*'s

couple of the year, profiled in *Fortune.* Maybe I'll even get into the gossip section of *W! Elle Medina was seen at Oprah Winfrey's sprawling Montecito estate—*

"...and with your contacts," he's saying, "we'll be unstoppable. Remember Philip Michael Thomas?"

"Used to be on *Miami Vice* with Don Johnson?" I say absently, thinking that I most want to be seen attending gala fund-raisers.

"He got three million bucks in a settlement, for his phone psychic commercials. Big money. You have to trust me, love. DRM is the key."

"What?" Takes me a moment to remember DRM is the company that owns Psychic Connexion. "DRM?"

"It's totally understandable, being reluctant to lift this paperwork we need, Elle," he says. "But we have to be bold. We have to overcome all obstacles. Together, you and I, we can—"

"I got fired."

He flicks me an exasperated look. "This isn't about Super 9. It's about DRM. Focus, honey. The 900 number racket is open season. With your inside information, and my—"

"I mean, I got fired from Psychic Connexion."

"You *what?*"

I emit a nervous giggle. "It's sort of a funny story. I was working on my Task-Oriented Readings..."

"Your *what?*"

I tell him.

"Un-fucking-believable, Elle. Hanging up on paying customers?"

"It was all part of my plan," I say in a small voice. "I was helping a lot of people."

He stands and grabs the raisin bagels.

"Where are you going? Don't you want to have breakfast?"

"Not anymore," he says, and closes the door behind him.

"I hate raisin bagels!" I scream at him and throw my cup of coffee at the closed door. Which turns out to be a bad idea because it takes me half an hour to get the stain out of the carpet. And I could have really used the coffee.

chapter 31

Back to memorizing the Help Wanted section every day. Back to composing bright, hopeful, misleading cover letters. Back to calling Sheila at Superior. Today, she recommends I try another employment agency.

The phone rings. Stupidly hoping it is good news, I pick up.

"Eleanor Medina," he says.

"Hi, Carlos. You got my check?" I sent a hundred dollars, even though I promised four.

"Elle, I like you. But this is serious. This can screw your credit for a lifetime. No credit cards. No home loan. No car loans. No job that requires a credit check. This can—"

"I got fired again."

"—mess up your…again? What happened?"

I tell him.

There's a long pause. "Listen, Elle. I shouldn't tell you this.

But if *you* can get fired for trying to help people, so can I. There's only one thing for you to do. Declare bankruptcy."

"Bankruptcy?"

"Yeah. You're not gonna get out from under this. You need to start over. It's a bad option, but it's the best one you have." He tells me how it works. I won't have to repay anything, basically, and his company is out six thousand dollars or whatever.

"And what about IKEA? They lose fifteen hundred dollars, for trusting me with a card?"

"That's exactly what happens."

Oh, God. What kind of person am I? I tell Carlos I'll think about it, but as we hang up, I renew my determination to get a job, *today.*

I sneak downstairs to steal Merrick's newspaper for the classifieds. This is nothing new; I've been doing so every morning for a week, too depressed to leave the building. I'm sure he knows it's me pilfering his paper. I don't think I care…until I meet him in the hall.

"Hi," I say.

"Hello." He steps into his office and shuts the door.

Oh, *God.* It's the way he says it. Indifferent and uncaring. I get halfway upstairs, my cheeks burning with mortification and his paper crumpled in my hands, before the tears start. I fall into bed weeping.

I am a failure. As an employee, as a credit risk and as a person. All I want is to be a child again, and have someone tuck me in and kiss me on the forehead and tell me it's all okay. But it's not.

I stay in bed for two days, sick of myself. Sick of my life. Just sick. What can I do? I mean—what *can* I do?

Then this happens:

Hunger drives me to Super Ralph's. Where poverty leads me to inspect economy-size cans of kidney beans with great care.

Someone nudges my cart. I turn, ready to battle a pushy aisle-hog, and find Todd, manager at Nordstrom and high school date.

"Hey, Elle," he says. "How's it going? We never got a chance to catch up."

"Oh, no. I—I've been busy."

He looks at my cart: family-pack of recycled toilet paper; family-size frozen coconut cake; five-dollar bottle of Zinfandel; one banana; economy size Advil; backup auxiliary family-size frozen coconut cake; and, monster tub of chocolate ice cream, to go with coconut cakes.

"That's my favorite vintage," he says about the wine.

He's sort of cute. Employed, presentable and he's not Joshua or Merrick. I'm sort of demolished. Plus, I'm unemployable and a fucking mess and I hate myself.

"Cheap Zin goes great with coconut cake and self-pity," I say.

He humors me with a laugh, and says something bland. So I take him home and we have sex.

The good thing: we already fooled around ten years ago, so we're past some of the awkward stages. The bad thing: I no longer have the body of a seventeen-year-old, and I'm pretty sure he notices.

I wake the next morning disgusted. I don't especially *like* Todd. Hell, I don't even care enough to *dis*like him. All I want is for him to be gone. I jab him with my elbow to wake him.

He yelps like a little girl. "Eee! Oh—oh. I was having a nightmare."

Welcome to the club. "Rise and shine," I say, afraid he's going to start telling me his dreams. "You don't want to be late for work."

"What time is it? Oh, no." He scrambles out of bed and searches for his discarded clothes. One of his socks is draped over a half-eaten piece of coconut cake, which is a terrible waste of good comfort food. "I'll call you—maybe we can have dinner?"

"Sounds great," I lie. I'm sure he's a nice guy, probably. But...*yech.* A one-night stand? What am I doing?

His other sock is among my shoes. He gives my shoe collection a professional appraisal as he pulls the sock over his somewhat-unsightly foot. "Hey, where are the most expensive shoes in the world?"

"Huh?"

"The BCBGs. Three thousand dollars for a pair of shoes—I wish I could *sell* them for that much."

"What? Three thousand? What are you talking about?"

He looks briefly puzzled as he fastens his belt. "You know. The settlement."

"The what?"

"Three grand. For when the heel broke and you slipped in the store—that guy you hired to represent you was pretty convincing."

Three grand? Three fucking thousand dollars, and Joshua gave me $200, and I loved him for it?

"He's a smart guy," I say.

Fucking Joshua. I probably knew all along. He *did* pretend to shoplift Super 9, so he could sue. And he probably never paid Citronelle. Poor Meeshell Reesharrrd.

And now I'm the kind of woman who has one-night stands with high school boyfriends? No. So I abruptly escort Todd downstairs, the better to shove him out the doors and out of my life.

At the bottom of the stairs: Merrick. Dressed casual, expression cool. He looks good. And more than that, he looks like he knows what he's about. He looks like a man, not a grown-up boy. He looks like the man you wish were single, you wish were interested (and maybe you wish would dye his hair), but never is. I am abruptly aware that I've fucked up big-time.

"Morning," he says.

"Merrick," I say, my throat dry.

"You must be Joshua," he says to Todd. "I'm Lou—Merrick."

"Joshua?" Todd blinks. "No, I'm Todd."

"Right, Todd." Merrick nods politely, and I am going to be sick. "Sorry, I haven't had my coffee yet."

"I know the feeling," Todd says. "I can hardly walk without caffeine and I need to be on the ball. We're having the semi-annual shoe sale at Nordstrom's today. Good selection of men's—you ought to stop by."

He moves to kiss me, and I dodge.

"Have a nice sale," I say.

"Nordstrom?" Merrick says. "The shoe department?"

"Yeah," Todd says. "Nice meeting you." And he's out the door.

Merrick turns to me—the words *the shoe department* echoing in the air.

"We knew each other in high school," I say.

There's silence.

"We were in chemistry class together."

Another pause.

I can't stand it. I can't stand always being clumsy and wrong and stupid, always being the butt of every joke. My humiliation turns to something like rage. "Okay. Alright, *goddammit.* He's the one who caught me shoplifting. Except I wasn't. And Joshua ripped me off for like three thousand dollars, and all he wanted from me was help with some scam, okay? And I got fired again. From the only job I was ever any good at. From the only job I ever liked. From the only thing I, I… Okay? Are you happy now?"

"Elle, I don't—"

"No! Shut up, Merrick!" I run upstairs and slam my door. Then I pretend I don't hear when Merrick knocks. Which, you know, is a great way to show how grown-up and good-natured I am. Then I finish the second coconut cake.

So that happened.

And tell me, what can I do? What am I supposed to do?

I'm in a downward spiral, circling the drain. I can't get out of my own head, I can't think of anything beyond what an utterly unrelenting failure I am. I can't think of anything but the rejection and humiliation and mistakes and stupidity.

I hate myself. Even the one thing I was good at was fake. Being a phone psychic, without being psychic. Without a single fucking clue. Adele was right.

Well…but Adele thought I did good work. She said I was great with callers. And I *was.* People get so caught up in their own crisis they can't see that *anything* is better than nothing. That's what the tasks were all about. Break the cycle, get them moving. Get them doing something, anything, for themselves or someone else. Get them out of their own head and into—

I sit up.

I need a task. I know exactly what to do.

I speed to Goleta, frantic with anxiety. What if she's gone? Let her still be there, please God let her still be there. I need her. She needs me.

I screech to a halt in the parking lot and bound inside. Nobody behind the desk. I sprint to the kennels. Past cages of healthy, glossy, barking dogs. Past cute dogs and easy dogs and pedigreed dogs.

To her kennel. Scab. My Scab.

She's gone.

An eerie sort of calm descends. I was going to adopt her. I was going to love her and heal her, and put her needs above my own. I was going to stop looking for someone to rescue me, and rescue her, instead. But she is gone.

I walk, dazed, toward the car. And she is there. My hairless jowly lizard-rat dog, being walked—if you could call it that, the way she hobbles at the end of the leash—by a volunteer.

I kneel and open my arms, the volunteer drops the leash, and Scab staggers toward me like a toddler taking her first steps. I hug her gentle and close. She smells of illness. She is birdlike in her frailty. Her skin is warm and pebbled and she exudes a six-inch slug of ectoplasm from her jowl to my knee. I can't remember ever being so happy.

I croon to her. I tell her I don't care what she does or how she looks, I don't care if she ever grows fur, I don't care if she is ever healthy or happy or anything—she is mine and I am hers.

In the office, the volunteer who matched us tells me Scab needs to stay two more days, for another mange dip. There's only a fifty percent chance her fur will grow back. I tell the woman I want to take her home today, but she convinces me to wait. For the dog's health, she says. Plus, I can visit tomorrow. As I kiss her—the dog, not the woman—goodbye, a male volunteer asks, "Oh, you're adopting Scab?"

"No," I say. "I'm adopting Miu Miu."

Because she may look like Scab, she may look a mess and a failure and a pathetic huddled creature, but I know her for what she is: a gorgeous jewel of a thing.

When I pull into the parking lot at home, Neil is putting some sort of power tool into the back of his pickup truck.

"Hey, Neil," I say. "I just adopted a dog! She's a boxer. She's bald, though, with mange. Her name's Miu Miu."

"A pound dog. Way to go. You know what I can't stand?" he asks me.

"You mean besides politics, people, places, popcorn..."

He makes a face. "I can't stand people adopting foreign babies. What's up with that? Like it's fashionable to adopt a Chinese or Romanian baby—you can't adopt a local child? These people buy local produce, for fuck's sake, they can't *adopt* local? I mean, it's a *trend?* Adopting a kind of child, like it's a poodle. You have a Jack Russell? I have a Korean, and I'm considering getting a Czech or Albanian."

"Neil," I say. "I'm adopted. From Canada."

"Oh, shit. I'm sorry—I just start talking and—" he eyes me, then chuckles. "Oh, bullshit! From Canada." He gets in his pickup and slams the door. "I hate Canadians, too." He starts the engine. "Oh, there's some old woman looking for you. She's inside."

"What woman?" I ask the back of his truck as he pulls away.

So I creep to the front door and peer inside. Sure enough, there's an old woman in the foyer. Wearing a canary-yellow Chanel suit. I try to think how this can possibly be good news—like maybe a rich uncle I've never heard of died or something—but fail.

So I browse at Anthropologie and Borders, and come back in two hours, and she's gone. Ha.

The next morning, I sell every bit of designer clothing I own, except for two outfits. Possibly three. Or four, depending on what you mean by "outfit." But definitely almost everything.

I drag three suitcases to the consignment shop. I'm wearing jeans and a ratty Limited T-shirt. I'm sweaty and determined, and the beady-eyed woman behind the counter greets me with a smile, and tells me how well I look. She also gives me $2200. The clothes cost Louis almost ten times that, over about four years.

I loved those clothes, but it strikes me that that's an awful lot of money. And having parted with the outfits, I feel light. Light-headed, maybe...but unburdened, too. Those were clothes from a different life, and they were gorgeous; but they no longer fit.

I pack all my IKEA furniture in the original boxes. Except for the stained chair and the kitchen stuff and two accent pillows. I send it all back, with a note. I will pay for what I kept. I don't know when, but I will.

I buy a huge bag of dog food. Solid Gold, it's called. Holistic doggie health food. It has lamb and yucca and blueberries and comes in a shiny gold shrink-wrapped bag. I can get by on rice and beans; I have hair. But Miu Miu needs all the help I can give her.

I send Carlos four hundred dollars.

I go to Shika.

"Billy the," I greet Kid. "What's shaking?"

"Martini," he says, and he serves it to Mr. Goldman. He's sort of literal.

I slip onto the stool next to Mr. Goldman and Monty. "Lost my job again," I tell them. "Who's buying me an iced tea?"

"As a psychic person?" Mr. Goldman asks. "Maya told me you were talking on the phone, but I never really understood...."

I tell them the whole story, except for the bits about Joshua. I'm not sure if Mr. Goldman understands what the job was, but when I finish, he says, "You're a good girl, Elle. Helping those people."

"I don't know," I say. "I tried. Anyway—if either of you hears of a job, let me know. I don't care what it is. Anything. And Monty...this is for you." I slide him an envelope with next month's rent. So I have another month free and clear.

He slides it back. "I can't take this."

But I insist. It's not for him, not really. "Besides," I say. "Six hundred a month for that apartment? You can't even pretend the market value's less than eight hundred."

Monty and Mr. Goldman exchange a glance, and I get the impression they've been plotting behind my back. "Nine-fifty," Monty says, pocketing the envelope. "But who's counting?"

"Not me. I couldn't afford nine-fifty even when I was employed." I finish my iced tea and ask when Maya's coming in. She's not due for a couple hours, so I call her from home and tell her how much I love her. She asks if I'm drunk. Yeah, I say. On iced tea and freedom.

I have a month, with no expenses but food and gas. I have an empty apartment, an empty calendar, an empty social life and empty closets.

I check the classifieds in Merrick's newspaper, and dash off four letters. House cleaning, receptionist, retail clerk and even the home health aide job. If I have to stick a hose up someone's butt, for $6.50 an hour, I'll do it. Because it's not about me. It's about Miu. It's about paying debts—not just to the credit card companies, but to the people who believe in me: Maya, PB, Monty, Mr. Goldman, even Carlos. And I guess it *is* about me. I'm ready to believe again.

chapter 32

I spend the morning at the shelter, reassuring Miu that I'll be back tomorrow, and telling her about the apartment. It's Spartan, I tell her. Clean lines and surfaces. Uncluttered. A white linen chair for me, and a den in the corner for her, with a folded cashmere blanket and two throw pillows.

I tell her about her exciting new bowls and her exciting new food and my exciting new job prospects. She doesn't seem reassured. I kiss her goodbye on the forehead—one of the few patches with fur—and leave her in the capable hands of a vet who looks sixteen years old.

I (speedily) complete applications at Manpower and Kelly Temporary services. In "previous employment," Martha Washington has been joined by Spenser and Superior, which means I fill all three spaces. I'm absurdly pleased.

Back at home, I'm famished. Fortunately, about thirty pounds of rice is left in the sack. I slip into something more comfortable—a gray Georgetown sweatshirt and DKNY leggings—grab the measuring cup and go downstairs. I pop my trunk, unfold the edge of the rice sack and dig inside.

I am filling the cup to the three-quarters line when I hear footsteps. I don't bother turning. It can't be Neil. It can't be Monty. It can't be some anonymous person. It can't even be the old lady who's stalking me. It can only be Merrick.

He has his portfolio and car keys. "That bag of rice," he astutely observes, "is still in your trunk."

I hide my face behind my hair. I tried carrying the bag upstairs, but another rice eruption threatened. So I've been sneaking downstairs and carrying it up a cup at a time. It's a system. "It seemed like a good place to store it."

"I see." He beeps his car door open, and puts his portfolio on the passenger seat.

Goodbye, Merrick. Drive away. Goodbye. I liked you.

I stick my head in the trunk, eyes stinging, and nudge a few spilled grains into the measuring cup. I'll have to sort it before cooking, but can't afford to let it go to waste. I have a sense that I've let too many things go to waste already.

Merrick's car beeps again. I look, and he's standing beside me.

"Out of the way," he says. He grabs the bag of rice and heads for the house.

"What if I want it in the trunk?" I ask.

He stands at the top of the front steps. "Open the door."

I do, and silently follow him upstairs, where the door to my apartment is already wide open. He places the bag on the kitchen counter and looks around.

"I like what you've done with it," he says.

I can't tell if he's teasing. The place is empty, except for the chair and pillows, the three-wick candle and a few little accent pieces.

"I'm serious," he says. "I like it. It's clean. Brings out the lines."

"Spartan," I say, and risk a smile.

He grins back, and I'm more relieved than I should admit. He raises an eyebrow at Miu's corner, with the dog bowls and cashmere throw.

"For my new dog," I say. "She's a boxer. She comes home tomorrow."

"You actually found a purebred at the shelter?"

"Well…she's a mess. She has mange. She's bald and she's twenty pounds underweight. She's sick to death, but she has the sweetest little face, and she's… I'm going to—" I shrug, embarrassed. "I like her."

He squats at her doggie den, and lifts one of the bowls. It's covered in a sort of mosaic-design of stamps. "Pretty bowl," he says.

"I made it myself."

He looks closer. "Um…Elle? These look valuable."

"Don't tell me you're a stamp-collector. Please, please don't tell me."

"My nephew is. He badgers me for them, on birthdays. Where'd you get these?"

"Ex-fiancé. He collected."

"Ah." He nods.

I prepare myself to be scolded, but he says: "Looks good."

Should I blurt something? Should I tell him something? I think I should, but I'm afraid.

He puts the bowl down. "I was on the way to my house. You want to come?"

He's asking me to his house?

"If you have a minute, I mean," he says.

I glance around the empty room. "I'm kinda busy with things here."

He smiles. "I can see that."

"Wait five minutes?"

He nods and settles into my ink-stained chair. He looks good sitting there—plus he hides the spot.

I race to the bathroom thinking about Merrick's dream

home. The key to his inner life. I can't wait to see it. I put on mascara and lipstick, twist my hair into a knot, and change out of sweatshirt and leggings into a TSE sweater and Marc Jacobs denim mini. I emerge from the bathroom, flushed and excited.

We take his car. Riding with him again reminds me of driving home after our date. We take Cabrillo Boulevard along the ocean, up to the Mesa, down a side street, through a bland neighborhood, to the ocean. His house is a charming little gem, perched on the cliff over the beach.

"And you live in your office instead?" I say, as he parks in the drive.

"The office is finished."

I look more carefully. The house is a soft gray two-story, with lavender and Mexican sage planted around it. The roof is covered in whimsical shingles, which remind me of the Moody sisters, these architects who designed fairy-tale cottages in Santa Barbara in the fifties or sixties.

"What does that mean?" I ask. "Unfinished? Walls, a roof, windows...looks finished to me."

"You'll see."

"If it has no kitchen, that doesn't count," I tell him. "I saw three places for rent without kitchens, and nobody seemed to care."

"It has a kitchen." We walk up the stone entryway. A warm gust of wind swirls the scent of the ocean at us, overlaid with lavender and sage. I stop a moment, listening, and Merrick waits.

"I can hear the surf," I tell him. I love the sound of surf.

"I love that sound," he says, and leads me inside. "It's why I bought here, I can barely afford it."

Windows span the ocean side of the house, floor to ceiling. Cream walls, accented with dramatic but unaggressive modern-type paintings. Oil pastels, Merrick tells me, by a local artist. Warm terra-cotta tile floors in the kitchen and bathrooms, with a light beige carpet in the rest of the house.

An island in the kitchen, which opens into the living room. Open beams along the ceilings. Talk about clean lines—my mother would applaud the feng shui. The energy, the light and air, flows clean and sweet through the house. I can feel it on the back of my arms.

"You like it?" he asks, a little unsure. The first lack of confidence I've noticed in him. I find it endearing.

"You know I do. The outside reminds me of…do you know the Moody sisters?"

He smiles. "The perfect thing to say."

"But the inside—"

"I know. Everyone says I shouldn't have carpeted."

"Not as elegant as wood floors, but that's not what I was going to say. It's comfortable. Livable."

"That's what I thought. Carpet is more livable. With wood floors, you get dust stuck to your bare feet."

"I hate that," I say. "Plus, you can't roll around on wood like you can on carpet."

"Carpets are definitely better for rolling."

I'm sure I'm blushing. "I don't see how you can say it's not finished. Windows and doors. Two toilets. Running hot and cold."

"Let me show you." He leads me to the master bathroom. The clawfoot tub is roughly the size of my ex-trolley. The window extends below the lip of the tub, so you can soak up a bath and the view at the same time. The walls are sand. I suppose it would be wrong to ask him to leave me alone for an hour so I could have a bath. Or he could join me. That would work, too.

"See?" he says, pointing to a window frame with a combination of triumph and frustration. "There. The wrong color."

It's white. Exactly the same white as the other two window frames. "The other ones too?" I ask.

"No. Those are right."

I squint at the windows. "They're exactly the same."

He insists they're not, blathering on about color samples and paint mixing.

"Even if they *are* the slightest bit different," I say. "There's no way anyone could ever tell."

"I can tell," he says.

"That's it?" I ask, dumbfounded. "That's the reason you're not moving in?"

"No, there's more." He leads me to the kitchen. "Notice the knobs?"

They are unpolished nickel and beautiful. "Are they antiques?"

"Well, yeah. But don't you see it?"

"What, are they a millimeter crooked?"

"No, they got that right the third time. But look. They messed up the color gradation. This one, in the middle, is darker than these two. It should have gone at the end. Now they need to redo all the knobs, starting here."

Bubbles of delight rise within me. The ocean, the house, his company: I laugh. "Merrick, you're *neurotic!*" I say it like it's the most wonderful thing, and maybe it is.

"You think so?"

"You are obsessive-compulsive, with borderline ridiculous disorder." I open a set of French doors and step onto the patio. It's Jerusalem stone, surrounded by palms. An oasis, overlooking the ocean. "In fact, it's a miracle you can live here at all. I think the waves break in an irregular pattern."

He stands beside me and we watch the waves. He seems satisfied with himself. I can't tell why. Because he showed me how anal he is? Because he discovered that I don't share his obsession? Did I just pass a test, or fail one?

But I don't think he's the sort for pop quizzes. More the sort to try to send a message. I give him a sidelong glance, and he's looking at me. I know there's some perfect thing to say, to figure him out and send a message of my own, but instead I point to three white wooden boxes perched on the cliffside. "What are those?"

"Bees."

"Neil got his honey from the sea, huh?"

"Temporarily."

"You know you're never gonna get rid of them now."

"Yeah. I won an argument with Neil exactly once, and that's because he passed out."

"Did he build the house for you?"

"Most of it."

I give him a thoughtful expression. "Ah, now I get it. Things are all starting to make sense—now that I've seen your house, I mean."

He gives me the gray eyes. They match the color of the ocean in the sunlight. "I'm afraid to ask."

"Neil's argument group," I say.

"You mean discussion group."

"Right. Anyway, he started the argument—"

"Discussion—"

"—group because of inner rage, right?"

"Well, that and his wife," he says.

"Now I know where his rage comes from." I smile. "Clients like you."

"Sure," he laughs. "*I'm* infuriating."

Is he saying I'm the infuriating one? Probably. But it doesn't matter. We stand, in a comfortable silence, watching the surfers and dog walkers on the beach. That will soon be me and Miu. The thought makes me happy.

"I heard how you got fired," he says. "Monty told me."

Monty told him? Is nothing sacred in that bar?

"I wanted to say, that was really decent of you. You should be proud."

"For getting fired?" I ask.

He doesn't answer, but I know what he means.

"Thanks," I say.

"And now you can get a real job." He must see something in my face, because he immediately says: "I mean, instead of a *surreal* job, like that one."

"Easy for you to say. You're good at everything. Look at this house, your career. Meetings in New York." I pick at the pins holding my hair back, and stare out to sea. "I suck at everything. Real employers don't want to hire me."

"Well, if you could do anything, what would you do?"

I'm surprised to hear the same question I asked Nyla. It sounded good when I said it, but now it's clearly crap. "I don't know. I was really good at the psychic thing."

"Elle." He says it like he's been taking lessons from Maya.

"No, seriously. I was good at it. Maya says I should go to school to be a therapist. But I don't want to deal with real problems. I want the silly stuff, you know—the little, girl-friendy things they need another perspective on. Things they're too embarrassed to tell their therapist, because they think they're supposed to be doing serious Freudian work. I'm good at that stuff."

"You're good at a lot of stuff."

I snort. "Sure. My fiancé married another woman. I'm six thousand dollars in debt and have no income or prospects. I've been fired from two jobs in three months. I—"

"Your fiancé did what?"

"You didn't hear about that?" I look at him. "I thought everyone told you everything about me."

He shakes his head. "He married another woman?"

"After six years," I say, bitterly, and it all comes tumbling out: "Six years, and we're planning the wedding, and he leaves town for a business trip, and in like a week comes back married to another woman. And so I…I mean, how ready was he to get married? Totally ready. And we'd been together six years. But one short trip to Iowa—*Iowa!*—and he finds someone he loves more than me. And all I know are people from his firm, and my parents are no help, and it's like I don't have anyone, except Maya, so I come back here, and I can't find a job or a place to live or…or…" I suddenly want to be naked in front of Merrick. I want him to see who I am, who I really am. I want to strip away all the crap and bullshit, and just tell him.

So I do. At length.

I start crying halfway through, but keep talking. He keeps listening. I finally end with a sobbing: "…I suck. I just suck. I fail at everything, and every time I think it's gonna work out, it falls apart."

I cry into his shoulder. The sun sets. Pelicans skim the waves. The scent of seaweed hangs in the salt air.

My tears dry and I pull away from him, embarrassed.

He takes my hand and squeezes. "He didn't even know, did he?"

I look at him, confused.

"You leave D.C., you come here and live in a trailer—"

"Trolley," I sniffle, but he doesn't hear.

"—because that's all you can afford, and you try the investigation thing, and that doesn't work, and you try the psychic thing, and that *does,* except you're not going to screw people for money, so they fire you. You think you're some kind of pathetic loser, but you get knocked down hard by your fiancé, and you stand up tall. You get knocked by the psychic place, by the lawsuit and the landlords, and the credit cards and whatever, and you're a fucking Weeble—you wobble, but you keep getting up and up." He takes my face in his hands. "You should be proud, Elle. It doesn't matter, what you've failed at. That's just stuff that happened. What matters is *you*—and *you* are something to be proud of."

Silence descends. The world consists of him and me—the world is empty and full, overfull, and I feel everything all at once, and I'm not sure if I remember how to breathe. Well. Apparently I'm in love. And I think: how long has *this* been going on?

"Merrick," I say. "I think I'm falling in love with you."

The words emerge like the tide, soft and relentless. I hear them as if they were spoken by someone else, and I don't even regret that I said them.

"Louis, honey?" A woman's voice from inside the house.

"Are you here?" She steps onto the deck; petite, neat, contained and pretty. Everything I'm not. And suddenly it's true: I *have* forgotten how to breathe. I am suffocating. This cannot be happening. There must be some explanation.

"Your sister?" I choke.

"No, she's my—"

"Girl Friday," the woman says, and puts a possessive hand on Merrick's arm.

"Elle," Merrick says carefully. "This is Betsy."

chapter 33

I lock my apartment door behind me and stumble for the phone. Must call Maya. Must call Dr. Kevorkian. Must call *someone.*

I pick up the phone, and a male voice says: "Yo."

"What? Hello? I didn't hear the phone ring. Hello?"

"It rang," the voice says, "Bitch."

Dingle. Not the someone I had in mind.

"Now I know where you live," he says. "I want my suit, bitch. Now."

"You really gotta work on that *bitch* thing, Dingle. How about you say asshole, instead. As in *you're an asshole.*" I hang up.

I don't feel any better. I call Maya. She's not home. I call Rusty's and order an extra-large pineapple-and-garlic pizza. I eat every piece but one, and continue to not feel better. I spend the rest of the night obsessively conditioning my hair, cleaning my apartment, and trying to forget what happened after Merrick said *Elle, this is Betsy.*

The next morning, I wake partially renewed. Screw Merrick and Betsy and Oprah and everyone. Today, I get Miu Miu.

I check the parking lot from the kitchen window. Merrick's car is gone. I grab the last slice of pizza and go.

Twenty minutes later, I'm filling out paperwork in the shelter office. The nice volunteer brings Miu on the leash. When Miu sees me, she hunches her left shoulder and swipes the air with her right paw.

"Ohmigod!" I say. "Did you *see* that? She made a punch at me! Who's my girl? Who's my Miu Miu?" I look at the volunteer. "Did you see that?"

She nods. "Boxers do that, when they're excited and want to play. It's why they're called boxers. But I've never seen Sca—Miu Miu do it before. She likes you."

Boxers do that? They box? I had no idea. It is *so* neat. And of course she likes me. I love her. She has to at least *like* me. I hug her and she looks into my eyes with her big, brown, pathetic, needy eyes, and…

I panic. I mean, what am I doing? She needs serious help. She needs a real person, a responsible person. Not *me.* Is it fair to her? I didn't even know boxers boxed. What if I can't take care of her right? What if she's unhappy with me? What if she gets sicker? What if she dies?

Miu leans against me, in what is an obvious plea for support. I can feel her ribs. Her skin is warm leather. A globule of drool bobs below one of her jowls.

"She'll be doing doughnuts in no time," the volunteer says.

"Doughnuts? Is that a drool thing?" I ask. "Or a poop thing?"

She laughs. "When she greets you, she'll probably curve into a circle, like a doughnut. Or a kidney bean, some people call it the kidney bean. Boxers do that, too—just so you know."

She's a hairless boxing kidney bean. She's pathetic and overwhelming and hopeless. And once I sign my name and pay the fees, she's mine forever. God. This is scary. My face freezes in a petrified smile. It's so permanent. And I don't know if I can do it. Nurse her and love her and everything, forever. I mean, it's marriage. It's marriage to a bizarre and demanding freak.

"Now you know how Louis felt," the volunteer says.

"What?"

"Her coat," the volunteer says. "It'll grow back in no time."

Oh.

I sign my name. This hopeless and overwhelming dog is now mine.

She likes pineapple-and-garlic pizza. She likes to stick her snout out the window. I glance in the side-view mirror, and she looks like a regular dog, because all that's visible is head. And one flapping jowl. I speed up, and the jowl gets stuck in the "up" position. It's bright pink inside. She doesn't seem to care it's stuck, but I slow down anyway.

We go to the Wilcox Property for a walk. Well, technically, it's the Douglas Family Preserve now, because Michael Douglas donated a lot of money, but it was the Wilcox while I was growing up, so that's what Miu and I call it. I park on the street, refusing to acknowledge how close I am to Merrick's neurotically obsessive-compulsive house, and tie Miu's horse-blanket-type cape around her. Well, she has no fur. She needs *something.* I tell her she's the hardest-working dog in show business as I fiddle with the cape. She drools.

We slowly creep along the trail, sniffing gopher holes and admiring the view of the ocean from the cliffs. Halfway around, a swarm of small yappie dogs encircles us and Miu stands with a sort of noble patience, allowing herself to be sniffed. The yappie dogs' owner tell me what a cute sweater she's wearing. I don't want people thinking I'm the sort who puts sweaters on dogs for no reason, so I pull it back to reveal her scaly pebbled skin. The woman recoils in horror, and I'm satisfied.

We're almost back to the car when a big male rottweiler bounds over. Miu sits. No aggression. No fighting. No hard-to-get. No growling. But no sniffing allowed. I like this dog.

Four days later, Miu and I pick up a sandwich at Tuttis in Montecito and have lunch at Butterfly Beach. Miu sleeps during the car ride home, then hobbles fairly spryly upstairs. She heads straight for her doggie den and settles onto her cashmere.

I curl up in the sitting nook and watch her as she sleeps. It's scary, being responsible for two when I've totally failed to be responsible for one. But I can do this. It's like I told people who called when I was a psychic: Do it, then think about it, not the other way around. So I completed my first task. Now I've got to think about it.

I do my finances. My costs are $600/month for rent. $100 for utilities. $100 for food and gas. Maybe $250. Well, call it $450, including car insurance and magazines and random costs like $20 for a cab ride home from the Mesa. $350 to Carlos and creditors. That's fifteen hundred dollars a month.

I write $1500 in my notebook, and circle it twice. Miu Miu stands and leans against me and presses her dry nose against the circles.

"No problem," I tell her. "Plus fifty bucks a month for you—but that evens out because I don't have to join a gym for exercise." Because between walking her and cleaning her ectoplasmic drool from the walls, I'm working both my lower and upper body. Oh, and I love her. She's depressed and needy and pathetic, and pees on the floor every time I come home. And I dote on her. Who'd have guessed?

"But that," I explain, "is before tax. We need $1500 after tax. So say…$2000 a month? Does that sound fair? They can't take more than five hundred bucks from a single poor woman with one dependent, can they? So that's $500 a week..." I do the math. "Twelve dollars an hour."

Oh, God. I can't make twelve dollars an hour. I was making ten at Psychic Connexion, and that was stretching it. I'm going to have to get two jobs, and I can't even get one. I lay on my back and stare at the ceiling. I don't know what to do. Miu stands over me, the bottom of her chest three inches from my nose. Her skin is gross. I rub it.

Earning twelve dollars an hour for eight hours a day for five days a week is the minimum necessary to put dog food on the table. Maybe I can work weekends. Seven days a week. I can do this, because I have to.

So I throw on my best leftover clothes and tell Miu I'll be back in an hour. There are a dozen stores in Santa Barbara I love. I'll hit each one, and ask for a job. Start with Honeysuckle, the little garden shop. Then I'll start again, with restaurants. Always wanted to be a waitress.

I do a Merrick-check as I head downstairs. I know he's gone, because his car's not here, but I peek outside from habit, and my stalker is standing on the steps. Wearing what has to be a mink coat—a sort of old-fashioned brown chubbie. It's sixty-eight degrees out, and she wearing a chubbie? Up close, I see her hair is the unlikely shade of cherry cola, teased beyond endurance, and her fuchsia lipstick bleeds into the lines around her lips.

I try to slink back inside, but she spots me.

"Elle? Elle Medina?"

I want to say, *who's asking?* I say: "Yes, I'm Elle."

"Oh, thank goodness! I'm Valentine. I called you at the Psychic Network?"

Oh, no. *Very* bad. This is the Montecito woman with the broken dog—and I recommended doggie acupuncture. Probably the dog died, and she's suing me. "Valentine—of course I remember. What a lovely coat!"

"This old thing? A present from my second husband.

After he died, I mean—he was too cheap while alive to buy me more than a new apron every anniversary."

I laugh, mostly to cover my discomfort. "Well, you must have quite a collection of aprons."

"Not at all. We were only married sixteen months."

"Oh. Yes. I see. Well…this is a surprise. Um, how did you find me?"

"I called to speak with you, and they told me you were *fired!* Well, I gave the woman a talking-to. *Fired,* I said. How could you fire the best psychic you've ever had? And the woman—Adelaide?—she agreed, and gave me your address."

"Ah." Not a lawsuit, then. "Well, here I am."

"I am so *very* glad I found you. You saved Rowdy's life. He lives for romping, you know. Without use of his legs…*quelle rapprochement!* That means, 'what good is life?' Two visits to the acupuncturist, and he is quite almost back to his old self. I so deeply appreciate it. I wanted to thank you in person."

"Thank *you,*" I say. "I'm glad to hear Rowdy is feeling, um, rowdier."

We stand silently for a moment.

"Anyway," I gesture toward the front door. "I've gotta—you know."

"Oh, you can't! Not yet. I need a reading. I'm desperate."

A *reading?* It's one thing pretending to be psychic on the phone, under the aegis of an organization which encourages that sort of playacting. But face-to-face? Out of the question. "Well, you see, Valentine. The trouble is that I'm not really a, I mean…of course with Rowdy I did get something of an intuitive, uh, message, but in fact I'm not—"

"I'll pay, of course. One hundred an hour. Does that sound fair?"

—*psychic.* Dollar signs explode before my eyes and keep me from saying the word aloud. I hear Carlos whispering into my ear with his Latino accent: *Take the money, Elle. Take it and run.*

I'm a fraud. What will I say to her—for an hour? What if it's all wrong and she sues me? What if *60 Minutes* does a feature on psychic scams, and features me? What if...what if I'm forced to move to Sedona and live with my mother because I can't afford rent? What if I can't take care of Miu Miu because I don't have any money?

I smile. "One hundred is fine. Why don't you come upstairs?"

Into my parlor.

chapter 34

A hundred dollars. *Cash.* For telling Valentine what she should wear to the Art Museum Gala Ball: "I'm seeing a long, flowing dress of white silk."

"I don't own a white silk dress."

"Yes, I know. You're going to buy one for the ball."

"Oh, of course," she smiles. "Why didn't I think of that?"

"Not all of us have the Gift." I don't know where to look. In her eyes? Out the window? Really I'm just imagining what she'd look good in, but it's hard not to be too obvious that I'm only doing her colors. This is why crystal balls must be so helpful.

She was impressed with my apartment. "So clean," she said.

"Good Feng Shui. It helps me concentrate during readings. I find that clutter and distraction leads to—"

"Oh, my goodness! Is that a *dog?*"

Then we had fifteen minutes of dog stories. She recommended her veterinary acupuncturist, then looked abashed and said, "But of course you already know that."

So I was twenty-five bucks ahead of the game before we even started the reading. I think I should charge for an hour, no matter what we talk about. It's like a lawyer. Besides, I could be reading her aura or something the whole time, couldn't I?

We discuss possible designers for the dress, then she wants to know if Mr. Tupner will ask her to dance.

"Hmm. I definitely see you dancing together..."

She brightens.

"...but the decision is yours. He's worrying that you're not going to ask him to dance."

"He *is* shy," she admits.

I close my eyes—much better. "Well, dancing is quite likely—a waltz?" I open my eyes and pierce her with a serious gaze. "But Valentine, it's up to you. You must ask him to dance."

"Oh, I couldn't do that," she titters.

"You *can,* Valentine. You *do.* I've seen it."

"Well, I suppose...you've seen it?"

I offer a silent prayer to the saint of fake psychics that Mr. Tupner not be in a wheelchair, married or utterly boorish, and nod. "I see you, Valentine, asking a handsome man for a dance, and I see him accepting—and I see your smile."

She smiles wistfully, and looks almost girlish. "Why not? If it doesn't hurt, and it makes us happy?"

Moments later, I smile too, putting her cash in my wallet. "I couldn't have said it better myself."

Miu Miu's not officially allowed inside Shika, so I sit at the end of the bar, with her around back. Before settling onto her blanket, an old beach towel of Maya's, she shakes thoroughly—and is so well-behaved that she doesn't even spray gobs of spittle in every direction. The front of her body finishes shaking about three seconds before the back, so her bony hairless butt shakes alone for a moment, sufficiently energetically that it almost knocks her spindly back legs from under her.

I call Maya and Monty's attention to this cute attribute of boxer engineering, but they ignore me.

"Lizard," Maya says. "Though it does look like ostrich skin."

"Rat. Looks more mammal than reptile," Monty says.

"As long as her landlord doesn't find out she's a closet herpetologist," Maya says.

Monty looks confused. "What does that have to do with anything?"

"Because the dog has scales, Monty."

"So that means Elle is a man-woman?"

They become increasingly baffled until I step in: "That's a hermaphrodite, Monty. A herpetologist is someone who studies snakes. And she does *not* look like a snake." I call to her, in a singsong voice: "Miu-Miu. Miu."

She looks up, her wrinkled brow quizzical, her eyes alert, and her string of drool bobbing. "See?" I say triumphantly.

"You're right," Maya says, cocking her head. "She looks like Winston Churchill."

"Put that in your cigar and smoke it," Monty says, before excusing himself for a meeting of some sort.

When he's gone I say: "You know my *Charlie's Angels* fantasy?"

"Not entirely." She fills a bowl with water and puts it in front of Miu.

"Well, I'm thinking Monty can be Boz."

I want to have a heart-to-heart type girly chat with Maya, but I'm afraid to tell her what happened with Merrick. "So one of my clients from Psychic Connexion tracked me down."

"Oh, *no,*" Maya says. "Another lawsuit?"

"It was only small claims. And I won."

"So another small claims suit?" She giggles. "I just realized that you were involved in a suit suit."

"Very funny. Anyway, I just earned a hundred bucks. Cash." I show her the money. "For fifty minutes of my time. I'm getting paid a hundred bucks an hour, and it's not even a whole hour!"

"For what?" Maya asks, her voice nervous.

"To be a psychic. Face-to-face. In living color. She tracked me down for a reading."

She looks me straight in the eyes, attempts solemnity and bubbles over with laughter. "A reading?"

"It's not funny! I'm good at it."

"B-being a psychic!"

"Not really a *psychic.* An intuitive counselor. That way people won't ask about palms and horoscopes and stuff."

"With a shawl and a crystal ball..." She finds this far funnier than it is.

"A pashmina," I say, and don't tell her I'm actually considering the crystal ball.

When she settles down, she says, "Oh, Elle. Thank you. I needed that."

"I live to be the subject of your scornful amusement," I say.

"I didn't mean it," she says. "Well, only a little. It's just that I've been kinda depressed."

I make sympathetic noises as she comes around the bar and sits next to me. I feel bad. When I have a crisis, I immediately turn to her, but when she has hers, I'm off in my own world.

"It's not the miscarriage, really," she continues. "But it got me thinking. I want to take a break from the bar. Figure out what I'm doing with myself. But we can't afford someone full-time, and my dad isn't feeling well—I'm worried about his health. And I don't know, do I want to be bartending the rest of my life?"

I am about to offer her some pearl of wisdom, when I

think it might be best to keep my mouth shut. Every now and then, when I worked at Psychic Connection, I'd get a caller who just wanted to talk. Just wanted me to listen. I have a feeling that's what Maya wants, so I shut up and wait.

She talks. For half an hour, about Brad and her father, about the bar and going back to school. About her mother, and falling into a rut—even if it was a rut she was pretty happy with. I continue to keep my mouth shut, until she finishes. She wipes her eyes and says, "You know, maybe you're right. You're not so bad at this. Now if only you could read my palm."

I take her hand and squeeze it, and smile at her; she has to know that whatever she does and whatever she wants, I'm there for her. "That'll be a hundred dollars," I say.

She swats me, then asks about my client, the one who tracked me down.

"I saved her dog's life," I say. "With long-distance veterinary acupuncture." I tell her about Valentine and Rowdy.

"So now you're taking money from old ladies?"

"She can afford it," I say. "Montecito money. Anyway, I told her to tell her friends. It's gonna be like that old Fabergé commercial. She'll tell two friends, and they'll tell two friends, and so on, and so on." I try to make my voice sound stereophonic at the *so on* part.

"I loved that shampoo," Maya says, nostalgically.

"Do they still make it?"

She shakes her head. "Wouldn't be the same, anyway. But aren't you worried it's illegal? Like practicing therapy without a license?"

I give her an incredulous look. "You're telling me that? A *bartender?*"

She grins. "Good point."

"And I have a hot-sheet of crisis lines, just in case." But I don't want to talk about this, because I'm afraid Maya will convince me not to daydream about it. And it's all I have, in terms of employment possibilities: a daydream about Valentine in a shampoo commercial. So, I say: "I went to Merrick's house."

Ten minutes later, Maya is staring at me in disbelief. "She called him *honey?*" she asks in stunned horror.

I nod. "And I ask if she's his sister. Grasping at straws. She says she's his girl Friday and slithers up against him, and I flip."

"You flip? Like a…an Elle Medina special?"

"The special-est. A shrieking fishwife, hair-pulling hysteric, eye-gouging special."

"Eye-gouging? You didn't—"

"No-no. No ambulance was called. Strictly verbal abuse, until Merrick made it clear that she was his new assistant, they were not sleeping together and he was not, in fact, a scumbag bigamist Chernobyl-headed fucktoad."

She looks at me with something approaching awe. "You called him that?"

"And worse."

"And…and, what did you say after?"

"After it became clear *I* was the fucktoad? What could I do? I fled. Raced up the street to 7-Eleven and called a cab."

She considers. "Wow. Classy."

"With a capital *K*."

So, Miu Miu and I were talking, and it's not like I'm stupid. I can see now that maybe I had too much invested in Louis and expected him to rescue me from my life. I wanted my parents to rescue me, my job to rescue me, my fantasies about Joshua and *L* and everything to rescue me.

I've got no money and no skills and no magic wand. The phone has not rung with referrals from Valentine. I suspect that if she told two friends, who told two friends…that someone along the line was not wearing her hearing aid. My run as a $100/hour psychic included precisely one client.

Manpower had a one-day job for me, answering phones

for a real-estate broker. I answered the phones. Then I went home, $52 richer after taxes. Coincidentally enough, I calculated that I need $52 after taxes, seven days a week, to support my little family. Manpower had no more work.

I get a call from one of my applications. It looks like I have a fifty-percent chance of being hired to deliver newspapers. It's early, *early* morning, but that means I can work afternoons, too. And I do own a car, might as well exploit what resources I have.

I finally crush my fantasy about IKEA; the one where a gorgeous Swede, possibly Sven Ikea himself, knocks on my door with a large check. They were so impressed with my honesty they think I deserve a reward.

So yes, I'm still falling apart. But no, nobody is going to rescue me. Nobody can. All they can do is postpone the inevitable. And even if they postpone it six years—I'm still me. This rescue, I have to pull off myself.

Miu Miu thinks I've taken the first steps. With Carlos and IKEA and with her. She thinks I ought to stop avoiding all the unpleasant realities. She thinks I ought to come clean.

About Merrick, for example. Am I falling in love with him? Have I fallen in love? Well, maybe. Maybe I have. And do I *still* want him to rescue me? Sure I do. But I know that's not how it works. So maybe I'll knock on his door. Maybe I'll apologize and—if he doesn't laugh me out of his office, if he doesn't tell me I was right about being a pathetic loser—maybe we'll talk. But I know he can't rescue me. Not really. Nobody can, except me.

I ask for only one thing: When I knock on his door, please God, do not have cool, collected, itsy-bitsy Betsy answer.

I knock on his door.

"Oh, hi," Betsy says. "Elle. Are you…okay?"

I attempt not to die. "I'm fine, thanks. Is Merrick in?"

"Louis? Yes, but Neil's picking him up in a few… Well,

let me get him." She retrieves Merrick from his den and discreetly disappears, and Merrick and I are left alone staring at each other. Eventually, I figure I have to say something.

"I—I wanted to apologize. For…the condoms and the doggie bags and your *newspapers* and…everything. I'm sorry. And I wanted to thank you. And…and…"

He inspects me steadily. His eyes crinkle, but his eyebrows don't move either direction. His hair catches the light, and glows a hideous orange.

"…and I haven't been myself, much—I mean, maybe I have, but I'm just getting to know me, really, and—" shut up, Elle "—that sounds stupid, I know. I mean, this whole thing—" I gesture, indicating my entire life "—has been new to me, and I'm still figuring it out. And you've been good to me, for no good reason, and I wanted to thank you and…I mean…"

He runs a hand through his hair and I see it: *his roots aren't red.* Oh, my God. His roots are definitely brown.

"I mean, I wanted to say, to say…your roots are not red." I freeze in a stunned silence at the fact that I've said this aloud.

"Forget my roots." His lips quirk. "I want to hear more about my newspapers."

He doesn't hate me. Must not weep in relief. Instead, must focus inappropriately on his hair: "Your roots are brown! Is this…vanity? But red, to cover the gray?"

"I am not going gray, Elle."

"Of course you aren't." I nod solemnly. "But still…you dye your hair. You *dye* your *hair.*" I sound like him, talking about a *lawsuit.*

"It's not like that," he says. "I didn't do it because I wanted to."

"Oh, no. I've heard about that. Mysterious abductions, people forced to dye their hair. The only thing they remember is the smell of Clairol number thirty-six."

He laughs, and my heart expands.

"It was for my niece," he says. "She's in beauty school here. She had a test and the girl whose hair she was supposed to dye backed out. She called me at the last minute, frantic for a replacement—and so I went."

I shake my head. "If you expect me to believe that—"

"I swear to you…"

I look at him in wonder.

"You don't believe me."

But I do believe him. And I think it is the sweetest, most selfless act I've heard, well, ever. Yet I'm too giddy to let it go. "How old is this alleged niece? You're not old enough to have a niece in beauty school."

"My sister's twelve years older. My niece just turned eighteen. I wanted her to go to college, but she chose cosmetology school."

It only made the whole story dearer—that he disapproved of her choice, but supported her anyway.

"It's *true!*" he says.

"Of course it is. I believe you. I couldn't…I couldn't not believe you. You're so utterly…*right.*" The words come out the wrong direction, and stick in the air. They hang between us, heavy with meaning.

"You're right," he says. "I am right. And you're right. And—"

—and I kiss him.

Nine hours later—after romantic walks on the beach, making passionate love under the stars, sipping lemonade on the front porch loveseat and exchanging heartfelt vows—the front door opens.

"Santa Barbara Municipal Airport," Neil says scornfully. "You pull into the parking lot, they charge you three bucks. Even if you're only gonna be there—" He looks between me and Merrick. "What are you two doing? Charades? I hate charades."

Merrick kisses me.

"Oh," Neil says.

"I'm going to New York, Elle. For five days," Merrick pulls away. He's gorgeous. "Promise you won't do anything…*anything*…while I'm gone?"

"I promise."

The only *anything* which even tempts me is the job delivering newspapers. I tell them I'll take it. Because though I've been sick with elation and dread about Merrick's impending return from New York, I will not allow myself, even in my most fantastic fantasies, to consider that he'll rescue me.

As I tell Maya during a love-maddened midnight phone call: "I don't want to fuck this up over that kind of ancient baggage."

"No?" she says. She can't really emote, because she's at work and—for once—has customers. So I pour out my heart, and she replies telegraphically.

"No. If I fuck *this* up, I'm gonna do it with brand-spanking-new baggage!"

"Louis Vuitton?"

"Kate Spade. No—I'm just not going to fuck this up. Because I'm going to be me from the inside out, I'm going to—"

"Please." Heavy on the scorn.

"I know it's stupid, but it's true. I'm going to make it happen for me, and until I do, he's going to have to take a back seat. He'll understand. Oh, God, what if he doesn't understand? What if he meets some woman in New York and *marries* her?"

"Elle."

"Don't *Elle* me! It could happen. Nobody knows that better than I do. But if this isn't about being rescued, if he actually *can't* rescue me, where's the line? I mean—do I not take anything from him? Dinner and stuff is okay, right? But I don't *expect* anything from him, maybe that's it. I make my own life work, and where we overlap, we overlap, but I don't leech onto his life and—"

"Kid," she says.

"Kids? Jesus, Maya. We've hardly even kissed. All he said was I shouldn't do anything until he gets back. He probably meant I shouldn't flood his apartment from my bathtub. Oh, God. What if that *is* what he meant?"

"Was talking to Kid. Billy the."

"Oh." And so on. *Ad nauseum*—but it was Maya's *nauseum,* and my delight. He returns in three days!

chapter 35

The phone wakes me.

"This is Elle," I say, disturbingly chipper despite the hour. Because it might be a job. I'm expecting a call or two.

"I want my suit. Today is fucking payback day."

"Mom!" I exclaim. "Lovely to hear your voice. How's Sedona? The Red Rocks still, uh, rockin'?"

"Today. You don't want to piss me off, bitch."

Today? Dingle's the last person I want to see today.

"What's that? The yeast infection? Much better. Luckily, I have this seersucker suit I'm using to clean the—"

Click.

Ha! All insecure men are vaginophobes. The best way to clear a crowded elevator, or taxi, or—

The phone rings again. I pick up, and am about to say *vaginal mucous* when I realize that I'm trying to put my Calamity Jane days behind me. If I did say that, it would merely guarantee that Merrick, Carlos or a job were on the other end of the line. So I say: "Good morning!" Even if it is the Dingle again, at least I will show him he can't ruin my mood.

But it's not the Dingle. It's a job. They want to hire me. I handle myself with calm and professional élan, and hang up the phone with serene dignity.

Looks like the New Elle is not only a newspaper delivery girl, but also a desk clerk at a residential hotel. Not precisely the level of glamour I had in mind—and two jobs may actually kill me, if the hotel residents don't get there first. But still: I am rescuing myself.

First steps in self-rescue? Long hot shower. Makeup. Outfit. Rub tea-tree oil on Miu Miu and take her for a walk on East Beach. She boxes fairly regularly now, but each time I thrill to see it. She also eyes seabirds with a certain predatory gleam. Soon she will be chasing them, and my life will be complete. Almost.

We return home to clean beach tar from feet and paws, using cottonballs dripping with nail-polish remover, but are distracted by open notebook. Two circles surrounding: $1500 a month.

I can make this work. I take pen in hand for haphazard arithmetic, but am ambushed by dread. Both jobs start next Wednesday. I will hate them. Of course I will. I am sick thinking about it. This is me? Newspaper-girl and desk clerk? I doodle in the notebook, yearning for the oblivion of the Neiman Marcus catalog or, failing that, an anvil dropping on my head, à la Wile E. Coyote. But this is my life we're talking about. My life, and Miu's life. And Merrick? We'll see what happens. I'm not counting any chickens.

The phone rings.

"Eleanor Medina," he says.

"Carlos, my man."

"Elle," he says in his official credit-guy voice. "They're getting serious. They're going to repossess your car."

"My car! They can't take my car. I use it for work."

"You got a job?"

"Delivery."

"Pizza?"

"Medical delivery. Hearts and kidneys and..." I sigh. "Newspapers, actually. And I got another job as a desk clerk. So I'll start my payments again soon and they don't have to—Miu!" I drag the phone across the room. Miu has something unnatural-looking encased in one of her jowls.

"What?" Carlos asks. "Is she okay?"

"She was sticking her snout in—" Oh, no. "In a suit."

"A suit?"

A seersucker, dry-cleaned, un-bagged suit. "The Dingle's suit..."

I burrow into her wet drooly jowls and unearth a sodden white stick capped with a glutinous red blob.

"Miu!" I scold, "not for you!" She slinks away, furtively licking her chops, and I tell Carlos: "A lollipop. She dug a lollipop from the pocket of this suit."

"Did you say Dingle?" Carlos buzzes in my ear as I assess the damage to the suit.

It's fairly total. Slime trails of drool, a tarry paw print, and even a layer of dog hair which the furless wonder somehow managed to shed. The lollipop has slimed the pocket and the credit card receipts and nudie matchbox.

There's a knock on the door. "Carlos, I gotta go. Don't let them take my car!"

I hang up. The knocking has stopped. It's Dingle. I know it is. There's no way he didn't hear me talking, either. He's going to break my elbows. He's going to make me dance at Café Lustre to pay for his suit.

I toss the suit in the bathroom and shove Dingle's sticky stuff in my pocket. Will tell him the suit is due back from the dry-cleaner's in an hour.

I open the door, and it's Joshua.

He smiles blindingly. "Elle, I missed you."

He's still the most gorgeous man I've ever seen, but he's not Merrick. "You sure did," I say.

He blinks, unsure for a moment, then invites himself in and closes the door. "Hey, great place. Lots of space. Prada?"

"Is there something you wanted, Joshua?"

"To see you smile again."

I give him a fake smile. "There you go. Next time call first, and I'll be sure not to be home."

"Elle, I don't know what to say." He looks crushed. "I'm sorry. How have you been? Found new work?"

"I'm doing private readings."

"Private readings? That's great! I knew a palm reader in Tucson who did that. Made a fortune double-charging credit cards. Nobody complained because they didn't want to admit they'd been to her. Worked it a year before the cops took an interest."

"Go away," I say. "I know about the three grand you got from Nordstrom and how you set me up at Super 9. I don't like you. *Josh.* I don't think I ever did."

He gives an injured-puppy look. "I'm sorry I was out of touch. I've been working. There's actually an opportunity for you, too, love—start-up money for your new business. I was thinking about DRM, how they fired you. You ever consider a suit for wrongful termination? I got a hold of their annual report, and they're minting the stuff. What we need to do is—"

There's a bang on the door. I want Joshua to leave, so I open it.

A hulking form fills the doorway. "Fuckin' bitch," he says. "Where's my suit?"

My eyes narrow. "Hello, Dingle."

"Tony?" Joshua says.

"Yo, Joshua."

These two know each other?

"You haven't been in for a while," the Dingle says. "Got

a new girl. Blond and blue. Flexible, too. And stacked like Jenna."

Oh, *Jenna*. They have mutual friends, of course.

"Girl defies gravity," the Dingle says. "Not like this saggy-tit bitch who ruined my suit."

"Lay off, Tony. Elle is very special to me."

"She's special, all right. Rides the little bus."

I consider hurling abuse at them, but honestly, why bother? Neither of them deserves the effort it takes to invent good invective. "Your suit's not ready, Dingle. The cleaners said five o'clock. If you want—" Behind them, Miu Miu begins dragging the suit toward us from the bathroom. Her stub-tail is wagging furiously. She is clearly trying to contribute. "You have to go!" I tell Josh and Dingle. "*Now!* Goodbye!"

Joshua shrugs and takes a step toward the door, turning to Dingle. "Comp me a lap-dance?"

The Dingle stands unmoving, the human boulder. "If it ain't here by five, I'm gonna…" He spots Miu. "What the fuck is that?"

"That's—that's my *dog,* you mouth-breather. She's a Canadian Hairless." I step in front of her, and she leans against me. "Purebred. Goodbye."

"What kind of lame-ass breed is that? I got a golden retriever—now that's a dog. Hey—my fuckin' suit!"

Oh, boy.

He lunges for Miu. I frantically grab him, but he shrugs me off. Miu shows a spurt of speed and scurries toward her corner. Dingle kicks at her, but misses and puts a dent in my wall. I scream and claw at his back. Joshua watches, no doubt wondering who can be most profitably sued. Dingle lumbers toward Miu Miu and she darts away.

She thinks he's playing.

"Your fuckin' dog ate my suit," he roars, and lunges for a flapping sleeve. She dances out of reach. I watch, stunned. This is as lively as she's been. She's having a grand time. She teases him with the suit, allows him close enough to grab at it, then squirts away.

"That's not your suit!" I shout, because if he *does* get a hand on her, I don't want to think about what'll happen.

"It fucking is."

"It's not. It's *not,*" I say, trying to get between them. "It's my…my slipcover!"

He lunges and gets a hand on Miu Miu, and she barely escapes.

"Joshua! Stop him!"

Then everything happens at once:

The phone rings. "Are you going to get that?" Joshua asks.

"You bitch! It's ruined!"

"Ellie?" At the door. A familiar voice, a familiar face. It's Louis. Not Merrick. *Louis.* My Louis. My ex-Louis. My six-years-and-gone Louis.

"You want *me* to get it?" Joshua asks.

"You're gonna fuckin' pay this time—"

"Ellie, what on earth is going on?" Louis asks.

Behind him, holding his hand, is a mousy woman. Dressed in a pale-lavender silk shirt and matching skirt I recognize from the Armani Emporio collection. I'm wearing a white sweater from the Gap. Her shoes are Gucci. Mine are New Balance. But still, she's definitely mousy. She notes my inspection, and smiles tentatively. Her smile transforms her into Julia Roberts.

Ducky.

"This is Lisa," Louis says. "Lisa, Ellie."

Fuck it. "This is the Dingle," I say. "He's a bouncer at a strip club. And Joshua here's a grifter. This is Louis. We lived together for six fucking years, then he married this—" I'm going to call her a serious name, but she's got this doe-eyed mousy thing happening "—woman while on a business trip."

"No fuckin' shit?" the Dingle says. "I want my goddamn suit." He lurches for Miu. She races away.

I pretend it's not happening.

"Good to meet you," Joshua says, also pretending. And to Lisa's feet: "Gucci?"

"Your phone is ringing, Ellie," Louis says.

"If you don't want to end up in the hospital again," I begin, then realize I don't care. I'm not mad. I'm not angry at Louis anymore. There's nothing. He seems like a nice guy, a stranger. "What are you doing here?"

"We're in L.A. We came up for the day—mostly for my stamps."

"Fuckin' dog!" the Dingle bellows.

"Elle. Sweetheart. I won't take more of your time," Joshua tells me. "I just need your signature—for that DRM thing, then I'll be out of your hair."

"Your *stamps?*" I say to Louis. "*Your* stamps?" This nice guy, this stranger, could easily piss me off.

"Bitch! Call your hairless fucking dog—"

"I'm really getting tired of that word, Dingle."

"Hey," Neil says from the door. "I heard arguing. You having a party?"

Oh, here we go. This is all I need—Neil in a manic rage.

"Please don't use language in front of my wife." Louis is stern and lawyerly toward Dingle. Of course, *I'm* the one being called a bitch.

"Hope you don't have any clients coming," Joshua tells me.

"Bitch has clients?"

"Language? Don't use *language?*" This is Neil. "Who talks like that? You want me to get the phone, Elle?"

Woorf. Roorf. Miu's barking! She's never barked before.

"For psychic readings. It's good money, mostly cash." Joshua holds out his papers. "Now if you'll sign here..."

"Elle's residence, Neil speaking. Carlos? What? No, I can barely hear you, it's crazy here."

Carlos. Of course it's Carlos calling back. Who else would it be?

"You know how I feel about my stamp collection, Elle."

The Julia Roberts smile again, this time apologetic. "I told him we shouldn't come, but you know how he gets. This is clearly a bad time, Lou."

"Fuckin' psychic *this,* bitch." The Dingle shows me his meaty middle finger.

"Carlos Neruda?" Neil asks. "Like the poet? Did you see that movie—*Il Postino?* I liked that movie."

I glance, shaken, at Neil. He actually *likes* something?

Then: "My stamps!" Louis spots Miu's stamp-decorated bowls and stares in shock and dejection. "My stamps!"

I stand fatalistically in the eye of the storm. There is nothing to be done. What will be will be. I wipe sticky lollipop from my fingers with the Dingle's credit card receipts and stare dully at the matchbox and receipts. I wish *I* had Jenna's tits. Hell, I wish I had the Dingle's credit. Each receipt is from a different card, purchases from Stan Storkin Jewelry, Sharper Image, Autos-Online, Goleta Car Stereo, Ameson Kennels, CompUSA, Good Vibrations... Shit. I can't even get a *single* card, and the Dingle's a major card holder.

"—a windfall from DRM, for wrongful termination, all you have to do is sign this complaint I drew up—" Joshua presses a pen into my hand.

"*Desperado?* Another great movie," Neil says to Carlos. "Have you seen *13th Warrior?* It was poorly reviewed and not well received at the box office, but I quite liked it."

"My stamps, my stamps," Louis moans mournfully. "They're ruined. I never thought you were spiteful..."

Something nags at me about Dingle's receipts. *Car Stereo? Good Vibrations? Ameson Kennels?* I can't quite put my finger on it...

"—only need your autograph, right here..."

"Louis, forget your stamps," Lisa says. "You owe Elle an apology—and not just for dropping in like this."

"—bitch dog, I'll rip your throat out—"

"Elle," Neil calls from across the room. "It's Carlos. He says he forgot to tell you, your check bounced."

Well, at least things can't get worse. Then I catch a flash of ginger freak-hair at the door.

"What are *you* doing here?" I say in horror. He's not due for days. Oh, God. He said I shouldn't do anything, and I'm doing *everything!*

"Lucy," he says. *"I'm home."*

"Oh, do you live here?" Louis asks him. "I just came to get my stamps." He holds out his hand to Merrick. "Louis Ferris. Elle's ex-fiancé. This is my wife, Lisa. And you are?"

"I'm..." he looks from Louis to me. "I guess I'm Merrick."

He smiles at me, calm and centered, as the barrage continues. He's a comforting and familiar touchstone amid the craziness. And it hits me: Dingle's credit card receipts.

I uncrumple them from my sticky fingers. They aren't Dingle's receipts at all. Not only are the numbers all different, but the names are, too. Why would he have other people's credit card receipts in his pocket?

"—would somebody..." the Dingle pants. "Grab that... *fucking*...dog!"

"So the crème brûlée hospitalized you, but you didn't sue?" Joshua says to Louis.

"I had no idea her credit was so bad," Neil says. "She told me she was an eclectic consultant."

"SHUT UP!" I shriek.

The room quiets. Six pairs of eyes turn toward me. Seven, including Miu.

I glance at Merrick and say: "You might be wondering why I called you all here today."

chapter 36

The next evening, I'm at Shika. Miu Miu is on her towel. Maya, Perfect Brad, Mr. Goldman and Monty are all here. Neil came along with some of the people from the argument group. And Merrick is here.

He came home two days early from New York. I asked why.

He said: "You know why."

I've been tingling for a full day from those three little words: *you know why.*

Haven't had a chance to do much more than tingle, though. I've been busy. Phone calls, mostly. Hey, you can't expect fame and fortune to be served to you on a silver platter with a watercress garnish. You've got to do it for yourself.

"So tell us what happened, Elle," PB says.

"What makes you think I had anything to do with it?" I ask, as we all watch the old TV over the bar. "Maybe they just have excellent investigative reporters."

Neil flares up about the state of reporting in the world today, but everyone shushes him as the TV says: "Up next, we have the local psychic who found Holly-Go-Lightly, the dog-napped puppy."

"How *did* you know?" Perfect Brad asks again.

"Pillow talk, probably," Maya says, with an evil grin. "You *know* she had a thing for that Dingle."

"Maya!" her father says. "Elle's a good girl. She'd never do anything to be ashamed of."

Universal groans.

"She wouldn't!" he insists.

"What I want to know," Monty says, "is if you got the reward. The check cleared?"

I'm about to answer—it did, indeed!—when the segment starts. "Wait, wait! There I am—oh, God. I'm *fat*. I'm huge. You need a wide-screen TV to see all of me. Look at my neck! I'm a linebacker, I'm—"

This time I'm the one who's shushed, as PB turns up the volume. On TV, I'm standing next to Sally Ameson, in the YSL suit I got at the vintage store downtown. I went light on eye makeup, and used red matte lipstick. I think it works. I look vaguely old-world—and chock-full of the Gift. Oh, and I'm cradling the cutest golden retriever pup in creation. I had to fight Ameson for the privilege, but I've been tooth-and-clawing it so long, she didn't stand a chance.

"Do you like my suit? I wanted to wear a pillbox hat, but couldn't find one. Sort of a Jackie O meets Miss Cleo thing. Does my hair really *look* like that? Oh God, kill me now."

I'm shushed again, as Merrick takes my hand under the bar. He squeezes it tightly. I tingle. But quietly.

"I'm just happy she's back where she belongs," the me on TV says. "That's the most important thing. I hardly feel I deserve all this attention. It's all in a day's work for an intuitive counselor."

"I nailed that!" I crow. I was afraid I'd call myself a psychic.

"You're a big fat liar," Maya says. "All in a day's work."

They shush her. Ha! Maya is shushed in favor of me. That's a first.

"—could hardly believe it when Miss Medina called," Ameson says on TV. "As far as I'm concerned, she's an angel. An absolute angel."

When she said that, I attempted to look angelic, but merely achieved a sort of colicky expression. The TV cuts to a clip of the Dingle being shoved into the back of a cop car as the anchorman wraps up the details of his arrest.

"That wasn't really Holly-Go-Lightly," I say.

"The puppy you were holding?" Maya asks.

"Yeah. Holly's all skinny and teenaged now. The producer insisted Sally substitute a more photogenic puppy for the story."

"I'm not surprised," Neil says.

"Okay," PB says. "Now you *have* to tell us."

Merrick smiles at me. He's the only one who knows the whole story. And it's just been a blur. It started with my epiphany during the fiasco in my apartment: all those credit card receipts. The golden retriever Dingle owned, the receipt from Ameson Kennels. And realizing that the Dingle was just a white-Mike Tyson version of Joshua.

I shoved Neil off the phone to speak with Carlos, my credit card expert. I called Spenser for Hire. Then Sally Ameson. Then the newspaper and local TV. Oh, and the cops got involved, too, of course. I had to let them take *some* credit.

I offer PB a mysterious smile. "It's the Gift, Brad. I am merely a tool in the hands of a higher power, which—"

I am hooted down. Anyway, I keep him guessing for a few minutes, then spill. My version is quite a bit more accurate than what appeared the next morning in the *Santa Barbara News-Press:*

Local Psychic Finds Missing Puppy

After almost five months, the kidnapped golden retriever puppy, Holly-Go-Lightly, returned home late yesterday.

Acting on a tip from local psychic and intuitive counselor, Elle Medina, the Santa Barbara Police located the dog at the home of Anthony Dingle, 32, who has been taken into custody.

"She was abused and neglected," said Sally Ameson, the owner of the dog. "If Elle hadn't found her, I don't know what would have happened."

After receiving what she called "an intuitive auric transmission," Medina put together a team consisting of James Ross of Spenser Investigative Services and Carlos Neruda of National Credit Affiliates. She then went undercover at Café Lustre Gentlemen's Club. Posing as a stripper looking for employment, Medina obtained the evidence needed for Spenser and Neruda to identify Dingle as the dog-napper.

"I kept picturing naked women dancing," Medina said.

In addition to the missing dog, investigators at the Dingle residence found evidence Dingle had been involved in an ongoing credit card scam. Employed as a security doorman at Café Lustre, Dingle has allegedly been stealing customers' credit card information for months.

Investigators long suspected the dog-napper of involvement in a credit card scam, authorities say, as a stolen card was used during the initial attempt to purchase the puppy. But it took the psychic prowess of Elle Medina to connect the missing puppy with the strip club bouncer.

As for Holly, she's safe at home. "She took her medicine well," said Veterinarian Dr. Anna Van der Water. "It was a close call, but with quality veterinary care, she'll be fine."

* * *

Quality veterinary care, and the psychic prowess of Elle Medina! Though I'm not sure about that "naked women dancing" quote. Surely they could have used something better. Still, it's the Sunday edition, and there's a color picture of me with Holly and Spenser.

When I told Spenser he'd get some credit for the collar, he forgave me for the lawsuit and offered me a "consultant's fee," which I turned down. Well, I was getting the reward anyway, and it didn't seem right. I did get a great testimonial from Sally Ameson, though, for the ads I'm gonna run in the local paper.

In the meantime, Maya and Merrick have convinced me to reapply to graduate school in psychology. There are four schools that offer programs here in Santa Barbara, so I won't have to leave town, and I've decided maybe they're right, it's time to take myself seriously.

Carlos is trying to convince his bosses to reward me for stopping the Dingle scam, with a check in the exact amount of my debts. We'll see. He says it's a done deal, but I'm not counting on it. I don't have to. I'm counting on me.

I am feeding Miu when the phone rings.

"Elle, this is Nyla. You probably don't remember me, but—"

"Don't be silly! Of *course* I remember you."

I'm not even surprised to hear from her. I had coffee with Darwin and Adele—well, Adele had herbal tea—and I gave them my phone number. They've referred a bunch of old clients to me. So I do phone consultations in addition to my regular appointments. I'm averaging eight clients a week. One hundred bucks a client. There's tax, of course, but I'm just starting out and work should increase once I get my degree and...well, you do the math.

"We got separated," Nyla says. "Well, really, I left him."

"*You* left *him?*"

"Temporarily. You know, I think he was taking me for granted. And I guess I was taking him for granted, too."

"You sound pretty okay with it."

"I'm really okay with it," Nyla says. "I'm working at the bookstore, and we're dating. Getting to know each other again."

I laugh. "And getting to know yourself, too, right?"

"It sounds stupid," Nyla says, "but you know…I have a feeling it's gonna work. What do you think?"

"The cards tell me," I say, "it's all gonna be okay."

chapter 37

"Elle! What are you doing here?"

"Bathing," I say.

"How did you get in?"

"Neil."

"I knew he'd abuse his key privileges." Merrick tries to sound disappointed, but can't keep the grin out of his voice. "This is a terrible betrayal of trust."

I smile as I sink beneath the bubbles in Merrick's bathtub. It's as good as my fantasy, soaking in a gigantic vat of steaming water overlooking the wide blue sea.

Merrick steps into the bathroom from the hallway. I like the way he walks across a room. I like the way his hand feels trailing though bubbles on my arm. I like the way his eyes crinkle when he notices the three-wicked candle. I like the way I don't have to pretend when he's around.

And I like the way his hair looks. Under the skylight I notice it's a natural dark brown.

"My niece finally got it right," he says.

Oh, my. Ginger Freak-head has turned to Mahogany Adonis.

"Speaking of getting things right," I say, glancing at the windowsills. "I see what you mean. They *are* different shades. You better get your painter back in here—they're ruining my bath."

"I don't think so," he says, his hand moving deeper into the water. "Because you know what I learned?"

"What's that?"

"The best things in life are always a little different."

Hey! He learned that from *me.* I'm not only learning lessons, I'm teaching them. I tell him how wise I am.

He leans over the tub and I kiss him, pressing my wet body against his chest. A tidal wave sloshes over the edge.

"Whoa," he says, laughing and drenched. "Settle down there, Medina."

"I never settle," I say, and pull him in.

It's all about me!

Coming in July 2004,

Harlequin Flipside heroines tell you exactly what they think...in their own words!

WHEN SIZE MATTERS
by Carly Laine
Harlequin Flipside #19

WHAT PHOEBE WANTS
by Cindi Myers
Harlequin Flipside #20

I promise these first-person tales will speak to you!

Look for Harlequin Flipside at your favorite retail outlet.

HFFPT-TR